To my brother
Ben

FLOATING ON THE
WOW

TIM YEAGER

To my wife Emily, whose words and wisdom have taken me
to places I could never go without her; to my brother Ben
for all the mischief he kept me out of; and finally to my
children, Matt and Amy, for every kindness, great and small.

Acknowledgments

I would like to acknowledge the following for their help in getting *Floating on The Wow* out the door: Ingrid Powell for her editing suggestions; Andrew Nicholas, Shane Keaney, and Echo Keaney of City Pool Design Collective for their whimsical illustrations and website help; Helen Monroe, Deb Dunham, Charlie Coleman, Tom Silverio, Annie Eckert, and Caitie Hetchka for their encouragement; Terri Wright for her thoughtful advice; my wife and children for their support throughout this project; and Nica, our cat, for sleeping on top of the pages to make sure they were safe.

Chapter 1
END OF STORY

Fall, 1947

More than anything else I wanted to be a pirate captain but settled for what came next, a bumpy ride to the Five and Dime. Our car engine wheezed, struggling to find its next breath. A plume of smoke rose from under the hood. Not surprising really; most of our family's mechanical devices seemed incapable of completing the simple tasks we asked them to perform. Our freezer, for example, only made ice on Tuesdays, and even then it was never enough to fill a pitcher of lemonade. My family had learned how to take life's disappointments in stride.

"Come up with any good ideas, sweetie?" My mother's question floated down over the top of her belly, ripe with my brother. I nodded back in reply. She pulled into one of the empty spaces by the front door and waddled inside.

The Five and Dime was a worn-out store with merchandise no one else really wanted but was just the sort of place our family liked to shop. For one thing the clerks were all wide-bodied ladies, in large flowery dresses, who smelled of drugstore gardenias. They moved gracefully between narrow aisles calling everyone "Dearie." This was heaven, especially if you were five and didn't get out much. Mom busied herself with baby supplies. I headed back to uncover my destiny.

Okay, so the outfit selected was a bit cheesy, point taken. The bandanna was real enough, and the eye patch fit comfortably in place. But my saber was made of a flimsy plastic, like the utensils found in fast-food restaurants, so the only real danger it posed was spreading too much secret sauce across the bottoms of hamburger buns. My victims, if there were any, would be dying from a greasy cardiac arrest rather than blunt force trauma. I was left to do what we all did in the late 1940s: fill the holes that the 99¢ made-in-China pirate suit left uncovered. It didn't matter. *Most things don't, I say in hindsight, having seen pictures of myself with the fluffy cowlick sticking out the top of the bandanna.*

Two weeks later our elementary school held its annual Halloween carnival. The PTA had only one mission: bleeding loose change out of grandparents' pockets, in order to buy more books for the library or a set of drapes for the nurse's office. We were merely the wallet-opening eye candy. The homeroom mothers spared no expense on our big night out. Crepe paper hung over every doorway, and their choice of orange and black balloons was nothing short of genius. After a spaghetti dinner in the cafeteria, we paraded around the school's playground for the amusement of our parents. Pictures were taken, compliments given. It was still hot in Tampa in late October, and standing next to the bread warmer some of my charcoal face paint began to slide.

"It's the pirate's life for me," I said to Mary Ellen Roseboro, a bumblebee by trade.

"I see that," she replied, her response seasoned with disinterest. She must have thought this to be only a temporary affliction and that next year I'd be returning as a can of tuna or a famous bullfighter.

"No, really, Mary Ellen, this is for always."

She curled her lower lip and said, "Peter, always is a long way off. Things will change."

"Really? You think so?" I replied, sharpening my glare but not buying her myopic conclusions. *Time is merely a concept people lug around on their arms, telling them where they're supposed to be in an hour and if they made it.* I considered unsheathing my plastic sword and teaching my annoying little insect friend a thing or two about proper pirate protocol. But then Mrs. Jackson, the music teacher, said, "Okay, children: it's time to march."

Our discussion cut short, we left the cafeteria line one bad interpretation at a time. On the way out of the cafeteria I leaned over to her large yellow and black fluffy head and said, "No, Mary Ellen, I am a pirate. End of story!"

Spring, 1964

Some dreams never die. My pirate dream was one of them. All the way through college I secretly hoped to find a way to spend the rest of my days chasing wenches and drinking beer. A few weeks before graduation a group of my fraternity brothers and I discussed what we wanted to make of our lives. John said he wanted to be a doctor—his father was one; Kevin, a chemist; and Jim, a veterinarian. All good jobs these; they just were not for me.

"How much do you actually know about pirating?" John asked, staring straight into my uncovered eye.

"Well, John, not all that much actually…. Okay, fine, nothing really, but it sounds neat. Of course, while pirating is my first choice, selling office copiers in the Midwest might make good sense as well." I made eye contact so he knew I was dead serious.

"We need more beers before we can settle this," John advised.

"Yes, more beers!" we shouted, clinking bottles together in a hearty toast. *Let's face it: There may be problems in life for which "more beers" isn't the best answer, but honestly I wouldn't want to tackle any of them without a few more beers.*

A case of beer and two hours later, John offered his reasoned response: "Hell, yes, Peter! Be a pirate. There are way too many copier salesmen out there already. What the world needs are more adventurers."

. . .

"Are you shitting me?" Dad angrily cracked back over the phone. Apparently Dad was still several beers shy of reaching John's insightful conclusion. My mood was now completely ruined by his sour response, and I waited to hear what was coming next.

"We're not paying thousands of dollars to send you to a pirate school in Barbados after college. No, sir. You're getting a real job, mister, and soon."

In my opinion, this was information he should have shared with me sooner. My best recollection before leaving for college was hearing him say, "Good luck, Peter," not, "Good luck, and don't come home with a scruffy beard or a gold ring stuck in your ear." Dad thought I needed an encounter with the career placement office. But Mrs. Cartwright's office sign read "closed" the afternoon I passed by, and I never made it back across campus to see what tantalizing offers she could find for me. It was doubtful she could have come up with anything more than a training job at Impervious Life and Casualty, and they'd hire anybody.

Dad laughed nervously, realizing he'd made a bad decision investing so heavily in my uncertain future. He wanted me back in Tampa working in his seed stores.

Less than twenty minutes through his hour-long rant, I imagined firing a cannonball over his eight-foot-high "buy four and get the fifth bag free" fertilizer display just to let him know what I thought of his useless suggestion. Instead I went with "Arrr." It was all I could manage, not wanting to get out of character. Why did my opinions matter so little?

Even though it was a career path not taken, I have no regrets. Being a pirate is hard, very hard. When I was five, I had a big growth spurt shortly after Christmas, and those black plastic pants, which had fit so generously only months earlier, were now halfway up my shin. Gaucho pirate? No, thanks. It's not a good look for me. Be careful, people. Our lives are defined by the costumes into which we no longer fit, so choose wisely or you'll end up in a training seminar at Impervious' corporate headquarters, or worse yet, standing in a seed store next to your father.... Shiver me timbers.

The time had come to take control. I looked over at my buddies, took a last swig of warm beer and said, "Places, gentlemen, our curtain is about to rise."

•   •   •

Chapter 2
VASCO DA GAMA WILL WORK FOR FOOD

2009

My name is Peter Dreeton, and I spent six wonderful years in Whitfield, Massachusetts. This small Cape Cod town was the sort of place you never forget, though my memories have indeed blurred all these years later. Was the post office next to Kaman's Drugstore, or not? Was it really as quiet and innocent as I remembered? It was likely some of both. What I can say with certainty is that Whitfield's past is tied inextricably with my favorite fruit, the cranberry. It is home to some of the largest cranberry producers, and every year it celebrates its relationship by putting on a gigantic fall festival, Back to the Bogs, which takes over the whole town and brings in weekend tourists from all over New England. But perhaps even more than this is that Whitfield is known for being the home of the Cape Cod Reds. This project was started in 1942 at a local Catholic girl's school, St. Anne's, to raise money for families of local soldiers, injured or lost in the war. The students boxed and sold dried cranberries throughout the Cape and Boston. They raised thousands of dollars and gave help to many needy families. During my last year in Whitfield the university sponsored a retrospective exhibit on the Reds and the good that the project did. What you are about to hear are actually two stories. The first is about what I learned from days of wanting to be a pirate to finding out who I really was and the other is about the goodness of cranberries.

From May through September Whitfield summers tourists, who rummage through dusty antique shops. On warm Saturday nights, teenagers walk the hormone gangplank of the town's pier to meet the most important romance of their lives—the next one—and the town's only movie theatre adds a late show to accommodate the crowds. Families wander under the shade of the tall sycamore trees protecting Front Street from the late afternoon sun.

In 1964 Whitfield was chosen to be "August" on the Impervious Life and Casualty's wall calendar, sandwiched between Jackson Hole, Wyoming and the famous covered bridge in Stowe, Vermont. The photograph, shot from across the bay, showed fragments of my world during my time on the Cape. But then that August was torn off, and Whitfield began her slow turn to another season. One by one the inns closed, the traffic grew lighter; the wait time for a table at Griff's became shorter. The air began to cool, and students arrived at the University of St. Jerome. Whitfield found a new purpose and an unspoken sadness. Parents unloaded their prized possessions, and in one afternoon learned how to say goodbye.

On those golden Saturdays, the sounds of the Crusader Marching Band filled the air with the kind of unsettled noises babies make at the end of long naps. I sometimes imagined a single Crusader—myself perhaps—breaking free and heading into a soft sea of green and blue banners at the far end of Kiley field.

June, 1964

When it came time for me to graduate from St. Jerome's, I had nowhere to go, nothing else to do. No carpools came to deliver me to grad school, or jobs, or whatever. No one came. No one! I waited for hours out on the curb of life, shuffling my feet, hoping opportunity might drive by and offer me a ride. I even constructed a "will work for food" sign on the back of a poster used for my Vasco da Gama presentation. I held it up until my arms got tired, before having a sinkin' spell, the kind that came after sleeping through a mid·

All that passed by was an empty van from Impervious Life & Casualty looking for stragglers. Just before commencement the vice president of operations said they were looking to fill a position in the admissions office, and he asked if I would be interested. I said, "Sure, Mr. Dawkins, does it pay money?"

By this time my parents and my brother Cory had arrived for my graduation, but our post-graduation meal was less than celebratory. "This was your last chance to dig yourself out of this hole, and you couldn't get your fat ass out of bed, could you?" Dad's disgust turned my head. You could still see small chunks of disappointment between his teeth—or maybe those were part of the seafood loaf he was eating for lunch. Whatever the case, it was unpleasant. And honestly if Dad had a better understanding of how hard it was to be me, he probably wouldn't have asked such loaded questions.

"Are you fucking nuts?" Dad continued.

Mom did her best to cool him down. "At least he's not a pirate, Bernie." Frankly, I was surprised she remembered my age five career goal.

Mom always sees the best in me, even when it's not really there. Dad's hope chest is filled with doubts.

"Peter, are you fucking nuts?" Dad said a second time because he either hadn't heard her or didn't have it out of his system. It usually took several tries for things to sink in, and even then he never went down without a fight.

"I don't know, maybe," I answered.

·   ·   ·

Chapter 3

ERIC THE RED ON LINE ONE

Fall, 1963 – Fall, 1965

One of the advantages of taking the job in the admissions office was getting to continue working on the Cape Cod Reds retrospective. During my senior year a group of town residents came to meet Dr. Tiller, the head of the history department, to see about the university's sponsoring an exhibit. As a history major, I had a part-time job filing papers and doing odds and ends for her.

When I first came to St. Jerome's, I had no idea which of the many invaluable liberal arts degrees to pursue. Economics looked good until my mid-term grade came in below the poverty line. I toyed with political science but couldn't really see the point of politics, since all politicians are liars. One night at Griff's a fellow crew member told me to cover the dartboard with letters and choose a major from the one I landed on.

"It's an H," Rusty said, taking a swig of beer and slowly pulling my future out of the cork board. I went back to our table to review my H options. I ruled out horticulture because that would have only made my father happy. I rejected holistic healing because I wasn't that fond of working with snakes, and sadly hopscotch was only offered as a single three-hour elective. In high school I had loved history because there were no surprises. Henry the Eighth didn't wake up one morning with a fresh attitude and start paying alimony to his divorced wives. No, sir, history is fixed, unchangeable. Learn it once, and you get an A. Take a few minutes reviewing your notes out in the hall prior to the test, and it all falls back into place like riding a bike. There is no slippery slope like the ones in math or science, where today X could be one number for some unexplained reason, something entirely different tomorrow.

At St. Jerome's my time was too valuable to waste studying. History was an easy match, never burdening me with unreasonable expectations. Someone was always getting poisoned or shot at a tiny sidewalk café in Paris, and soon a war would break out in some distant land. Or a new religious movement was stirring up trouble in Bogotá or Cairo, so that made it fun. Over the four years I learned a great deal of completely useless information, like who won the Boer War, and why.

Dr. Tiller had been the chairman of the department for only two years. She came from one of the branch campuses of the University of Illinois system, and she knew only a little about the Reds and the money the project had raised.

Dr. Tiller taught two of my senior courses. I always did my best to keep things fresh around the office.

"Dr. Tiller… It's Eric the Red on line one. Do you want to take his call?" I said, sticking my head in her office.

"Oh, Peter, you're sweet, but seriously not very funny."

"Me, not funny, Dr. Tiller? Now that's funny."

"Well, Eric never calls me at the office, so the joke doesn't really work. And that goes double for these messages from René Descartes and Helen of Troy. Please thank them both, but I can't go white-water rafting this weekend. I'll be tied up at Gregory's soccer game."

"Whatever, Doc, but you're making a huge mistake. The Green River is amazing, and René is a fun guy."

"I'm sure. Ask them for a raincheck."

One afternoon in late September the ladies showed up for a meeting about the possibility of creating an exhibit about the Cape Cod Reds. The idea excited Dr. Tiller. She was able to secure a large amount of money from the university as well as grants from the State Historical Society and the Smithsonian. Once the project was given the green light, there was always stuff for me to do. Shortly after, I was promoted from paper-filer and coffee-fixer to administrative assistant. It didn't make any difference in my hourly wage, but still it was good. She needed me for more hours, and I needed the money. She had me working a couple of nights a week and sometimes on weekends. I'd come in after crew practice in jeans with my hair still wet from the shower and not leave sometimes until eight. On her way out the door, she would stick her head in my cubby, and say "Don't stay all night, Peter."

"Don't worry, Doc. I'll be out of here before my hair dries."

"That may take a while with all the hair you've got."

Dr. Tiller wanted me to go to graduate school and become an historical writer, but I guess the dreams she had for me were a bit larger than my own. In the end, I think she was glad I took the job in admissions so that I could keep helping her with the retrospective.

The exhibit was scheduled to coincide with fiftieth anniversary of St. Anne's, the local Catholic girls' school that started the project. The whole town jumped on board. We sent letters to every Whitfield resident asking for souvenirs or information about the Cape Cod Reds. The athletic department had two large storage units behind the gym, and Dr. Tiller talked them into loaning us one to keep all the artifacts we were collecting. Each item had to be tagged and filed and given an exhibit number. Then a thank-you letter was sent out. The Smithsonian loaned us documents and photographs, and local residents donated some interesting objects, including a pair of formerly white gloves the workers wore while boxing the berries. Over time they had developed a rich red stain from the handling of so many dried cranberries.

One afternoon, I came across a handful of boxes, no longer containing cranberries. When I looked more closel at them, I found a curious item. Inside one was a note read "You're cute. Do you want to meet later at Kaman's for a soda?" signed by a girl named Carrie. It made me think about what those lives long ago must have been like.

Dr. Tiller had oral histories recorded so that guests could hear personal narratives of the times and how the actual process worked. It took two full years of gathering and planning, of design meetings and changes, to get everything the way it should be. The actual exhibit was housed in the library annex in a massive room with a fifteen-foot ceiling. We constructed a replica of the warehouse, complete with faux bricks and the actual banner that hung over the building, reading "Home of the Cape Cod Reds." We gathered photographs from many sources, and some of the best ones were enlarged to hang over the beams in the exhibit hall. There were guided tours where each guest was assigned to one of five teams and asked to participate in actually boxing and labeling berries for shipment as well as other hands-on displays. Old radio broadcasts played over the loudspeaker system, and war-time posters covered the walls. Three classrooms were set up for lectures about the project, the teams, and the money they raised. In a fourth we created a home economics kitchen where docents could prepare recipes from the *Cape Cod Reds Cookbook* for the visitors. Once the exhibit opened, schools from all over the state came to relive history.

Whitfield embraced the project, and it was a major tourist attraction during my last year there. Articles appeared in all of the Boston papers, and we even got a brief mention in *The New York Times*. Dr. Tiller wrote a book called *Guns and Berries: America Goes to War*, and we sold copies in the gift shop along with every other form of gift item: from T-shirts to key chains; cookbooks to aprons, adorned with the five different logos from the project. A local cranberry supplier even provided berries in boxes with replicas of each of the five original designs.

Dr. Tiller felt it was important to get the local elementary school involved. In the spring of '65, after all of the college acceptance letters had been mailed, she sent me over to

Whitfield Elementary to talk the school into participating. Dr. Tiller came up with the idea of having the students give stage presentations in the town's square the following fall, during the first month of the exhibit. The principal was very nice and decided that the school would also sell reprints of the cookbook and boxes of the berries to raise money for new playground equipment.

June 26, 1943

The pavement had worn thin in front of the boatyard. An early morning light rain pooled in the low spots, causing a splash when the truck's tire rolled over it. The two small boys in the front seat cheered. Puddle-chasing was a good way to spend a rainy summer Saturday with their dad. Another was to go see what treats Uncle Frankie had for them. Their dad pulled the truck to a stop right below the sign reading: Bellini's Boatyard, serving Whitfield, Mass. since 1921. The two boys were out the door and stomping in the puddles before the engine turned off.

"What's up, Frankie?" the dad said as he got out of his truck.

The man standing just outside a small office replied, "Hey, Leo, I got your boat repaired. You were lucky. They're not manufacturing more of those drive shafts until the war's over, but I was able to pull a used one off Abernathy's old trawler."

"Thanks. You don't think he'll mind?"

"No. I'll think of something to stick on if he comes by, b' he hasn't been getting out much since he busted up his '

Anyway, the park service boats come first," he responded as the two boys, now slightly wet, approached. "Hey, bambinos! How are my two favorite nephews?"

"Great, Uncle Frankie. Is the boat fixed?" the older boy asked.

"Of course, Ricky, we've got to keep the park service up and running," Frankie was middle-aged, short, and spoke with a heavy Cape Cod Italian accent.

"So how much do I owe you?" Leo asked.

"Make it twenty plus the part. Let's say thirty-five all together." Frankie wiped grease off his hands and patted Tony, his younger nephew, on the head.

"Are you sure that's enough?" Leo inquired.

"You're family, right? Don't worry about it. I'm doing my civic duty." Frankie held the worn wooden office door open for the boys to go in.

"Can we get candy?" Tony asked in an excited voice, looking up at his uncle.

"You're just like your mother was when she was little, Tony. Just pick out something from the rack."

The little boy smiled and began looking over the selection of candy. "Geez, thanks, Uncle Frankie, you're the best."

"That's what they tell me," Frankie replied.

"Hey, wait, boys. Let's get some of these instead," Leo said picking up two small boxes of dried cranberries labeled Cape Cod Reds. The display rack contained twenty-four boxes which all appeared to have a drawing of a lobster across the front.

"Your father is right, boys. The cranberries are yummy, and you are supporting the USA when you eat them."

A man in his early thirties wearing a baseball cap came into the office.

"What can I do for you?" Frankie asked, surprised to see a customer this early in the morning.

"Well, I might be interested in seeing a couple of the used boats out there, if the price is right."

"Sure, let me finish up with these guys, and we'll take a look."

Leo handed his money to Frankie and turned to his boys. "Come on. You guys ready?"

"Hey, look, Ricky. I got the only starfish box. I got the only starfish," Tony chanted while raising the box up over his head.

"I want it," Ricky said, trying to grab the box out of his younger brother's hand.

"Boys, they're all the same cranberries on the inside."

"Are those good? I've been meaning to buy a box," the stranger behind them interrupted.

"Cape Cod Reds? Yeah, they're great. Here have a box on me," Frankie said handing him one.

"Thanks." The man opened the box up and tossed a handful of dried berries into his mouth.

"Hey, look. This starfish one's got no trading card inside, just this old paper," Tony said holding up a piece of torn notebook paper for his uncle to see.

"That's weird. What is it?" Leo asked looking over at his son.

"Hey, Dad, what if it's full of secrets? I bet that's what it is," Ricky said, snatching the paper from Tony. "See; there are drawings of something. I bet it's a submarine or something."

They all laughed including the stranger.

"Here, let me see," Uncle Frankie offered, taking the paper from Tony. He examined the note, turning it over in his hands. "Well maybe Tony is right after all. Like here at the top in red pen is written, 'Hey, Brenda, are you going to take Harry to the summer dance?' It's signed 'Becky.' That certainly sounds fishy to me," Frankie said, breaking into a smile. "It's okay, boys. It's just a note some girl scribbled on the back of her school work. No spies this time. Anyway, how crazy is that, boys? Secrets in a box of dried cranberries from a Catholic girls' school. What are those nuns up to now?" Frankie teased. He tossed the paper into t[

trash can. "There, we stopped the secrets at the boatyard. Now you boys need to get going in case the storm comes back."

"But I want a trading card," Tony complained.

"You can have mine," the man in the baseball cap volunteered, holding out the card from his box.

"Gee, thanks," Tony said appreciatively.

"Thank you, sir. That is very kind of you," Leo said. "Come on, boys."

They headed out the door. Frankie turned, looking over his shoulder at the other man, and said, "I'm going to walk them down to their boat, and then we can go take a look at what might interest you."

"That's great. Take your time," the stranger replied, as Frankie and his relatives headed out the door. The stranger realized that he should have arrived earlier in the morning. He hadn't figured on customers being at the store before 8 on a Saturday. It didn't matter now, and he felt relieved. He reached down into the trash, picked up the notebook paper he needed, and stuffed the secrets into his shirt pocket. Out the window he watched the boys jumping into puddles on their way to the boat, and he smiled.

•　•　•

Chapter 4

DR. DEATH MAKES A HOUSE CALL

What I have for you here are unfortunately only scraps of small stories, that took place at different times in my life—some far back; some more recently. These stories are tied together loosely, the way a mattress is fastened to the roof of a roommate's Volkswagen, allowing it to shift from side to side without falling off. Your job, dear reader, is to hold on tightly, to see that our story doesn't come undone, to help me finish thoughts, complete sentences, before our time runs out. This story is a team effort, and you're riding shotgun.

It may be nerve-racking to hear only parts of an idea; to be shifting back and forth in time. I wish it were different. I have wished for many things in my life: good grades; no more car payments; a Swedish girlfriend who likes handcuffs. None of that happened. Same deal with this story. Fragments are all you will get, small stones thrown across still waters. A torn autograph with only half of Babe Ruth's signature appears worthless, but it is still not without value to those who understand its origin. Our lives can only be understood in pieces, and even then it takes somebody else to put them all in place for us. My story picks up in my father's store when I was nine.

Spring, 1952

My dad ran a chain of seed stores called Florida Seed and Supply which my little brother struggled to pronounce "Foreeda," and we all got a kick out of that. What makes a family is the commonality of experiences shared and repeated and then finely pasteurized into family lore. For years, we asked Cory, "What is the name of Dad's store?" and he answered, "Foreeda," on cue, like a dog reclaiming a thrown stick. Cory did that for us, until he got older and realized that we were having fun at his expense, which of course we were. *I have to say it. I love that guy.*

If Dad ever possessed a functioning imagination, it must have been dismembered in some gruesome shredder accident. Whatever else I could say about him, Dad was tough as nails. At the time of his injury, he probably wrapped the open wound with oily rags from the ground in order to stop the bleeding and chugged a bottle of hydrogen peroxide to help fight off infection. *Arrr, mateys.*

When I was little, it seemed as if we lived at one of the stores. Mom ran a cash register when they were shorthanded, and I performed chemistry experiments with the pesticides on aisle three. Cory served as my all-too-willing patient.

During that period, I was known as Dr. Death, a code name assigned by the U.S. Army chemical research unit in Flatsville, Oklahoma. My responsibilities called for developing secret mind-altering cocktails to be use on captured spies. Unbeknownst to the rest of my family, the government agreed to keep my father's struggling business afloat in exchange for the fruits of my research. My government contact, Millard Watkins, promised to send just enough customers to keep us from going under and told me to leave samples of my handiwork outside the back door in a brown paper bag.

"Bottoms up," I'd say to my imaginary customers, handing a glass of tap water to rinse down the white tablets large enough to choke a horse. "More is better, and more better is the best. Anyway don't be afraid to live a little, especially not in your condition. What's the worst that could happen to you?"

Sometimes, to raise a little extra cash, I even took on celebrity customers with special needs. The medications weren't exactly for *them*, if you catch my drift; rather, for a wife, perhaps, whom they wanted to disappear by, say, Thursday at three or three-thirty at the latest. My remedies, therefore, had to be swift, certain, and completely untraceable. *The practice of alternative medicine is not all fun and games; mostly it's just plain hard work. Of course, in reality much of it is just blind luck, though no one wants to hear that from their chosen health care provider. They want to believe that you're a god and can do no wrong.*

"We've got a schedule to keep here, Dr. Death," my client would say to me over the phone. "See what you can do for me, chop, chop. Bambi and I are planning to pick out our engagement rings on Friday but can't move forward on honeymoon plans until this little matter with Irene gets taken care of." The Hollywood producer cleared his throat but left no doubt as to what was to happen next. *Perhaps a chorus of "Goodnight, Irene" would be appropriate before she sets sail into another dimension.*

"I hear ya, friend, loud and clear," I responded. "Consider it done, and please give my best to Irene, while you still can."

Ours was the only clinic in town offering around-the-clock patient care, including a drive-up window for free refills. My thinking was light years ahead of the competition, and the best part, no prescriptions were needed.

"If we can't trust each other, what kind of relationship are we building?" I'd say to my customers. "And there's no need to make a special trip. You want someone to die, just see me first."

Frankly, I saw this career move as a better opportunity than the empty path my parents had chosen. Selling dime packets of pinto beans hadn't put our family into the inner circles of Tampa's beautiful people—far from it. The stores were an unimpressive collection of garden materials displayed on five aisles, with a warehouse containing peat moss, fertilizers, and garden sprayers. Our names only got mentioned in the daily paper if Dad was running late again on his property taxes. That never happened to Dr. Death, who made twice what he could spend, his social calendar spilling over in red ink. He was the toast of the town, a coup for any dinner party. Asked to chair several charity balls every season, Dr. Death was a snob's snob. He was seen with all the right debutantes, who gazed longingly into his deep blue eyes. He was everything I hoped to be and then some.

On most of those long summer afternoons, Dr. Death could be found mixing potions of questionable origin, with his imaginary lab assistant, Igor, who worked for him three days a week while studying for the pharmaceutical boards.

"Igor," I'd say to him, his stale breath beating hot against my neck, "go get me a vial of that most vile potion over in the corner, and hurry up." Igor would slowly shuffle off, saying, "Yes, master," over his left shoulder hump. "I love that guy," I thought.

My most famous concoction was a secret recipe, a house special called Strangler's Poison, served in a Dixie cup with a small slice of mint to cover the bitter aftertaste. My death certificates were preprinted with the words "Natural Causes" in the appropriate box, taking the guess work out of any inquest. To be a full service provider, I had to think of every detail.

"I wouldn't drink that, Cory," I said to my younger brother, putting a fresh cup of my handiwork down on the floor. I was in the process of filling an order for a new referral and didn't have the time to supervise his activities closely. But Cory never listened, mostly because he was only four.

"What am I going to do with you, little feller?" I said to him as he finished the cup, smacking his lips, and handing it back for a second helping.

"No, one's plenty for now. Maybe you can have seconds later, if it doesn't make you sick."

October 24, 1942

A small crop duster flew low over a cranberry bog north of town. The sound of the engine sputtering broke the stillness of early morning. A minute later it crossed back over the shoreline and into Whitfield's harbor. The plane moved higher and then banked slowly to the right towards downtown. Behind the plane was a large white banner that read "Back to the Bogs, 1942." Crowds along the parade route looked up and waved.

"Look, there's Kristin's dad," Mary said to Katie as they stood on the front steps of Kaman's. On the silver body of the side of the plane in dark red letters were the words "Kelso Crop Dusting Service." The street became a mass of waving arms and flags and horns. The fly-by was the opening event before the start of the parade celebrating the Cranberry Days Festival. Mary was wearing a new blue and white dress her mother had made for her, and she waved her small American flag furiously as if Mr. Kelso could actually pick her out of the crowd.

"Come on, let's go," Katie said grabbing Mary by the arm. "I want to see the start. Jenny Nelson's little sister is one of the berries."

Mary waved to Mr. Kelso, whose plane was now almost out of sight somewhere over St. Jerome's football field and said, "Okay, okay."

The two girls weaved through the crowd past Town Hall and up Center Street to the elementary school where the parade was about to begin. They heard the crack of a snare drum as the band began to play, and they tucked into a small opening by the school's driveway. Katie and Mary watched the parade go by and laughed together as girls who are sixteen will do. Then Mary left to go take pictures for the school yearbook. Katie looked down at the tiny watch her father had given her before he left for the war and saw she had a few minutes before she needed to meet Lucy. She was hungry and wandered over to the booths set up in front of the public library. She bought a powdered doughnut and soda and stopped to look at the arts and crafts exhibit. Her mother had entered a quilt, which Katie felt was very artistic and sure to win unless Mrs. Ellison's God Bless America quilt swayed some votes. She was having a wonderful day and most of it was yet to come. Now she had to find Lucy. The park was crowded with spectators and contestants milling about, but spotting her tall friend at the registration booth was easy. Katie rushed over and squeezed Lucy's sides.

"Hey, watch it!" Lucy said, turning around surprised by the gesture, but broke into a smile as she realized it was Katie. "Hey, I wasn't sure you'd make it. Where have you been?"

"Eating a doughnut," Katie said routinely.

"I can tell," Lucy said wiping the white powder crumbs off her friend's face.

"Hey, I was saving those for later," Katie joked.

"Come on. We need to sign up. The races start in ten minutes."

Behind the booth Katie noticed the sign: "Teenagers: try your luck with someone new. Enter the co-ed three-legged race and be paired with a mystery partner." At first Katie was disappointed because Lucy and she had talked about doing the girls' three-legged race together, and since Lucy was faster than a comic book superhero, there was no question they would win. Katie liked to win, but then she smiled to herself and said, "Lucy, let's do this. How many boys do we get to meet at St. Anne's Academy for Girls?"

"Are you kidding? What if I get somebody short?" Lucy questioned.

"You worry too much, and anyway I'll make sure they put you with a tall *number*, like eleven or even twenty-eight," Katie teased.

Part of her wanted to see who she'd get. There were a lot of cute boys from Catholic Prep, so after she thought for a second, she said, "Okay."

The two girls giggled about who they'd end up with before putting their names on the back of chips number five, Katie's favorite number, and number sixteen because Lucy had recently turned sixteen. Katie suggested that they walk by the bench where most of the boys were standing. One of the boys whistled. Lucy was sure that it was for Katie, but she didn't say anything. Another voice said, "I hope she's got my number."

"They don't look like the kind of girls who would choose zero, Clarence," another replied, and the other boys all laughed.

Katie smiled. Lucy turned to her and said, "Just for the record, if I get Clarence, you die."

The race director began speaking into the microphone, giving out general race instructions. "For the three-legged race this year we're adding a new twist. Each team will run to the end of the field and back blindfolded to make it extra difficult. When you get to the far end, volunteers will turn you both around. So without further ado I will ask all the high school boys who have signed up to stand in line and hold up their numbers. All right, girls, go find your partners. We'll give you each a couple of minutes to plan your strategy and then will get started."

"Well, Luce, here goes nothing," Katie said as the boys started forming a single line on the side of the field. As luck would have it, Kyle, number sixteen, was two inches taller than Lucy, and almost as shy. Number five was a slender quarterback with dark brown hair and blue eyes. Katie smiled as she walked up and thought to herself, "Gee, he's cute. Too bad we're going to be blindfolded." The boy's name was Josh.

•   •   •

Chapter 5
COLDEST MELONS IN TOWN

Summer, 1952

During the summer I turned ten, Dad and a friend of his, Wally Johnson, planned a deep-sea fishing trip to the Caribbean. Wally was a tall man with a lopsided mustache, on which he was forever chewing, and he smelled like an Italian recipe gone south. Mom said it was from all the garlic he ate.

Sometimes Wally came by the store at closing time and took Dad for a beer at the icehouse down the street. We loved how Dad smelled when he got home, an hour or so later, his mood smooth and mellow, his voice soft and reassuring. He scared me shitless growing up, but I mean that in a good way. I thought for several years that he was the voice of God in our Christmas pageant. That turned out to be Dr. Roark, the dentist, but that didn't change things for me. Dad was tough as nails, end of story. Sometimes after those trips, he'd take Cory and me over to the watermelon stand on the outskirts of town for a little one-on-one time with his boys.

"Coldest Melons in Town," the sign read. The melons soaked for hours in the deep wooden ice-filled tubs before being fished out with crab poles. On one visit when Dad stopped to talk with a neighbor, I told Cory to stick both hands into the tank while I counted very slowly to fifty. He was hopping on one foot before I hit twenty-three, blowing smoke out of his mouth before thirty, and I wondered if I had given Cory too hard a job. Once a challenge had been made, though, there was no going back, no quitting. Those were our rules, and we were bound by a code of honor to follow them for better or worse. So I held his tiny shaking arms down until he completed this task to my satisfaction.

He'd thank me later; that was for sure. Helping a younger brother build character was just one of the thankless jobs that filled up my days. We couldn't raise a quitter and bring shame to the family Dreeton.

Cory smiled as I slowly enunciated the numbers, "Forty-eight, forty-nine, and fifty. Okay, pull 'em out now. You're finished, little guy!"

I was happy for his success—our success, really. He couldn't have done it without my help. *But, I am entirely too modest to take any of the credit myself. Of the hundreds of gifts hanging from my tree of many talents, humility is the ornament I have chosen to place on top.*

Even now, Cory was hopping on one foot, looking as if he might wet his pants at any moment. Except I was reasonably certain his extremities, including that one I can't mention here, were flash frozen and thus completely shut down. So peeing was not an option.

"Good job, little buddy," I said, patting his head. Sometimes I assigned him tasks, back-to-back or even two at one time, but only if he could handle it; more importantly, only if my folks weren't looking. I thought he could relax now, his suffering done, until he held up blistered red digits for me to inspect. The blisters looked bad, and I decided we needed to find a hot car radiator to warm them on before Dad came back and saw what had happened. Otherwise Dr. Death might be forced to perform an emergency amputation with a melon knife before gangrene set in. I told Cory that we should get a free table while there was one. He was still shaking and turning kind of blue, and I told him not to mention our little "activity" when Dad got to the table. But my offenses hadn't escaped Dad's watchful eye.

"What did you do to him this time?" he asked sitting down on the other side of the wooden picnic table.

"Nothing much—and anyway he went along with it!" I offered as my alternate defense.

"Listen, Peter, I've told you this before: That imagination of yours is going to get you into real trouble some day; you hear me?"

I nodded just as the waiter came to take our order. The waiters wore starched white shirts and black bow ties, while carrying pieces of juicy red goodness on large steel trays. I have wondered over the years why they were so dressed up. All the customers came in dirty shorts and fish-stained sneakers right from the beach or the fishing pier nearby. All I can say is the world was a much more formal place when I was small and the melons much colder. We sat on wooden benches, trying to spit seeds through small slats on to the ground. Sometimes, one of us would spot a bug crossing below and would yell to the others, "Attack." And then we'd fill our jaws with bullets of Black Death and commence firing, on the count of three... two... one. . .

Dad talked business, because that was all he was comfortable with, and we listened intently without having the foggiest idea what he was saying. There were times growing up when I wasn't sure if Dad actually knew our names, or any details about our lives for that matter; he was so preoccupied with his business.

He often referred to me as "the booger" and Cory as "the little booger." With those names he could have been talking about any kid in our neighborhood. I never called him out on it, because he was buying, and he was our father, which in our minds made him the biggest booger of them all. *Let's face it: there are two things children never want to hear a parent say to them: the first is, "I can't remember your name," because that will make them sad forever; and the other is where babies come from, because that will make them wise forever. "You and Mom did what? How did it happen? How many times? Why? Where was I? Was seed spitting involved?"*

The stand stayed open all summer. We went ten or twelve times every summer, and Dad always made a point to take us on the last day of the season, Labor Day. Then one summer they didn't reopen. There was no sign or warning; they just never came back. I wondered if that was legal; for sure it wasn't fair. For several weeks I kept expecting them to reopen, hopeful of cold slices and good conversations still to come. Our psyche demanded it; our tummies craved it. But the lot sat empty; the brown tables stacked end to end behind the chain link fence. From that point on, our lives changed in ways I couldn't realize and didn't want to. "Dr. Death" closed the apothecary shop soon afterwards; Igor had already accepted a job with a pharmaceutical company in Oregon, and I didn't feel like training a new assistant. I asked fewer small favors of Cory and spent more time with friends. We lived in a world of fewer chilled melons, and it was not as good a place.

We didn't own a TV back then. Dad thought television was some kind of a fad. So our trips to watermelon land were some of the only entertainment we had growing up. Looking back now, though, I have to say it was all we needed. It is my single best memory from childhood. The watermelon was good, but that wasn't it. It was the time we had together. Seeing Dad smile, listening to him drone on to some far off place only one freeway exit down from endless, about things we couldn't understand and didn't want to. What did it matter? What does anything matter, as long as we were together? We had it all. He was talking, and we weren't to blame. Our lives were filled with a never-ending series of grunts and groans, and we wouldn't have wanted it any other way.

Of course, there was also the afternoon at the kindergarten lunch when Kimberly Lambert dropped her white underpants to the floor, and invited all the boys at the table to go under for a "look-see." And frankly that was fun as well, but I am sticking with the watermelons, so cold they made your teeth chatter.

Our seed business slowed during the heat. Even the bugs who served us well most of the year, couldn't find enough energy to chew on things. So off Dad and Wally went for days in the sun out on calm waters, and when they got back, red and roasted, they smelled of sea salt, suntan oil, and fish, which at least for Wally was a new aroma.

October 29, 1942

Lucy Grennan was the first one to arrive at Sister Margaret's office. She could see the nun on the phone, so she waited by the doorway before entering.

Sister Margaret looked up and motioned for Lucy to come in. Lucy put her books beside the chair and fixed her barrette, pulling thin blond hair off her face.Sister Margaret pulled the receiver back and smiled. "Nice to see you, Lucy. I'll just be another minute."

Lucy nodded. At lunchtime Mrs. Washburn had asked Lucy and four of her friends to report to Sister Margaret's office at the end of the day. Lucy hated being the first one here, but her history class was just down the hall. She tried calculating who would be next. She knew for certain Kerrie would be last. She noticed a piece of dried tomato from lunch on the blue section of her plaid school uniform and used her nail to clean it off.

"Hello, Mr. Pavito. Sister Margaret here, calling to confirm our start in a few weeks." There was a short pause. "That's great. This is such a wonderful donation. I'll call at the end of the week about specifics. And please give my love to Mrs. Pavito and the boys for me," she concluded and hung up.

Lucy couldn't take the pressure any longer. "We're in trouble, aren't we? This is about Mr. Dowling's math class?"

"No...at least I don't think so. What happened there?" Sister Margaret asked. Lucy realized she had created her own problem. Mary and Katie were always getting on her about that. She'd confess to a bank robbery if it would get an icy stare off her face.

"Oh, nothing, Sister, just wondering," Lucy smiled, turning her eyes down to her hands, hoping the nun would drop it.

"I see. Well, no, this is not about math class, but I hope you girls are working hard. Mr. Dowling's a very fine teacher."

"Of course, Sister Margaret, I have a ninety-three average, so far."

"Excellent, Lucy. It's important to do well in math."

Katie Welch and Mary Sealy arrived in time to overhear the last part of the conversation.

"What about math, Lucy?" Mary asked, giving Lucy a death stare as they came in the office.

Lucy knew they'd be upset and tried to cover it.

"Oh, nothing. I was just saying how much we all like Mr. Dowling's class, that's all."

Mary looked at her strangely. Sister Margaret picked up on the glance but let it go. She hadn't called them in about some minor incident involving numbers. She had bigger plans to discuss.

"Please, come in, girls. We're just waiting for the other two ladies."

"Well, Penny should be here in a second. I saw her in the hall, but no telling about Kerrie. Tomorrow, if we're lucky," Katie said.

"Very lucky," Mary added. "In fact, I think Sister Margaret would have to use up one of those." Mary pointed to Sister Margaret's glass jar on her desk with "miracles" written on the front and a selection of hard candy inside.

Penny Caulkins came in just then and sat on the sofa behind them.

"Sorry, I'm late. I had to come from the stables."

"Not a problem," the nun said. "We're still waiting on Kerrie."

"You know Kerrie. She likes to make a grand entrance," Mary whispered to Katie.

The four girls sat squirming in their seats wondering why they had been summoned to the headmistress's office.

.   .   .

Chapter 6

NO MORE MONKEYS
JUMPING ON THE BED

Christmas, 1953 - Summer, 1954

One Christmas our parents surprised us with a set of bunk beds. Cory and I shared a room because Dad needed the third bedroom for an office. Before the bunk beds arrived, we slept on two dark metal army cots Dad had picked up at a garage sale. They had been used, the owner told him, for interrogating captured prisoners during the Spanish American War.

"How great is this, boys?" Dad said. "It's like sleeping on a piece of history," as if that was supposed to make us feel better.

"Maybe so, but next time we want to sleep on the winning side, Pops," I replied. My cot had the name Rodrigo scratched into one of the side rails and below it the numbers 5518. I spent a great deal of time trying to figure out what it meant, but never got anywhere. The springs were wound so tightly they could repel the advances of Dad's bowling ball dropped from our roof, and we had the test results to prove it. Some nights I hunted for hours in the dark trying to find any soft spot and once in place wouldn't move until morning, unless I had to pee. Neither one of us was sorry to see them go, except for the fact that it ended forever our days of playing "no more monkeys jumping on the bed." The game had given us hours of good fun but drove Dad crazy and was probably the reason we got new beds.

Since I was older, they let me choose first, and naturally I went with "the more spacious upper berth." Cory, of course, threw a fit. Mom explained they were exactly the same size; later, when he asked me if Mom was just saying that to make him feel better, I said, "What do you think?"

The set was delivered three days before Christmas. It was my favorite gift. I found countless new ways to inflict pain to my lower bunkmate. Among these were: Peter's slow water drip; the midnight chocolate malt ball attack; and the evil death stick, which doubled as the hall closet broom.

We were home the afternoon Mr. Parker and his helper arrived to set it up. He asked Mom where she wanted it, and I said, "Upstairs, please." He looked at me funny since we lived in a small one-story ranch in the part of Tampa where the only second stories were rundown apartment buildings. But the idea of verbalizing my unfulfilled dreams felt satisfying even then. "The big bedroom at the far end overlooking the water. When you're finished, Mr. Parker, please come join us for a tray of hot hors d'oeuvres by the pool."

Mother dismissed my comments with a shake of her head and held the door as they moved the frame down the narrow hall.

My whole perspective changed the first time I climbed up to the top bunk. It felt like rearranging the furniture, only better. Discovering my newfound ability to leave dirty footprints on the ceiling was just a bonus perk. By proper positioning, I could get off twelve or even fifteen steps before hitting the wall behind my head. Cory asked, "Whatcha doing?" and I made up some lame story to entertain him. We'd set off on a dark adventure of searching for a mandarin orange containing the crown jewels of Butshia. Cory asked me where exactly Butshia was located. I explained it was near the Ivory Coast, and when he asked where that was, I said, "Stop asking so many questions. We're merchant traders, not junior high geography teachers, for God's sake."

Other times the story involved mountain lions chasing me along a narrow rock ledge, carrying a beautiful girl in my arms. Sometimes we made it across the crevasse safely;

sometimes, to keep the story fresh, my foot would slip on a loose rock near the waterfall, and I would hurl my body down to his bunk below. After regaining his breath, Cory asked what happened to the girl, and I would say, "Oh, no. I think she's still up on the cliff; shall I go back and check?" Groaning loudly, I ascended the side of the cliff.

From my new perch I had a bird's eye view into Mr. Prescott's backyard. A widower with two grown children, he seemed a shadowy figure. We rarely ever saw him to speak to. A large vegetable garden occupied half his backyard, and he spent hours applying various chemicals to keep the hapless bugs at bay. He moved between the rows with a long-handled applicator, setting off billowing clouds of smoke and leaving a white powder coating the plant. I wondered who needed that many tomatoes or that much okra in the first place. Was he shipping them off somewhere or supplying an underground army about to take over the neighborhood? It seemed a plausible scenario, but I wasn't sure exactly who to trust with my discovery. About two or three times that summer he gave my father a big bag of green beans for us to enjoy, but I never dared eat any for fear his chemicals might cause damage to my brain. Shortly after we got our second installment of green beans, the explosion occurred.

An oil refinery across town blew up, and of course, my first thought was Mr. Prescott's army had fired the first shot. I was spending the night with my friend Mickey when the sky lit up, first red and then yellow. We were upstairs in his parents' bedroom watching *I Love Lucy*. Seconds went by, and we sat unsure of what had actually happened or why. We heard heavy steps on the back stairwell, and Mr. Miller appeared in the bedroom door. The room filled with an eerie stillness. He stood with his sweat-stained shirt pulled halfway out of his pants. We waited breathlessly for instructions.

"Put your shoes on, boys. The McDermott plant just blew," and before we had a chance to ask questions, he headed down the hall to Mickey's sister's room to tell Becky the same thing.

It was the fifties, and instead of people running from a disaster, they ran to embrace it, to be part of the experience. We all piled into the back of his dark blue Dodge and flew like fireflies into the light, after making a quick pit stop at the 7-Eleven to buy four cold cans of beer and a fresh pack of smokes. The usually stingy Mr. Miller told us we could get whatever we wanted, but just to be quick about it. We loaded up on a selection of chocolate bars and large sodas. After all, we had a long night ahead of us; who knew what might happen next. It was the fourth of July, just a month late. We sat on one of the side roads leading into the refinery, watching fire trucks from all over the city rush by and ambulances heading back in the other direction, their pitiful wails filling our ears with grief and sorrow. *It is sad, really, how one man's suffering becomes another's entertainment.*

Mrs. Miller worked as a nurse at County General, and she was on duty the night of the accident. Mickey's dad talked about how busy she'd be, and how badly burned some of the men must be, and how some of them wouldn't make it. We listened and watched as periods of quiet were broken with wild activity. About a half an hour in, the second explosion occurred. It was not as big as the first one, but it was still powerful and rocked the car as if it were a toy. We buried our heads into the plastic mesh seat coverings, and when we looked back up, a second smokestack was engulfed in flames.

We were willing to stay all night; in fact, we hoped for such an outcome, but Becky said she had to pee, and the mosquitoes began feasting on bare arms and legs. We went back to Mickey's house and watched the coverage on the local news.

Nothing much ever happened when I was growing up, so being this close to a major news story seemed strange and wonderful and sad. I waited for days for Walter Cronkite to fly down from New York to interview the four of us, as first-hand observers.

"You had three tall ones, Mr. Miller, or was it four?" Mr. Cronkite would ask in his authoritative voice to his national audience.

"Yes, that's right, Walter. It was four, actually, and half a pack of smokes," and the three of us would be there to back up his story. That was the summer between sixth and seventh grades. I spent much of the rest of my vacation biking past my junior high hoping it would meet the same fiery end so that I wouldn't have to face teasing from the older boys in the school shower. I even left a copy of our school's media guide on Mr. Prescott's front lawn, hoping if he had been responsible for the refinery accident that he would consider the school a worthwhile target.

October 29, 1942

The four girls continued to wait uncomfortably in Sister Margaret's office for their tardy friend. Finally Kerrie Mason, a petite redhead, showed up. Genuinely surprised at being last, she said, "Oh, everyone's here already." She took the last chair next to the window. It wasn't as if she was that late, not really. Kerrie looked out the window to the athletic field and the grove of trees beyond and remembered another time when being behind schedule had definitely been a good thing.

In the summer of 1938 Kerrie was running late to work at her father's bakery. As she biked down Milford, Kerrie thought she heard the faint sound of banging. She turned her head and saw two men replacing the clapboard siding of a house on the far side of the street. Momentarily she thought that was the source of the noise. Then something made her think again. The banging hadn't come from that side of the street, and the carpenters' noise had mostly been nails driven with a hammer. The sound she had heard was softer. She passed a green one-story brick with a big wide front porch and a pitched roof. There didn't seem to be anything going on there so she rode on to a small yellow cottage. There was a black Ford in the driveway and through the large kitchen window a woman was making breakfast. *Oh, well,* she thought, *I must have been hearing things,* and she turned around to leave when she faintly heard the sound again. It was coming from the green house. She biked up its driveway and got off her bike. Kerrie knew stopping would make her even later to the bakery, but she felt she had to check things out first. She got a faint whiff of something as she walked up the front porch. There was no sound coming from inside until she rang the bell, and then the banging started again. No one came to the door. She waited another minute, before walking around the side of the house. The banging grew louder. When she reached the frosted glass bathroom window, she heard a voice saying, "Please, help me, please."

Kerrie grabbed a baseball bat laying nearby in the neighbor's yard and broke the bedroom window with it. Once inside the smell of gas was everywhere. She covered her mouth and turned the handle to the bathroom door, but it wouldn't open. She lifted the bat over her head and like a club swung it down hard. The handle cracked but didn't break. She swung again, and this time the knob fell to the floor. Kerrie kicked the door open and found Mrs. Walcott, a woman her grandmother's age, lying on the tile floor. The woman tried to get up but couldn't stand. Kerrie helped her up and outside through the kitchen door.

The next day her picture with Mrs. Walcott appeared on the front page of the newspaper. The headline read "Twelve-year-old Saves Retired Teacher's Life." Kerrie framed the article and hung it in her bedroom.

"Kerrie, welcome to our meeting," Sister Margaret said, bringing Kerrie back to the present.

"If this is about math class on Tuesday, I wasn't there. I didn't even get to school that day until third period," Kerrie volunteered.

`"Ladies, I want you all to help Mr. Dowling. He's new this year and feeling a little overwhelmed at the moment. Can I count on you?"

All five girls nodded.

"Good," she said. "Now that we have that settled, let's get down to business."

. . .

Chapter 7
TROUBLE ON THE RANGE

Summer, 1955

We never traveled much as a family, which was both good and bad. But during the spring of seventh grade, Dad started making plans to drive us out west to see "God's country," as he liked to call it. Cory took him literally and asked Mom if that was where God spent summers trying to escape Tampa's oppressive heat. Mom said, "Not exactly."

"Geez, Cory, it's an expression," I said, shaking my head, and later asked if Cory had been adopted.

She said, "Not exactly."

Dad stopped by AAA one night after work, bringing home a handful of maps and brochures about places to visit and things to see. We spent several nights sitting at the kitchen table strategizing the best routes to take from Dallas to El Paso, and about how many nights to spend in Arizona. It was fun I guess, but I wasn't sure we'd ever pull it off. Up until that summer even a family outing to the water tower seemed worthy of a diary entry. Now Dad was talking about heading to places about which I'd only dreamed.

Much to my surprise, when the summer heat hit, off we went. We had as much fun as four people, trapped in a loaded down Plymouth station wagon with only modest air conditioning skills, can have. And remember, whatever amount of fun you come up with, divide that number by four. As Miss Atkins, my math teacher reminded us, "If you only work part of the problem, boys and girls, you'll end up with only part of the solution." *Her words, not mine; half an answer seemed like all we needed.*

I looked out the window at the flat stretches of open road and blue empty sky, filled with complete nothingness for as far as the eye could see, other than occasional billboard invitations to buy Burma Shave. Looking back at the interior of the car, I also saw the vast stretches of complete nothingness and announced, "It's the same everywhere, isn't it? Nothing ever changes around this place."

Mom, not understanding the context in which I meant this, said, "Yes, dear, you're certainly right about that."

Mom was busy making a needlepoint winter snow scene, as a Christmas present for her mother. As the towns and miles rolled over, and heat swelled up from the highway, desolate and never-ending, leaving us in a semi-daze, we watched her village snow scene take shape before our eyes. The big spruce tree came alive, fresh on the hill. The tiny boy and girl figures, which she named Jessie and Tom, were sledding down a background of white yarn. I wondered if it was entirely healthy for Mom to establish such a strong familial bond with a piece of yellow yarn named Tom and a red one named Jessie. But as long as they kept her busy and out of my hair, it was all that mattered. On more than one occasion Mom and Dad joked about how refreshing her snow looked and how they wanted to jump inside the scene to cool off.

Dad only spoke to us when we called his name, or if we mentioned not going to the bathroom during the last pit stop as he had instructed us to do. Instead we chose to spend our time out of the car stretching our legs and contemplating the proper candy selection. "Plain or nuts?" Cory asked at the counter, and I said, "Always go with the nuts." And he did.

"I can't hold it, Dad," one of us would say meekly a few miles down the road to nowhere and the other would immediately chime in, "Yeah, me too, Dad. I got to go real bad."

"I don't care, boys. Pee in your pants. We'll be in Fort Stockton in four hours, maybe less."

We moaned, and Mom got mad at him. Finally, he pulled the car off the road but only after several more miles, choosing to make us sweat until the last possible moment. He timed his exit seconds before our bladders were set to explode. We rushed into the brush or behind a broken tractor, as if someone had set the backs of our pants on fire.

Occasionally—heaven forbid—he would start off on one of his lectures on responsibility. Of course, it all made sense now: That's why he brought us along. He couldn't have cared less about seeing the "Grand Fucking Canyon," as he often referred to it. Dad had fourteen days of nonstop lectures planned, in order to turn our still forming minds into worthless mush. Cory and I should have read the fine print before signing on to this road trip to the outer banks of sanity.

Usually his lectures started late morning, caused from too much acid in the coffee he drank endlessly from his old yellow thermos. Once he started, we were pretty much in for it until lunch break. Our collective hope was that he would opt for a sugary dessert and blow off the afternoon session. Or maybe he'd fall asleep, and we'd become an oil spill on the road to nowhere.

One particularly painful lecture dealt with family chores. From Flagstaff to Phoenix, Dad never came up for air.

About half an hour in, I was laying my cheek against the warm windowpane, trying to see how flat I could squish the skin—important scientific research, which could bring fame and fortune to our family, two things sorely missing from the Dreeton chronicles. I would no longer be just another pretty face; now I'd be a pretty face with cheek skin covering my nose. Was this possible? Many had tried, but always, their nasal passages remained exposed. *But that's what testing the bounds of science is really about.* My mind was considering the possibility of winning the Nobel Prize for Science, when Dad's voice said, "You boys better be listening."

Mostly we stayed at relatively nice motor courts, where we always found clean, comfortable rooms at affordable prices, but sometimes we ventured into what could best be called

Bates Motel territory, like the Teepee Inn in Tempe. *Do you think I am making this up? I only wish I were that good.*

Cory and I were in teepee number five, which just happened to be my favorite teepee number, and our parents stayed in teepee number six, which just happened to be my least favorite teepee number. Each was a concrete freestanding unit, painted in Indian colors with feathers hanging over the door. The rooms were small and had pointy ceilings. If you were tall, like Dad, you had to bend your head to one side or risk knocking the crap out of it, which he did while bringing bags in from the car.

We had planned on eating at the Campfire Grill next to the office because Mom had read to us about it in a guidebook, "*Arizona, My Way!*"

But when we walked over from the lodge, we found the Tempe Health Department had beaten us to the punch. Or, to put it correctly, they had removed the punch bowl altogether.

"Health code violations: 113 B, 124, and parts of 129 and 31." The sticker on the door warned of a whole string of broken promises. The Campfire Grill, suffering from a bacterial overload, would no longer be featuring their fresh salmonella buffet bar. The write-up in the guide book said: "Weary travelers must stop at the Campfire Grill for a once in a lifetime dining experience. Come hungry and bring a bag." Did they mean doggie or barf? The article didn't specify, and now we'd never know for sure.

Cory said he was glad it was closed, because he didn't like Japanese food, and Mom explained that salmonella was a state of being, not a cuisine choice. And later when Mom asked me if Cory had been adopted, I told her, "It certainly looks like it." So instead we went off reservation to a hamburger stand in town. We each got bags of grease with ketchup and ate back in our rooms.

After dinner, I talked Cory into a little test. On the ceiling of our room was painted a blazing yellow sunburst; I stood on the bed and put Cory on my shoulders to see if he could touch the top of the teepee.

"Cory, let's see if that sun is really as hot as it looks from here, want to?" He was panting before the words got out of my mouth. I made him put two pairs of white socks on his hands for safety reasons, just in case I was right.

"Just a couple of more inches, stretch!" The tips of the white socks brushed the edges of the fiery red flames, but that was as close as we got. His unwashed feet wiggled in front of my eyes. I swatted them aside to see what I was doing, but lost my balance, and we came crashing down on top of the other bed, almost breaking the frame in half. Dad heard us all the way from teepee number six.

"What's all this commotion?" he asked as he barged into our teepee. "Behave yourselves or Mom will come in here with Cory, and Peter, you'll have to go sleep with me in teepee number six."

"Yes, sir," we responded. Just the thought of that unhappy alternative put an abrupt end to our space exploration.

We stayed up late watching the only movie on the TV, with commercials every five minutes. The movie was sponsored by a local car dealer who claimed to have severe brain damage. Big Bob's Cars and More interrupted to show the features on a 1948 DeSoto with a leaky transmission. That planted an idea in Cory's head. He said we should trade in our heap and get ourselves a new one cheap.

"With deals this good, you'd be crazy not to," he said, repeating Bob's line from the commercial. I explained that Big Bob didn't really have brain damage and would most certainly get the better of us in any financial transaction, no matter what his disabilities might be. Outsmarting people was not a feat for which our family was known, but Cory seemed unconvinced.

One good thing about staying at the Teepee Inn and Guest Suites was the picture we took the next morning. Out near the parking lot they had one of those large painted tableau boards with holes to stick your faces through, and bingo, you were a frigging Sioux or some such tribe. Of course, we made Dad, with his day old beard, stand in the hole for the squaw with pigtails, just to be funny, because in our family, funny was never more than a car length behind and closing fast.

Mom loved the picture, though Cory pointed out that if you looked closely you could tell those weren't really our outfits after all. My response was, "No shit, Cory, you can? Aren't you perceptive?"

But I tried to go easy on him now that I knew he had been adopted.

October 29, 1942

Looking at the five girls sitting across from her, Sister Margaret continued, "We have a lot to go over. I want to talk to you about an important matter . . . concerning cranberries." The girls all looked at each other questioningly. Sister Margaret elaborated, "I've had an idea for a while, and this past weekend at the Cranberry Days Festival I was able to work out some of the details. We are going to package and sell dried cranberries to raise money for families of soldiers lost in the war. It's a project we'll call the Cape Cod Reds. I hope you five juniors will accept the challenge to be in charge."

Sister Margaret was asking a lot of these girls, who already had busy schedules. Katie was president of the junior class; Mary, yearbook photographer; Penny, a member of honor council; Lucy, a star athlete; and Kerrie, a leader in the theatre group. To make this plan work, Sister Margaret needed girls with energy to get the other students involved, and she needed juniors who would be with her for two years.

She hoped the war would be over by then and their work complete.

"It's wonderful. I'd love to be involved in it," Katie said.

"I bet my father could help out with some of the expenses to get us started," Penny volunteered.

"Like what, buying a building, Penny?" Mary replied.

"Gee, Mary, what's that about? I didn't mean it in some bad way," Penny responded, hurt by the comment.

"No, of course you didn't, dear," Sister Margaret responded. "We would all appreciate his help. Mary, I think you owe Penny an apology."

"Sorry, Penny, I didn't mean it that way," Mary said.

"Thanks, Mary. It's no big deal. Let's move on." Penny understood that Mary had a chip on her shoulder about Penny's family having money. This wasn't the first run-in they'd had, and she was sure it wouldn't be the last. Penny realized that it wasn't easy to be struggling to make ends meet during the war, and she always tried to be sympathetic without sounding condescending.

"Since we will be running shifts, maybe we should divide the students into teams to make it more competitive. We could give them each a name," Katie said, hoping to turn the conversation back to a positive.

They all agreed and, after considering a series of choices, settled on Cods, Starfish, Clams, Lobsters, and Whales. Then they drew the names out of a bowl to see who got to be in charge of what team. Mary, who struggled with her weight, drew the Whales and unhappily complained, "Gosh, Sister Margaret, do I have to be a Whale?"

Lucy, who was thin, jumped in, "I'd like to be a Whale. Would you be a Lobster for me, Mary?"

"Okay. Thanks, Luce," Mary gratefully replied.

Sister Margaret refilled the bowl, this time with slips of paper, each containing the name of a St. Anne's high school student. The girls spent the next few minutes selecting their team members, while Sister Margaret recorded the names.

"This project is going to take time out from your classes, but I'll talk with your teachers. Some things are more important than math. Even I can see that," Sister Margaret said.

All the girls looked at each other and smiled. Any time they could get out of class was a good deal.

•   •   •

Chapter 8
WHY YOUR FEET SWELL UNDERGROUND

Summer, 1955

Sometimes it's good to let yourself go. And the Dreetons did. Most of the places where we stayed on our trip had swimming pools, and after a long day of lectures, a cool splash in the water felt great. Usually Cory and I stayed in too long, turning our feet into long white prunes. Mom and Dad sat by the edge of the pool in yellow plastic chairs. Dad read the evening paper from whatever little town we were in, while Mom worked on her needlepoint. It seemed in that moment, we would forever be lost in the warm evening twilight of time, that we would never grow any older, or even get out of the pool, with the big wide sky opening above our heads and the small golden mass of sun folding behind the mountains. Sometimes while we were in the water, Dad continued his sermons. We'd come up for air from our penny diving, and he would ask if we were listening. We'd turn green goggled faces towards him giving a friendly wave that meant, "Oh, hell, yes, Dad, all ears. Can't you tell?" The side straps of our masks pushed our earlobes forward, making us appear to be the newest arrivals from Chlorine, a mysterious dark planet at the edge of our solar system.

"You'll see a whole new me when we get home, Dad. Just you wait," I said before diving down into the cooling blue waters searching for another round of buried treasure. I wondered how much loot we'd have to find to strike out on our own, two brothers in search of their fortune. Could we make enough someday to get married, to buy homes and raise families from our winnings? Our business plan seemed simple enough:

quality cleaning service to homeowners throughout the western states and Canada...Peter and Cory's Pool Service. Our slogan: "We remove your unwanted copper debris fast! Call for a free estimate." Then we'd nail them with our catchy finish, "We work for pennies!" and hope they wouldn't bother reading the fine print: "Ten penny minimum."

Some mornings we got to sleep late, but generally we were up at the crack of dawn and on the road to some pothole miles away. One thing I never figured out was why it was so urgent for us to be in Cow Springs by lunchtime. Was our hometown paper awarding cash prizes to the family who got to the most "somewheres" during the summer of '55? Would the winning picture appear in the *Tampa Evening Sun*?

"Congratulations: the Dreeton family, pictured above, got to more worthless places than anyone else!" I could see it now with the number eighty-four written in bold type next to our photo. We'd be standing in the background smiling at the camera with large dark raccoon rings under our eyes, and empty packets of NoDoz stuffed in our shirt pockets.

Mom read the maps as we flew by what might have been an interesting stopping point that we'd all enjoy as a family, but we'd never know. From the back seat one of us would holler, "We really, really, really want to see the Natural Stone Caverns." What we really wanted was to spend our hard earned money on miniature ceramic renderings of the cave filled with fun facts printed on the back for us to ponder, like the number of visitors entering the cave each year, and the number who left, or why your feet swell underground, which I believe has something to do with air pressure. *After all, learning first-hand the mystique of tourist trap gift shopping is a rite of passage.*

"Not this time, kiddoes, can't stop now. We need to push on. We'll see it next time, when we're back out this way," Mom responded, looking as if she'd been hit several times over the head with a large metal bat. This seemed especially true when she was routinely engaging her two yarn spots in lengthy conversations.

Sometimes we listened to a radio broadcast of a minor league ballgame from some small town we were passing through. We all loved baseball, and we would hear part of it and become involved, wanting to know if the Bisons could push home the winning run from second base. Mom would tell Jessie and Tom to "shush" until the inning was over, and then we went back up in the mountains, and it would go fuzzy, and on and off again until finally it was lost altogether.

In the backseat I spent hours looking through boxes of my prized comic books until one day we stopped for lunch, and all hell broke loose just after crossing the Utah border. The roads were windy and steep, the meal in Cory's stomach uncertain, and as we started descending a sharp slope, he blew beets—actually, bits of hot dog—over a box of my favorite comic book heroes. Superman was now soaking in my brother's upchuck. My life was ruined. My secret plan of selling my collection, moving to Arizona, and changing my first name to Carlos, was now down the drain. *Adios, mi familia.*

My heroes were covered in an unappetizing brown glaze, and they looked to me for redemption. I socked Cory twice in the arm, once *por mi hermano,* Carlos, and once more for me. Cory started crying, and I knew I was in for it.

Dad jumped on me, Mom joined in, and then Cory. Nothing was fair about this fight. Nothing. A few weeks earlier at Tommy Smith's birthday party in the Tampa Coliseum we watched El Diablo get the stuffing beaten out of him by not only Uncle Tio, but Tio's business manager, Gloria Alvarez, as well. The crowd loved it, but El Diablo took it hard. This felt like the same kind of mismatch. My prized possessions apparently meant nothing to them at all.

Later that night I apologized to Cory, and we moved my box of superheroes into the trunk to dry out.

One night we went to the Thunderbird Drive-In, located in one of the western states. With the screen huge and rising above us against the blackened sky and charcoal mountains, John Wayne stood twenty feet tall. It seemed as if he might at any second ride right off it and over us. Frankly, I feared a stampede would crush our station wagon. The car was hot and smelled of too many days on the road. Plus I wasn't entirely sure that we had recovered all of Cory's unfortunate accident, and I began looking between the seats for doggy bits. Before the movie ended, a big electrical storm lit up the sky in short angry bursts. The lightning cracked behind the screen, up in the mountains, and then worked its way down to us, but what precipitation we got was mostly hail. The temperature dropped sharply in a matter of seconds. We scrambled to get all of our windows up, giving us the chance to enjoy our family bouquet together. Then we watched breathlessly as John headed for the last showdown with wet ammunition.

We made it as far north as South Dakota and held my birthday at the foothills of the presidents. Mom said that I could tell everyone back home I had four presidents to my birthday party. *That should go well.*

"Will you come visit me in the hospital when the big boys beat the crap out of me for being a pantywaist?" I asked, wondering if she had been left out too long in her snow scene without protective gear. *It made me realize this spot of yarn had become the daughter Mom never had. It was sad really.* She and Dad chuckled over her joke as we stood staring at our stoned-faced birthday guests. Dad asked if I could name the presidents up on the mountain. But I said, "Not really. Curly and Moe are the only two I know for sure."

After our birthday party with the stars, we turned east and came back across the northern states, and then dropped down to come home. Cory said he wanted to go through Kansas and see the capital, but Dad said he was in a hurry, and there was nothing special about Kansas, except for lots of wheat.

Once home, we spent the rest of the summer messing around, trying desperately to find trouble. My friends and I hung out at the ball fields, went to the beach, and chased girls at the drive-in. We waited for days for the movies to change. Life came unhurried and yet unconcerned about our needs. Days spilled out in front of us, unused and unremarkable and then forgotten. All I had to show for that summer was a picture of a plump squaw named Father.

While we were on our trip, it seemed as if the tedium would never end, and then something funny happened. That fall when we were back in school, I came home one afternoon and said to Mom, "You know, I miss the time we had together in the car."

"I know, Peter; so do I."

"Dad looked funny as the squaw, didn't he?"

"Yes, dear, he did," she replied.

October 29, 1942

"All right, ladies, let's go inspect our workspace for the Reds," Sister Margaret said. The nun stood up and motioned to the girls to follow her. On their way out of the office, they saw Mr. Walters, the custodian, painting trim in the reception area. "Please join us, Mr. Walters, on our tour of the barn," Sister Margaret invited.

The campus, originally a summer estate for a family from Connecticut, had been left to the local Catholic diocese in the early part of the century. The school had opened in 1915. There were a couple of athletic fields, a stable with four horses, three small classroom buildings—one with the administrative offices—a cafeteria, and a gymnasium.

On their way to the barn, Sister Margaret and Mr. Walters discussed what needed to be done.

The girls walked by themselves, a little behind the two adults. "Explain how math class came up in the first place, Lucy," Mary demanded, nudging Lucy in the back. "Did she make you recite the times tables or ask when a speeding train heading from New York to Chicago would stop serving dinner?"

"I can't say, Mary, but we got out of it, so what's the big deal?" Lucy protested.

"Luce is right this time, Mary. But it was a close call, and the next time you give out sensitive information without our permission there will be consequences. That goes for you, too, Kerrie," Katie warned.

"Are you talking a tickle session, Katie?" Mary asked.

"Exactly: bare feet, two feathers. We can't have people going south on us," Katie answered. "Remember our pact from our camping trip with Penny's parents. We are the five fireflies forever."

The summer the girls were ten Penny's parents took them to Bird Island for an overnight camping trip. On the sail over, the girls' romantic notions were in full swing, and they imagined they were traveling as far away as Zanzibar. When they arrived in late afternoon, they excitedly set up two tents, the large green one for the girls and a smaller blue one for Mr. and Mrs. Caulkins. They picked a spot facing the lighthouse and high enough on the bluff to catch the breeze. Penny and her dad gathered firewood while the other girls began pulling out the dinner provisions of hot dogs, buns, and homemade baked beans. They ate their main course and sang songs and laughed. Eventually the light faded enough to reveal a starlit, cloudless sky. Fireflies joined them for slices of cold watermelon. Mrs. Caulkins gave each girl a jar with holes already punched in the lid, and they set out to capture as many lightening bugs as they could. The girls fanned out in all direction. By the time Mrs. Caulkins called them all back, their five jars were glowing. Mr. Caulkins declared Mary the winner with the most fireflies.

Mary frowned, "I really don't like sealing up these beautiful bugs in a jar."

"Mary is right. Let's let them go," Penny agreed.

"I know," Katie said. "Let's have a freeing ceremony."

"Yes!" the others all exclaimed together.

The girls took their jars to the bluff. As she unscrewed the lid to her jar, Katie began, "Dear fireflies, we love how you light the world." She raised her open jar to the sky, letting her prisoners go free.

All the rest of the girls followed, lifting their jars up above their heads.

"Tonight, on this place, we are the five fireflies forever," Kerrie stated with flair. The girls stood there, watching the fireflies escape from their jars.

"Boy, Kerrie, what is this weird 'five fireflies forever' business, anyway?" Mary questioned.

"Oh, I just thought it sounded good."

"It did sound good, but it was more than that. The five of us have been best friends since kindergarten. It can be sort of a club name. Let's call ourselves the five fireflies," Katie announced.

The girls clicked their empty jars together, like a toast, and declared in unison, "The five fireflies forever!"

From in front of the barn, Sister Margaret waved to the girls. "Let's get a move on, ladies. There's a lot to see, and we don't want to tie up Mr. Walters's valuable time or ours."

"Come on, fireflies. Duty calls," Kerrie said as she began skipping towards the barn. The rest skipped close behind her.

· · ·

Chapter 9
LET THEM EAT DIRT

Summer, 1958

Until I was fourteen or so, my dad's business struggled. You couldn't say we were dirt poor, but times were tight, and we were known in the neighborhood as "dirt baggers." Dad began buying truckloads of topsoil from Green's Dirt Yard at seven dollars a yard, and we bagged the fertile mixture in plastic bags labeled "Florida's Finest." Finally our family had discovered the American dream: turning one pile of nothing into second pile of nothing and making money off it. Hallelujah!

We had three stores, and we filled all their needs from the Main Street location. I shoveled, and Cory held the bags open, unless something caught his attention causing him to let go with one hand. Then together we'd watch the dirt slide down the outside of the bag and back into the pile. *Tweedle Dee, Tweedle fucking Dumb.* My God, it was the world's ten longest fingernails scraping both sides of my brain.

Just lifting the big scoop into heavy soil hundreds of times a day was hard enough without running head-on into one of Cory's brain cramps. Nevertheless, after my motivational message, "Watch what you're doing, you worthless piece of crap," we would regroup and start over.

When we finished the afternoon's work, we loaded the bags onto a flatbed dolly for delivery to the other stores. It wasn't really hard work, just tedious, but by late afternoon it was very hot and messy.

But then something unexpected happened, and our lives changed for the better. The new store on Bayshore took off. It was out by a new home development, where sales had started booming a few months earlier. Dad ran ads in the weekend paper, offering the fruits of our labor for ninety-nine cents a bag. *Was he serious?* No self-respecting dirt bagger would accept such a modest appraisal of their work. Forget artistry; the sheer backbreaking labor of bagging made our effort worth much more. Even our regular price of $1.49 seemed puny. Cory and I wanted to charge $7000 per bag and get the suffering done sooner, but Dad wouldn't go along with our plan.

"You boys had best let me do the thinking around here," he said, chuckling to himself. This was unsettling news, based on the thinking we'd seen out of him so far.

About the same time the new store took off, Dad started carrying yard equipment, and opened a repair shop. *Bingo.* We had customers lined up out the door from the first day, and he made me an assistant manager. Cory got left behind as the family's only remaining dirt bagger, a fact I held over him whenever possible.

"Can you spell promotion?" I asked one night before dinner, as he peeled away the dark outer layers of grime off the back of his hands. He frowned but didn't say anything.

"Well, don't feel bad, neither can I, but now I am one… promoted, that is," I chuckled while patting the back of his sweat-stained shirt.

Suddenly, I had become lord and master over all my eyes surveyed.

"My mower will be fixed when?" A look of complete disgust crossed my customer's face when I broke the bad news.

"It looks like the eleventh, Mr. Keller. Yup… number eleven it is." Did I mention we had added rental equipment next door? So the longer his mower stayed in sick bay, the better our chances of making a secondary sale. *Understanding and capturing market share builds financial wealth.*

"Excuse me, son, but today is only the fourteenth. That's a month from now," he began spitting words, as only Mr. or Mrs. Irate Customer was capable of doing. I wiped away the small spray from my face and continued.

"Yes, sir, it does seem like a long time, no question, and I wish I could help… but…" my voice trailed off. "As you can see, we're kind of backed up right now. Call me in three weeks, and I'll try to dig you out sooner." We both knew there was no chance of that lie coming true, but it felt good saying it.

After a few weeks, I learned one of life's most valuable lessons: Those bearing gifts receive benefits. It was pretty simple really, *quid pro quo,* as we found ourselves saying in Latin class. *Seriously, I ask you, who knew more about timely lawn mower repairs than the ancient Romans? No one, right?*

Tickets to Tampa's minor league baseball team, good seats for the Florida State-Auburn game, or a Fats Domino concert sold out weeks earlier: all wound up in my hands and moved my chosen customers to the head of life's never-ending repair line. I even displayed my used ticket stubs up front with a note saying, "Thanks to all our good customers. Without you, I'd be nowhere."

Literally, this was the absolute truth, not some cheap sentimental drool designed to get repeat business, because who needed that? This message was about the here and now, and more importantly about the here and gone, about where I'd be spending my Friday night. I usually didn't have to make it any clearer. "My friendship is for sale, people. Make me an offer!" But if they still didn't get the simple message, I'd wave a stub in the air and say, "This concert was really great. Did you get to see them?" or "I can't believe that kid missed the field goal with two seconds left." Looking out the window at the dark clouds, I reminded my customer, "Sure looks like more rain coming, doesn't it, Mr. Keller?" *Nothing makes the grass or anxiety grow any faster than a strong line of thundershowers.*

Sometimes they'd asked for another place to take their equipment, thinking I'd bend under the pressure and move them up a couple of spots. Trying to be cooperative, I pulled down one of the used stubs, wrote a couple of our competitors' numbers on the back and said, "Good luck; sorry, we couldn't help." Mr. Irate Customer would load his mower in his trunk and go flying out of the parking lot in a cloud of hot dust and frustration, which only he was capable of making. But by morning he'd be blown back in on the cooling winds of humility, with treats in hand and a pitiful look of remorse on his face.

"For every action there is an equal and opposite reaction," Mrs. Casey, our physical science teacher, explained during science lab, and Mr. Irate Customer's action only confirmed her theory.

"That's more like it," I said as he pulled sheepishly into the parking lot, giving a big friendly wave. I could smell his fear and nodded back without a reply.

"Pick whatever you like, Peter," he said, holding a series of tempting treats for my consideration. "In fact, please take a couple. I appreciate your helping me out like this, and on such short notice. I mean, let's face it, you didn't have to." *Of course I didn't have to, but that's not the point really. It's important to treat customers as if they matter, even though we both know they don't—at least not when it comes to the repair business.*

"Heavens, Mr. Keller," I said, trying to make him feel better. "Glad to be of service. As you must know, we aim to please."

Once in a while I got multiple offers to the same event, which presented a thorny moral dilemma. In those cases I felt duty bound to turn down the second offer, unless—listen carefully now—the backup tickets were much, much better than the first ones. In those rare cases I picked up the phone and regrettably explained the term "back order slip" to my earlier suitor.

"Well, yes, Mrs. Mundy, it is surprising that the manufacturer didn't have a single one of your parts in stock. Maybe in another week or so; I've got my fingers crossed." *And here's some friendly advice, Margery. Next time don't go so cheap on your repairman.*

It was important to be honest with customers and treat them fairly, whenever possible. Fair play is an essential part of good healthy living choices. I learned this from a self-help book titled *Squeezing the Most out of Friends*, and it was true. To think I used to hang out with people just because I liked them. How crazy was that?! Who knew friends could be good for so much more than friendship?

October 29, 1942

Sister Margaret and Mr. Walters waited for the girls just outside the barn. "So, ladies, I know this may be a little crowded at first. Hopefully, if the idea takes off we can find a larger space," the nun stated optimistically.

They spent the next half hour going over where to put the supplies and the boxing tables.

Upon completion of their tour, Sister Margaret asked, "So, Mr. Walters, how long will it take you to make the space ready?"

"I'd say about a month, maybe a little less." He answered surveying the work involved.

Well in the meantime, we have to come up with designs to represent your team logos. Do you have any suggestions?" Sister Margaret asked.

"I'm sure we each ended up with at least one good artist on our team. Why don't we let the teams design their own logos?" Katie volunteered.

"Sounds good to me," shouted Mary.

"Sure, we can do that," the others agreed.

"All right, then. We've accomplished a lot this afternoon, but I'm sure you girls have a lot on your minds right now, including some math homework that needs to be done. You'd better get going. Have a good evening," Sister Margaret said.

"Thank you, Sister. Goodbye," the girls responded, as they waved and left the barn.

Sister Margaret turned to the custodian. "Well, Mr. Walters, with God's help and yours, our project will be a success."

"You couldn't have picked better girls to be your leaders," Mr. Walters observed.

"Yes, great girls. I needed them all, but Katie is the one I had to have. I knew once she was on board, the others would follow."

In the spring of her sophomore year, Katie made a last minute decision to run for junior class president. She only put her name in the race because Mary told her she should. At the election assembly, Alexis Burton gave a good speech. Then Katie walked to the microphone and put away her notes. She looked out at her forty classmates and smiled.

"There are lots of things I could say about wanting to be class president, but none that are any better than the speech you just heard. Instead I want to tell you about my mother and how important she is at this time in my life. She taught me first to respect myself and then to respect others, and that is how I feel about Alexis. We have been friends since third grade. She would make a wonderful president. We are all trying hard to get through this difficult time in our lives with so many of our fathers and brothers going to war. I know each of you is just as proud of your mothers who quietly struggle to make your lives as good as they can. I believe that leadership means understanding that we can overcome obstacles. I'd like to be your leader, but mostly I want our class to make a difference, to make our parents proud of what we can do."

Katie won the election by three votes. Her father, a navy doctor, had taught her not to get ahead of herself, not to count on things before they arrived, and she lived day to day with that same philosophy. After the election, Katie shared with Sister Margaret a note that she had written to her father.

Dear Daddy,

My class elected me president today. I wish you were here to celebrate the moment with us and enjoy Mom's favorite meatloaf. We dished up a plate in your honor, and I ate it for you. I miss you so much, Papa. I hope I make you proud.

Love,
Katie

"Indeed I can always count on Katie to make good decisions," Sister Margaret continued, as she and Mr. Walters walked back to the main buildings.

• • •

Chapter 10

CONFESSING TO A STRING OF UNSOLVED AX MURDERS

Summer, 1958

The Bayshore Boulevard store opened in February, and by June it was the top producer. My social life began hitting an all-time high. Girls who previously hadn't looked at me twice without laughing now found themselves walking into a Kingston Trio Concert, their arm wrapped tightly around my waist. The rich, too-cool-for-school guys now made sure I was included in their weekend plans.

We had cash to burn. Dad called it "positive cash flow," and we wondered why the hell he hadn't discovered it sooner. He plowed some of the profits into advertising on a weekend radio gardening show hosted by a local horticulturalist named Delbert Wells. The show was so boring it made my nose bleed. I wanted to listen to a top forty station, but Dad always turned it to the chinch bug channel when he came by the store to check on me.

"Son, I want our customers to hear our ads. It's called merchandising 101."

"Well, Dad, two things here. First, any more than half an hour on the treatment for spider mites, and I'm confessing to that string of unsolved ax murders over in Collier County. Second, the customers are already at the store. They're not going to say to themselves, "Oh, that reminds me to stop by Florida Seed and Supply after I leave Florida Seed and Supply." But he never listened, so I just changed the channel whenever his truck drove up.

My parents closed in the screen porch and bought a pool table and a new car. The old Plymouth station wagon finally got her walking papers. Walking was about all she was good for, with cataracts in both headlights; it was a wonder she hadn't wiped out the Benson boy. He was always darting out of dark corners, and there wasn't a streetlight at his end of the block.

We held a funeral service for the Plymouth, and each of us shared our favorite memories of our time together. She had been a grand lady and a trouper in her later years. She carried our family secrets gracefully to her grave. We would miss her dearly, Amen. But enough already, we were ready for something new to get life started. This was to be the first new car I'd been a party to, and I wasn't sure how the ritual worked. Would Cory need to bring his tom-toms? Would my unused slide rule come in handy? I couldn't say, but one night after work, we set off to the car dealership to find out.

The Ford dealership was on a freeway across town, so we stopped for burgers at Bud's Burger Barn on the way over. By the time we arrived, we were not only filthy from work but had onion ring crumbs hanging off our clothes.

We sat in every four-door on the lot and some of them twice. After an hour Mom and Dad narrowed the selection to a woody wagon and a full-sized car. Mom went back and forth. The car was several hundred dollars less, but the wagon was really what she wanted. She and Dad huddled like prizefighters going back to their corners between rounds. Cory bet on Dad, but I knew Mom would win. Dad was tough as nails, but Mom held the hammer.

Finally, they settled on Mom's choice, and Dad went inside to talk with the general manager. Back then it was a man's world. Women and children were just along for the ride, to be seen but not heard.

Mom waited out on the showroom floor with us, fixing her plain skirt, trying to make herself look as good as possible. I could see the gentle kindness in her humility and watched her try to brush out the wrinkles of her inexpensive life. She hadn't spent any of our new-found money on herself yet. I wanted her to get all the things she wanted in life. *What I could not possibly have known then, sitting in the showroom floor, was that she already had them.*

Mom told us it was important to keep the car clean, so there would be no food allowed in the backseat. She talked about how comfortable the car was, and we saw her glow. Forget a new housedress; I was going to buy her one of those fancy black ball gowns like the hostesses wore on *Queen for a Day.*

It was getting late, and we were glad when Dad got through the paperwork. On the way home we stopped at the A&W stand for root beer floats and laughs. It was the dead of summer, and the place was packed with people trying to cool off. It felt great finally to be part of the middle class, and nothing said it that better than a new car sitting in the garage.

November 9, 1942

Sister Margaret had good business sense. She felt that the look of the Cape Cod Reds packages would make a difference. She also felt that asking each team to create designs for the covers of the boxes would build team loyalty and togetherness. Today she would find out if she were on the right track with her ideas.

All of the high school students sat cross-legged on the floor of the gym, each girl in an area designated for her team. Sister Margaret stood at one end of the gym on a temporary stage. Behind her stood Lucy, Penny, Katie, Mary, and Kerrie, and beside each of them was an easel, draped with a cloth. An excited buzz filled the room. Sister Margaret raised her arms, and the room fell still.

"Today we are here to unveil the drawings that each team has created for its logo. I am very pleased with the results. I know they will build team spirit as well as attract interest in the Cape Cod Reds from within the community and beyond. Always remember that the dust of our deeds will be carried to places far away. So let's get on with our business of today. Lucy, if you please . . ."

Lucy raised the material to show the Whale blowing stars from his blow hole. Then Lucy, holding an atomizer behind her head, squeezed the big black ball so that a powdery spray flew above her. The audience applauded, the heartiest appreciation coming from the Whale section.

Each of the other team leaders went in turn, removing the covering from her easel. Penny's showed the happy Cod swimming under its slogan "May Cod Be With You," flying on a banner above his head, and she pulled out a banner with the same words written on it. The Starfish held an American flag in one of its points, and of course Katie waved a little American flag, too. The Lobster was a Popeye-like crustacean pumping one of his bulging claws. Mary made claw-shapes with her hands and pumped her arm muscles, a gesture copied by all of the Lobsters in the audience. Finally Kerrie, yanked the curtain off her easel with flair to show a Clam resembling Rosie the Riveter. Then she picked up a toy rivet gun from behind the easel and did a little dance to the wild cheers of the Clam section.

Again Sister Margaret raised her arms before speaking. "I can tell that you love the designs as much as I do. As you know, the cranberry growers in our area are donating a portion of their crop for our project. Gerald Hunnicutt, one of the growers, is also donating aprons and ball caps decorated with these logos to each of the teams." Loud applause once more filled the gymnasium. "You will have them by the time the barn is ready for the packaging of our Cape Cod Reds. Thus our project begins. May God find favor with our work. That said, I know you have to get to other activities as well as a lot of homework, so we are dismissed."

• • •

Chapter 11
CHATTERING TEETH

Summer, 1959

We went to visit our grandmother in North Carolina the summer I turned seventeen. During part of that time Dad took Mom on their first real vacation: a Caribbean cruise.

At Grandma's, fun abounded, or as close as you can get when spending time with a person whose teeth popped out after supper and were left soaking in a glass of salt water with part of the meal still attached.

"Hey, Grandma, you didn't finish your corn," I called out while looking at the physical evidence floating in the glass.

"No, sugar, but please help yourself," she replied.

My only hope was that her dentures would get picked to co-star in Sandra Dee's rumored upcoming thriller, *Chattering Teeth*, so I could finally meet my dream girl, but that seemed a long shot at best.

The first few days we were with her, Grandma had relatives for us to visit. Of course, Cory and I objected, but to no avail.

"Well, you can't come this far and not get together with cousins Ruthie and Stevie," Grandma countered.

"My sentiments exactly. In fact, they're pretty much the reason for our visit. What are their names again?"

"I can't sleep, boys, so we're going to get an early start," she said opening our bedroom door.

"Early start? It's 5:40 in the morning. Get back to us when the chickens get up," I said, pulling a pillow over my face.

"No, puddin', you boys can sleep on the way over."

What she hadn't explained was that she planned on sleeping as well during the thirty-minute drive. We piled pillows and blankets in the back seat and off we went. A short while later, the horn blasting, we saw Grandma's head lying on top of the steering wheel.

"Are you okay?" we screamed, as she swerved back onto her side of the highway.

"I'm fine, boys. Go back to sleep."

We said, "Okay," but I kept one eye open just in case.

Several hours later Cory spotted a sign reading Texas Bureau of Records next exit. He asked if that was a problem.

"Heavens, no, Cory. I'm pretty sure Texas and North Carolina share a common border."

Around lunchtime we saw Chilean children picking sparkling grapes high up on a mountainside near Santiago. They were colorfully dressed and waved for us to join them in the fields. Cory was hungry by then, and the grapes looked fresh and cool, so he asked if we could stop and pick a basket full for the road, but Grandma said no, because we were behind schedule. Fortunately moments later a state trooper clocked her doing 18 in a 60 zone, and he pointed us in the right direction.

November 21, 1942

Kaman's Drugstore was a popular destination for all of the townies, and high school students were no exception. The girls decided to drop by after attending a costume party at school. At Kerry's insistence they had not changed out of their costumes yet. Kaman's lunch counter was mostly empty except for a few residents getting a late night snack.

"Well, ladies, what do we have here?" Mrs. Kaman asked from behind the counter as the girls walked by.

"Just another slow night in Whitfield, Mrs. Kaman," Kerrie smiled back.

"Well, Kerrie, we don't often get Annie Oakley, Uncle Sam, Scarlett O'Hara, and could it be Fred Astaire and Ginger Rogers dropping by this close to closing. Where have you girls been?" Mrs. Kaman said with a wink.

"Our school sponsored a come-as-your-favorite-character dance with Catholic Prep, and we were all supposed to wear costumes," Katie responded.

"Well, you all look great," Mrs. Kaman said wiping the counter with a wet cloth.

The girls piled into the last booth, except for Mary whose hoop skirt meant that the closest she could get was to sit on a chair at the end of the table. Kerrie got up to go to the bathroom and on the way there did a little tap dance number to the delight of the sparse crowd sitting at the counter. Mrs. Kaman was impressed. "Kerrie, you should be on Broadway someday," she said.

Kerrie turned to respond to what seemed to her an obvious fact, "Oh, I'm going to, Mrs. Kaman. I'm going to."

It was the second annual "Pick Your Own Banana" weekend at Kaman's. A sign read "Pick, peel, and pay for a world famous banana split at bargain prices." The five of them agreed to share three banana splits. They selected the three biggest bananas and were pleased with the low prices hidden on little folded slips of paper taped to the bananas. Mary volunteered to eat one of the sweet confections by herself, but the other girls turned her down. The ice cream arrived, and the girls devoured it quickly.

"You know our school days together are numbered. We should plan to do something special after we graduate," Penny mused. "We could go on a sailing trip."

"That would be fun," Lucy agreed. All the girls began thinking about some kind of trip or adventure that they could share.

"Well, we have a year and a half to plan it. But maybe we could do something completely different. Let's think about something we've always wanted to do," Katie said. In these deliberations, as always, Kerrie was hyper, Lucy was quiet, Mary was opinionated, Katie was thoughtful, and Penny was just happy to be with her friends.

. . .

Chapter 12

SEEING HER HEAD EXPLODE OVER A BOWL OF POTATO SALAD

Summer, 1959

Our cousins Ruthie and Stevie were waiting for us in the front yard, Stevie waving his Blue Devils pennant. Ruthie was six, and Stevie was five. When one's age was more than the other two combined, it was hard to find much to talk about, so when I got out of the car, I said, "Nice shorts."

Uncle Bob taught creative writing at Duke. He had graduated fifteen years earlier, but it was as if he'd never left. Once inside their house we thought we'd entered the gift shop at the Blue Devils Stadium. Small figurines followed our every movement. Two of them were sitting on top of the television; another one leaning over the shelf peering from behind a box of cereal. It was kind of spooky, being watched so carefully. In the bathroom a Blue Devils toilet paper holder challenged me with, "Hey, Buddy, the next move is up to you." Fearing performance anxiety, I covered the holder with a small towel, but that just made him mad.

"Cheer up," I fired back, "Aunt Helen's just finished her second bowl of high fiber cereal; she'll be along any minute." But there was no consoling him, so I went back and joined the others.

Uncle Bob had taken a group of grad students to England for two weeks, leaving Aunt Helen at home with the kids and figurines, clearly a recipe for disaster. During our car ride Grandma had told us not to bring up Bob's absence, or we'd be having our own remake of Lady Macbeth starring Aunt Helen in the title role. The tension was stifling. My knowledge of the play was limited, but from what I'd been told, the woman goes mad. Cory, who either had forgotten Grandma's warning or just wanted to see what would happen, dove right in.

"Hey, where's your daddy?" he asked Cousin Ruthie, after giving her a big hug.

"On a trip," she said, a brainwashed frown appearing on her face.

"Oh, really? How come he didn't take you along?" He stretched his remark out for dramatic effect.

I have never been so proud of Cory in my life; seeing his darker side was a wonderful thing. Maybe all my years of training were finally paying off, or maybe the longer-than-necessary car ride put him in a foul mood. Either way he was moving ahead full throttle. Not twenty minutes into this family odyssey, Cory was introducing stuff that people sit through two acts of a play to see happen.

"Cory Dreeton is a tour de force," the drama critic from the Duke paper would later write of his stunning performance on Aunt Helen's porch. "He has raised the bar on family feuds, stirred the subtle undercurrents running through family disharmony, touched a raw nerve, broken the skin, and caused swelling to the glands. Bravo, Cory!"

I was dying to see what was coming next, and which one of us would be the first to go when Aunt Helen went on her killing spree.

"Aunt Helen, do you want me to go down to the courthouse and file the divorce papers for you, or stay here and stuff Uncle Bob's personal effects into smelly garbage bags?" Cory proposed, peeling back the outer coverings of civility. Aunt Helen, disarmed by Cory's questions, made a face.

I thought Cory was pushing the envelope, knowing what I did of Aunt Helen's predilection for violent behavior. She patted him on the head, code for, "Cut the crap, mister, or we'll be heading off to take a sponge bath soon."

It was time to eat, and we went outside to have a lunch of chicken salad sandwiches and deviled eggs. The eggs were overcooked. During lunch Aunt Helen told us about Bob's trip.

Maybe it was helpful getting it off her chest. I pondered if Cory knew more than he was letting on, and if he might not someday have a career as an afternoon television pop psychologist .... The Dr. Cory Show live from Raleigh-Durham where every problem, no matter how seemingly complex and insurmountable, would be resolved within the hour, commercials included. But since there weren't any shows of that kind on the air back then, and since I couldn't imagine anyone wanting to watch another person's life fall apart before their eyes, I gave Cory credit for breaking the ice and left it at that.

Bob had left on his trip two days before with twenty graduate students, pencils in hand, to learn how to write like William Shakespeare. Well, I guess that would work, but I wondered if there was really much of a market for "thee" and "thou" in today's prose. *I'd have to say it seems very doubtful, Uncle Bob, very doubtful. In fact you never hear those names in movies or books on the best sellers' list, do you? And isn't that the only list that matters?*

Aunt Helen broke an interesting piece of literary trivia over lunch. It turned out, according to Uncle Bob's research, that both Thee and Thou were gay. *No, I'm not kidding.* Throughout all of English literature they kept their personal lives private. In an interview for the BBC, Thou explained they didn't want to unduly influence the opinions of the reader. Apparently, one of the Henrys issued a "Don't ask; don't tell" policy, and they followed his wishes.

"I wish I could have gone on the trip," Aunt Helen said.

I thought, "Ah hah, the moment we've all been waiting for: full frontal family conflict, uncut and uncensored, flesh-eating human emotions ready to devour us. She might destroy every figurine in the house, blow a gasket, and go on a blathering rampage." My body was alive with excitement, but nothing came. Instead she remained calm.

"But at least when he gets back, we're going to visit friends in Colorado. I know the little ones will enjoy that," she added.

Talk about a big build up and then no pay off. It was as if she had talked herself into a good mood without our permission. What a waste of time this had been. Seeing her head explode over a bowl of potato salad would have been way more interesting than conflict resolution.

A new Disney movie that Ruthie and Stevie were dying to see was opening that afternoon. I think the phrase Aunt Helen used was, "They've been pissing in their pants all morning." I wondered how Thee and Thou would take to Aunt Helen's colloquial language. But Grandma, realizing no age difference between us, thought it would be fun if we went together. The theatre down the street was showing a Sandra Dee movie, which I saw as a much better use of my time, but Grandma said, "No." The whole time I dreamed about Sandra quietly in the dark while small animated characters danced in front of my popcorn box.

November 21, 1942

The girls sat quietly around the booth at Kaman's as they pondered possibilities for their post-graduation trip.

"Hey, sometimes magazines have ads for places to go. Let's each get a magazine and look through it," Kerrie suggested.

Mrs. Kaman couldn't help but overhear their discussion. "Kerrie, for your impromptu performance for my clientele and staff tonight, I will give you each a magazine of your choice from our rack over there," she offered.

"Wow! That's great, Mrs. Kaman. Thanks," Kerrie exclaimed, and they all raced over to the magazine display, with Mary's hoop skirt knocking a few chairs over along the way.

"Take it easy, girls. I may be giving you some magazines, but you are going to have to pay for any broken furniture," Mrs. Kaman joked.

"Sure, sure, Mrs. Kaman. I'm sorry," Mary apologized.

Having made their selections, they sat back down and began pouring over the magazines. Several ideas crossed in front of their eyes and were presented to the others: climbing in the Adirondacks; bicycling around Maine; working at a Victorian hotel by the ocean in Cape May.

"Oh, my gosh! Here's a great idea: We could join a stateside USO troupe that travels around performing at army bases," Kerrie squealed.

"That's a great idea for you and Penny, but the rest of us might not pass the round of auditions," Mary said sadly.

Katie looked up from her *Collier's Weekly*. "Well, here's an idea. A dude ranch in Jackson Hole, Wyoming is looking for college help. Doesn't that sound cool?" Katie enthused.

"Won't it cost a ton just getting out there?" Mary asked.

"Not really. This far in advance we could all work on saving up the money for the train ride. I think we should seriously think about this one," Katie said.

"It does sound good to me," Penny agreed. "A dude ranch would be wonderful, and we all know how good Lucy and I are with horses."

"Do we ever," Katie answered, thinking back to Penny's and Lucy's horsy adventure from several years before.

When Penny and Lucy were twelve, the two girls were paid to feed and look after the Jacobys' horses for two weeks while the Jacobys went on vacation. Penny's dad and Mr. Jacoby were friends, and in order to accept the job Penny needed to get a buddy to help her. She talked Lucy into doing the job.

As they were leaving the stable one evening, it started to snow. The Jacoby's farm was only a quarter mile from Penny's house along the main road, but Penny suggested that they take the trail through the woods. It was quicker, and Penny liked walking the trail. The girls made it to the end of the trail, when Penny remembered she had left one of the stall gates open.

"We have to go back, Luce. It will only take a minute. I promise," Penny said.

Lucy groaned, but they turned around retracing their steps. When they got almost to the stable, Lucy noticed the door was partially open. She saw a shadow moving inside the stable, and then another. She stopped Penny. "Wait. Something's wrong," Lucy said, almost unable to get the words out of her mouth. "Some people are in the stable. We need to get help. They might be stealing the horses."

"Let's wait until they come out to make sure," Penny replied.

The stable door opened, and two men came out leading the horses. Hearing a noise, one of the men pulled out a flashlight and shone it in the direction of the girls, but Penny dropped down in the snow, pulling Lucy to the ground with her. The man's flashlight made a long sweeping path across the birch trees above them.

Penny grabbed Lucy's coat, and the two girls started retracing their steps, racing as fast as they could. They heard the movement of horses and of the men mounting them. There wasn't time for them to make it back to the main road or to Penny's house, and they both knew it.

"In here," Penny said, pointing to a small opening between two birch trees. Lucy followed her, and the two girls ducked down and waited for the horses to pass. The man in front was holding his flashlight and checking the footprints. The girls held their breath as the men pulled up to survey the situation at the fork just past the bend.

The first rider pointed his flashlight up ahead towards the tracks the girls had made earlier. As soon as the men headed off, Penny said, "Come on. This way will take us to the Miller's backyard, and we'll be safe."

The girls made it there without incident and began shouting and banging on the door for help.

A day later the horses were found in a horse trailer at a truck stop in western Massachusetts. The horse thieves were apprehended inside the diner. The Jacobys were glad the girls were okay and happy to get their horses back. Lucy was just glad that Penny knew all the trails behind her house.

"Yes, with their equine expertise, I think we will all master the intricacies of the dude ranch quickly," Katie said, and the others all laughed.

•   •   •

Chapter 13
GRANDMA'S SILK KIMONOS

Summer, 1959

After our trip to Aunt Helen's, Grandma went into a slow glide pattern, leaving a soft white trail of smoke behind her. Her social planning came to an abrupt halt. Our one afternoon at the movies wore her out. We wouldn't have really cared if she'd have let us off the reservation. She had wheels. I had a license. But she wasn't able to put these two random thoughts together and come up with a good result. My suggestion of driving Cory over to the zoo fell on deaf ears.

"Too many wild animals, no telling what might happen to you boys," she warned.

Then I saw a notice about a prayer meeting and figured she couldn't say no to our religious callings. She seemed skeptical, however, of our family's conversion to Jehovah's Witnesses.

"When did this happen?" she asked, "and how come I never heard about it from your father?"

"Sure, Grandma, it's coming up on two years now. Right, Cory?"

"Nope. I think it would be better if you boys stayed around here. You go into town and no telling what might happen to you."

Really, Grandma, isn't that the point? We were ready for the challenge. In fact we welcomed it. What wasn't in town was boredom; she had the county's entire supply stockpiled in her living room.

"What do you suggest?" I asked, because watching her cat chase yellow butterflies through tall grass hadn't really gotten our blood flowing.

"Well, why don't you two wash my car? That's something good to do with your time. And don't forget the tires, boys," she hollered from the front porch sipping from an oversized iced tea glass. "I paid good money to get whitewalls."

Grandma had a television, and we watched her shows or nothing at all. She had opinions about every show she'd never seen and was eager to share her views.

"Nothing good can come from watching trash, boys." When she wasn't watching television, which wasn't often, she placed a white hair from the bottom of her chin across the dial, to make sure the channel wasn't changed.

Sometimes in the afternoons we got into extended domino games. She kept the dominos set up on a big table in the living room, with her seat positioned so she could watch her shows and play at the same time. *Let's face it; in this house it was good to be the grandma.* She knew every domino trick in the book; she saw moves before we thought them out in our heads. Simply placing my finger on the flat backside of the three-four or the six-five brought a questioning response.

"I wouldn't go that way, sweetie. You have much better choices. Try the blank-five from the other end."

How did she know what dominos I was holding? I decided then and there if I was going to join the professional domino circuit I would need to return to her temple of the holy blocks to learn the game from the ground up, to study at the foot of the master, to be at one with her spirit. *It is a wise man who journeys into the fields of knowledge to pick the fruit ready for harvest.*

I imagined Grandma would have dark red silk kimonos made for us, with a pair of leaping yellow dragons on the back surrounding a single black domino, the double sixes drawn on hers, as teacher, and the double blanks on mine, as student. After a morning of rigorous mental preparation, we'd rest peacefully by her newly completed rock garden and reflection pond.

Grandma would soak her dentures on top of a dark rock, next to the pool where the goldfish and koi played, and I would reflect on her teachings. My body would be wrapped in some spiritually contorted yoga position from which there was no hope of escaping. And when our rest time was over, Cory would bang the six foot brass gong announcing that lunch was served. Then we would retire inside to enjoy bowls of Minute Rice and steaming vegetables while watching an old kung fu movie. *To be in the moment, one has to live the moment.*

"Why don't we spice things up a little?" she said one afternoon, a wry smile crossing her face.

"What do you mean, Grandma?" we asked, naively playing into her hands.

"You boys win a round, and I'll let you take the car into town, stay out late, have some fun." She reached down deep inside her purse pulling out a crisp new twenty. "And maybe throw in a little spending money to make the trip worthwhile."

She rubbed the bill between her fingers, creating a crackling sound filled with the whispers of sin. We didn't question why she no longer needed Dad's approval for this road trip. For us, it was the devil calling, and we were all ears.

"But," she said, and we held our breath to hear the other side of her Faustian bargain, "if I win, you boys fix dinner and do the dishes."

Cory and I recklessly jumped at the opportunity to sell our souls for a night of pleasure. Later, as he was putting the rest of the meatloaf into the refrigerator, and I was scrubbing the Pyrex dish, we learned one of life's hard lessons: In dominos, the devil is always in the details.

"Why did we let her talk us into it?" he asked.

"Because, Cory, we're stupid, and caged animals don't think straight; they react."

During those games, with the stakes so high, she dusted us off in a hurry, no questions asked. As she put the winning black block into place, she laid her recipe on the table and said, "Easy on the salt, boys. It's not good for Grandma."

December 19, 1942

The train pulled into the commuter station a little after 8:48 AM, and the five girls got on the last car. They were spending their first day of Christmas vacation together in Boston. Penny's dad was treating them all to a fancy lunch at the Oak Room of the Copley Plaza Hotel, as a reward for all their hard work on the Cape Cod Reds. Before and after lunch they would do tons of window-shopping, and each would work on their own Christmas lists.

Their train car was filled with young sailors and a number of other probable Christmas shoppers. The girls took over the last two rows of seats facing each other, and began pulling off their mittens and hats.

"I'm going for hot chocolate. Does anyone want to come with me?" Mary said as she laid her blue jacket on the rack above their heads.

"I do," Lucy answered, blowing into her frozen hands.

"Me, too," Katie added.

"No, thanks. I had a big breakfast, and I'm going to try to finish my book," Penny said, holding up her copy of *Wuthering Heights*.

They all laughed. Penny could reread the same page four times and not notice or care, but she always had "a book" she was working on, the pages so dog-eared from being thrown in one book bag after another.

"If by 'finish,' Penny, you mean the chapter, okay then, we'll believe it. But please don't put us under the pressure of having to stay in the club car until you finish the whole book," Mary admonished.

"That's mean," Penny shot back. "I've only got thirty more pages."

"Really? Gee, it looks like more to me. Let me check," Mary said.

"Okay, just go. It may be forty, but it's not much." Penny opened her book and stuck her nose deep inside page 374.

"Good luck," Mary said in a softer voice. "We love you."

"Go now, I'm busy," Penny responded, giving her companions a dismissive wave.

"Yes, and we're proud of you. Kerrie, are you coming?" Katie asked.

"No, thanks. I'm going to hang out here and see if one of the sailors stops by."

"Okay," Katie laughed, "but you know it will be a short-term romance. They're probably leaving in a few days."

They spent the next half hour in the club car sharing stories and looking at the snow beginning to stick on the rooftops outside their windows. When they pulled open the coach car's door, they found Penny asleep with the book in her hand, and Kerrie laughing with two sailors at the far end of the car. Mary turned to Katie and asked, "So do you think Kerrie will ask us to be bridesmaids?"

"Absolutely, as soon as she figures out which one is the groom."

• • •

Chapter 14
ROUNDING THIRD BASE

Summer, 1959

During the summer we stayed with Grandma, our only salvation was the neighborhood pool three blocks from her house. We started going down there every morning and stayed most of the day, even when it was raining. The homeowners' association hadn't done any basic maintenance on the pool for a number of summers, and it showed. Behind the pool was a large children's play area with a sandbox, three swings, a slide, and a set of grip rings that kids use for doing back flips. But with one of the rings missing, the equipment could only work for one-armed gymnasts, something I hadn't seen too often at neighborhood pools. The playground equipment sat behind the pool on an open space of grass, though by this time of the summer, it had become a worthless mixture of dirt, grass, and weeds, reflecting the utter contempt the neighborhood had shown for it. Having vast experience in the weed and seed business myself, I knew full well a couple of bags of 13-13-13 would clear the problem up. But I didn't like bringing my work with me, so I never volunteered to help out, choosing instead to ignore the "We need help!" sign posted next to the pool check-in stand. "Please help bring the community pool back to what it can be," the note asked. It was signed "Bill Teague, President of Clearwood Homeowners Association." The sign gave both Bill's home and office numbers.

I thought about calling his office and giving a few tips, without leaving my name. I didn't do it, because from my experience, once you utter the words, "I'd like to be a volunteer," your life is permanently altered. Then when your parents send you to church camp and the counselors need a volunteer, it's your stupid name they call on for help.

"Why, Peter Dreeton, you seem like just the sort of lad who'd like to fold the white dinner napkins while the rest of the boys and girls go skinny-dipping down at the lake."

"Would I ever, Mrs. Johnson! Just show me how." *Listen; I'd made that mistake once, and it was not happening again.*

Cory made some friends at the pool, while a lifeguard named Lacy Dinkins decided I was worth spending time with. Lacy was my age with pixie-cut brown hair framing her seriously cute face. And like most lifeguards at public pools, hers was really the only body there worth saving. She had two different suits: a yellow one and a green one. They were both nice, but I liked the green one best because it was a size smaller and form-fitted her plump little behind. Sometimes in the evenings, if the pool was empty, she swam laps, while I sat on the side watching two green melons floating nicely just above the surface line.

She also had a driver's license and, more importantly, access to the forbidden fruit: her mother's car. *Now we were getting somewhere.* The days she had off from work, we met at the pool before heading into town. I left Cory with money for vending machine meals, knowing full well all of his nutritional needs were only a knob pull away.

"Look at number eleven … a Cheetos sandwich on Wonder Bread slathered with heavy mayo. Save me some, little buddy."

But soon Cory wised up. He started bribing me into buying him something better, in return for keeping his silence. It began innocently enough, and I went along with it, which was my big mistake. You know the old saying: "Once the camel sticks his nose inside a French menu all hell breaks loose." That was sure true in this case.

"Hey, Peter, could you bring me back a hot dog or some fries?" he begged the first week. At that point I felt sorry for him being stuck at the pool.

"Sure. No problem, Cory."

That worked the first couple of times, but then he upped the ante. I called him a snitch and a jerk, but he seemed completely unfazed with my raw character assassinations. The boy had no shame. When ordering a plate of nachos, he said, "Make sure they add extra cheese. I love cheese." By the end of our stay, he was dining from the finest establishments Raleigh-Durham had to offer. Sometimes Lacy and I wasted an entire lunch hour getting him "the special of the day."

"What exactly is Vichyssoise? And do you think I'd like it?" he asked one afternoon, while perusing the menu from a bistro called Chez New.

I smiled and said, "Sure, why not," secretly hoping he'd choke on whatever it was, but of course we filled his order; we had to. To get even, Lacy made sure that the soup was cold by the time we brought it back.

Now it seemed I had not only to admire him, but to fear him as well. I missed the happy-go-lucky kid with the go-fetch attitude to life. "Kids grow up so fast and then become entirely useless," Dad was always saying to our next-door neighbor. For the first time, I understood exactly what he meant.

Lacy was far more advanced than I, but that wasn't saying much since I thought "third base" had something to do with kissing. The afternoon she told me we were going to give that a try, I put on an extra layer of Grandma's moldy ChapStick just to be ready. *But isn't that what a summer at Grandma's house is all about: learning and trying new things.*

I didn't much care for any of Lacy's friends. Most of them smoked and seemed wild, and it made me feel uncertain. I was never sure if robbing a liquor store or blowing up the bank might not be on their night's things-to-do list. Would I be powerless to resist their commands for fear of looking weak?

"Just grab a couple of bottles, Peter. It doesn't matter, bourbon or gin, whatever you can take.

We'll keep the car running." She gave me her instructions outside Discount Liquors, a few blocks from the pool, the neon sign crackling over our heads. I saw this as something close to evil and feared that I would fall prey to their wishes, all in the selfish hopes of moving another ninety feet to uncover the golden treasures hidden beneath home plate.

Were these people satanic devil smokers with whom I found myself mixed up? Lacy got me to try one of her Pall Malls one afternoon outside her house, but it made me sick, so I didn't try it again.

Her dad also taught at a university, but their house had none of the trappings of team spirit that Aunt Helen's contained. We hung out there a few times, mostly babysitting her younger sister.

Lacy came over a few nights with friends and parked up the road from the house. She threw small stones at my bedroom window. As I left, Cory asked if I could bring him something back to eat.

"No way, Buster, room service closes at eleven," I said climbing through the open frame.

· · ·

By the time we got the train home, we had done our time, paid our dues, though I think Grandma probably felt the same way as well. I told Cory that she'd be hard-pressed to find two competitors less skilled at dominos than we had been.

Cory made pretty good friends with two of the boys from the pool, and one of them came to visit at the end of the summer. I learned most of my way around third base, all in all, not a bad summer, indeed. That was until we got home and found two big straw hats sitting on top of our beds. *Weren't we going to be popular at school with those on our heads?*

December 19, 1942

The girls were excited about dining at the renowned Oak Room but were a little awed by the fancy surroundings. "Oh, my gosh, Penny, do you eat in restaurants this fancy often?" Mary whispered loudly to the group.

"Some," Penny replied.

"You go first," Mary said, nervously shoving Katie in the back.

"Thanks, but I think Penny should do the honors," Katie replied.

"Relax, ladies," Penny instructed in a calming voice. "Just act as if we belong here."

Penny walked up to the maitre d' and said, "We have reservations in the name of Caulkins."

"Certainly, ladies. Right this way," he responded.

Once at the table, the girls settled in and considered the offerings on the menu. "I don't even know what some of these things are," Lucy said.

"Whatever they are they must be the most gourmet foods in the world. Look at the fancy prices," exclaimed Mary.

"Your father is so generous to treat us to this magnificent lunch, Penny," said Katie.

"He was happy to do it. Treating us to this meal is one of his Christmas presents to me. You are all so dear to me. Oh, and I can help you decipher the menu. Remember, we are the five fireflies. We can handle anything," Penny reaffirmed.

After lunch they went in separate directions agreeing to meet back at the train station by 4 in time for the 4:30 train home. By that time, the snow had piled up on the curb outside. The girls went inside to warm up and sat down on two of the long wooden benches facing each other.

A deep voice over the loud speaker announced a thirty-minute delay on all southbound trains due to the weather.

"Rats," Mary complained, as she took off her coat and mittens. "Hey, I know. Let's see the great buys we made." They all agreed, and promptly the girls opened their boxes to show off their purchases.

"Look, I found this scarf in Notre Dame colors for Josh. Do you think he'll like it?" asked Katie.

"Oh, yes, good choice," complimented Lucy.

"I agree, and I got this purse for my mother," Penny said.

"Oh, it's so cute. She'll love it," Katie said admiringly.

"Well, I have to confess. I got myself a present. How do you like this dressy little sweater that I'm going to wear to the Christmas dance at the community center?" Mary asked as she pulled out a blue sweater and held it up to herself.

"It will be perfect," Penny assured her. Katie and Lucy also made appropriate ooh and ah sounds, but Kerrie was silent, looking noticeably miffed.

Finally, Kerrie spoke, while taking the same blue sweater out of her bag. "And how do you like the dressy blue sweater that I am going to wear to the Christmas dance at the community center?" she said with emphasis on the "I."

"Oops," said Penny, as she and Lucy and Katie giggled softly under their breaths.

"Well, I don't see the humor in being twins. Look, I don't have anything else to wear to the dance," Mary scowled.

"Neither do I," Kerrie scowled back.

"Since the train isn't leaving for a while, why don't you run to Filene's and exchange yours for something else?" Mary suggested.

"Yeah, right. When did you get yours? It was the first place I went after lunch, and according to Emily Post, first sweater wins," Kerrie confidently retorted.

"Come on, girls. We'll figure something out," Katie said in an effort at peacekeeping.

"We could try a round of rock-paper-scissors to decide the winner," Lucy suggested.

Mary got up and went in one direction with her sweater, and Kerrie did the same, going in another direction. After a few minutes, they each returned wearing their new sweaters. They sat on opposite ends of the bench across from the other three girls. Mary pouted, Kerrie scowled, and they both sat rigidly with their arms crossed tightly over their chests.

"It's going to be a long dark ride in the snow," Lucy observed.

．　．　．

Chapter 15
I SERVE AT HER PLEASURE, NOT YOURS

Fall, 1959

"What happened to the last D?" I asked Mr. Donal Smart, my senior English teacher, as he finished writing his name on the blackboard. The other students chuckled under their breath.

"What D are you talking about?" he shot back.

"The D on the end of Donald?" I replied.

"Why, I'm saving it for you, young man, if you earn it. That could be quite a stretch, though, if your permanent record is any indication."

I assumed he was joking because I worked hard maintaining my strong C- average. Donal was a dapper dresser who had attended a snotty Ivy League school, and he branded our entire senior class "a bunch of hapless sub-humans."

There was no argument about that statement. Our events billboard proudly proclaimed our school's prehistoric heritage: "Cleburne High, Home of The Fighting Sub-Humans." Our mascot, a slow-witted woolly mammoth, showed up at pep rallies carrying a big club and no fresh ideas. If Donal hadn't bothered checking the school's low-rated credentials, that was his problem, not ours.

Mr. Smart announced that the more gifted among us would be enrolling in schools with state or tech tagged on the back end. The bottom half could apply to places named junior, and a few of us should not consider attempting anything more strenuous than a six-month stay in vocational programs involving large tools.

Let's face it; we Subs were by nature a passive breed and not prone to wild outbursts of either thoughts or emotions. We never took ourselves too seriously, and no one else in town did either. Every year before the citywide prep bowl, the school board always awarded Cleburne High ten courtesy points, but even that advantage never got us into the second round. So naturally, I was taken off guard by Mr. Smart's reaction to what happened next.

It was a Tuesday, and Heather Sweet, babe of all babes, leaned back dangling her long blond hair over the edge of my desk. Mr. Smart was droning on about some book so boring he'd lost any shot at keeping my attention.

All that mattered now was that Heather had invaded my space and taken possession of my glands. Not to put a fine point on it, but my glands were in her hands. We'd been warned about this danger in boy's gym class, two periods earlier. Coach Haywood showed a film presentation entitled *Cold Shower*. It presented a chilling account of what could happen to us if we pursued our dark dreams, and why it was so important that we not consider stepping out from the shower until we were at least twenty-five.

"Temptation is everywhere, boys; courage is in short supply," Coach explained. "First it gets really bad, and then you die."

Forewarned as I had been, I sat powerless to resist Heather's temptations. I stood ready to follow every sick deviant command my princess might require.

Mr. Smart's voice came and went from my consciousness. He said something, but I couldn't hear him clearly. Deeper and deeper I slipped into a place I shouldn't be but didn't want to leave.

Heather and I were out on the beach past the jetties. It was early afternoon, the beach strangely empty, the sand smooth and soft. We had just gotten out of the water. She was relaxing in a long white beach chair sipping a cool glass of hand-squeezed lemonade, and I was shampooing her hair. *Don't ask. I serve at her pleasure, not yours.* Anyway, she mentioned that she might want to give up her virginity the following weekend if I was going to be available.

"With me, your princess?" I asked. Naturally, to be a notch anywhere on Heather's black leather love belt was a dream come true and then some. Just as I was about to say, "Sure, Heather, that sounds like fun," it hit me. Where was Kenny Byers, her football-captain-going-steady-with-Heather-kind-of-guy, who never took his paws off her? I looked to one end of the beach but saw no one. I looked the other way, still empty. After realizing this really wasn't about Kenny anymore, I took him out of the equation.

I lathered my hands for the cream rinse, the most critical part of any hair care application. She explained that her hair was her most important feature, and failure now was not an option.

"Peter," she said in a solemn voice, "pretty doesn't just happen; it evolves. Sure, it's a gift, but there are needs." She gave her hair a light flip. That sounded right to me. I was just a worker bee. She was my Queen. One false step now and her highlights would be mere streaks, and I would be banished from the hive.

Just then, another voice standing over me was saying something. It sounded like one of those awful computerized shrieks that dinosaurs make in a natural science exhibit.

"What are you doing, Mr. Dreeton?" the voice asked again. I didn't answer, hoping the large reptile would fly off, or that our class would move over to the next display window featuring the discovery of the television by cavemen in twelve thousand B.C.

"What are you doing?" this voice said a second time, the words coming into focus. I looked down and saw my hands dancing above her hair, rising and falling in the sort of slow rhythmical motions one performs when conducting voodoo experiments over a dead chicken.

"I dropped my pencil," I replied.

"You what?" he asked, not buying any part of my excuse.

"I dropped my pencil, and I was about to pick it up." Maybe I would get out of this unharmed after all, before I noticed the pencil stuck between two of my fingers. The class broke into laughter. Heather turned around to see what the fuss was about and smiled dismissively at me.

Mr. Smart shook his head and dropped my failing paper in front of me, the "F" searing itself into the dark wood of my desk.

"This explains a lot, don't you think?" Mr. Smart asked to no one in particular, and I guessed he meant my present activities explained the grade sitting in front of me. But it didn't seem wise to respond, at least not without having a priest present.

"Yeah," was all I could muster.

Mr. Smart tapped on my desk with his stubby fingers.

"Come see me after school, Mr. Dreeton."

I guessed offering to give her a blow dry would be completely out of the question and disruptive to the rest of the class. Was this the end for Heather and me? I looked around to survey other possibilities for a back-up English class dream babe. Sure, there was Gretchen Mallows, and she could do in a pinch. But I didn't care for the name Gretchen, and to be honest her eyebrows were way too close together for my taste. If we had children together would this gene be passed on to them? When it hit me.... Get a grip, Peter. It was fall semester of my senior year. All my friends would be marking girls' lockers, while I was stuck in Mr. Smart's tutorials, having my way with action verbs. Nothing about this seemed right.

February 24, 1943

The last group of marine scientists took their seats in the meeting room. Dr. Arnold finished his conversation with the man sitting next to him and got up from his chair. "That's a good point, Bruce. I'll bring it up at our next board meeting." He smiled and patted the man's white lab coat and moved up to the podium. The room which had been filled with quiet, idle chatter became still. As he always did, Dr. Arnold began their weekly meeting with a review of what he did on the weekend.

"I hope you gentlemen enjoyed the good weather. We went for a long walk in the snow, and Maureen tried to talk me into helping her clean out some closets, but I managed to get out of that task by coming into the Institute to do some work. I recommend that tactic if any of you find yourself on the road to one too many quilting shows." A gentle chuckle went up from the audience. Dr. Arnold always managed to get in some reference to Maureen, his bride of almost thirty-five years. And more often than not it included some sweetly henpecked idea that she was trying to rope him into, and the only real suspense to these stories was whether or not he had escaped unharmed. Everyone understood the good-natured way that he intended it. These brief interludes were always followed by reports on the status of existing projects they were working on for the Navy, the War Department and public companies. At any one time the Institute might be involved with as many as a hundred marine research grants, and that didn't count special government projects which were dropped in their lap. Dr. Arnold called on each project head to give the updates and to answer questions from the other scientists. Today's meeting which began at 10 finished just before lunch and was concluded with a series of announcements.

"I know that everyone is ready to get out of here, but I wanted to pass on a bit of local news before we conclude. I'm sure many of you are familiar with the Cape Cod Reds, which my dear friend Sister Margaret has started at St. Anne's. Their sales have been so good that they are moving into a warehouse on DeCarlo Street, and they will be expanding their packaging operation to the community. This is a wonderful project, and I know that Maureen has already signed up both of us to work There is a meeting scheduled for tomorrow night at the school, and I'd like to encourage each of you to get involved."

"What time is the meeting at, Dr. Arnold?" a voice from one of the middle rows called out.

"It's at 7 in their gymnasium. So I hope to see you all there." Chairs started moving on the floor as the scientists got up and gathered their notes. On his way out the door, Dr. Schneider, a man of similar age, stopped Dr. Arnold to ask a question, and just as they were finishing, he added, "Oh, I guess I'll see you at the Reds meeting tomorrow night. That sounds like just the thing to do with my spare time."

"That's great. See you there."

At lunch Dr. Schneider went to eat by himself at The Broken Angler, a small seafood café at the south end of town. After he pulled into the parking lot, he stopped to use the pay phone and called a number in Boston.

"Oh, it's you, Professor," the voice over the phone said when Dr. Schneider spoke.

"I think we've found the opening you've been looking for, without the kind of risk that we have now."

"What is it?" the voice sounded anxious to hear.

"There's a project here in Whitfield that sends out dried cranberries to stores all over the Cape. I have some ideas about how we can move the information without being detected. That incident a week ago at the wharf was too close for comfort. I'll work out the details and give you the plan when I call you next."

The Marine Institute was a mixed bag of the mundane and unimportant, yet was very valuable because of that fact. White-jacketed lab technicians wandered halls with half-eaten ham sandwiches in one hand and top-secret files in the other. The FBI and naval security had simply too many other high-risk spots to put the necessary manpower on this sleepy Cape Cod research lab. The hardest part of Dr. Schneider's mission was sifting through all of the material to pick and choose the best goodies. There was too much information, and it was too risky to move every shred. Once in a while he got a whiff of projects from other labs or rumors about war strategy, so having him here served the cause, even when the information wasn't too valuable.

In 1942 German agents had identified the Institute as a worthy target. They had scrutinized the staff for someone who was sympathetic to their cause. When they found Dr. Schneider, they had needed to develop a foolproof plan to get the information moved with the least amount of commotion. He had given them that as well.

•   •   •

Chapter 16

GERMAN POETS FROM THE TWELFTH CENTURY

Fall, 1959

At 3:30 I made my way down the long, empty senior hall, banging open locker doors shut. At the far end Mr. Gillen, the custodian, stood sweeping loose papers off the speckled floor of broken dreams. When I got to him, I considered tossing my paper on the floor but nodded instead and knocked on Mr. Smart's door.

"Come in," said the spider to the fly.

I opened the door carefully just as he looked up. "Oh, it's you," he offered in a sour tone. I could feel the love. Right now, I wanted to be one of his fat toadies who sat in the front three rows, their hands always raised and ready, moist with anticipation, eager to please.

> "Oh, pick me, Mr. Smart, please. German poets from the twelfth century, know them all. Let's see, there's…. Goethe, Hansel, Gretel, and one more, don't tell me, is it Sleepy or Doc?"
>
> "No, no, Daniel, it's neither. Remember our topic today is German poets, so the answer is Grumpy."
>
> "Oh, so right, as always, Mr. Smart. My mistake, of course."

When Smart said to one of his pets, "Come see me," it was only to heap praise on their heads or to share a passage of some obscure British writer they both enjoyed, and of whom

I'd never heard. *Ass kissing was never my style. Opinions are everywhere; the really good ones, like mine, are much harder to find.*

"What can I do for you?" he asked, half-mockingly.

"Would drop dead be an option?" I thought. Instead, going for a kinder response than I wanted, I went with, "You said to come see you."

"Yes, yes, that's right. Sit down." He motioned to a chair in front of his desk. "I'll just be another minute," he offered.

I nodded as if I had any say in the matter. My next F minus minus was somewhere in the stack, so there was no rush. It was just something else for me to look forward to, a chance to break the Cleburne High record for the most F minus minuses in one semester. The current record stood at six.

"Live the big dreams," Dad was always saying to me. I was well on my way to completing my goal. I settled myself into the seat and looked for a way to pass the time. Like all things Donal, I was two chess moves behind and fading fast.

When he finished his grading, he put down his pen and asked, "So, now, young man, what do you expect to get out of senior English?"

"I want to write like Hemingway, to tell adventure stories. Can you help?"

Figuring there was no pay-off to small bettors, I moved all my chips onto a red square waiting for the ball to drop. Tic, tic, tic: It moved busily around the wheel. The shiny ball slowed to a thump for the last few squares.

"I don't know, Peter," he said accepting my challenge. "That may take more time than we've got. Hemingway is a very good writer."

"That's okay; I don't have to be at my dad's store until 6."

"Listen, Peter, storytelling isn't as easy as you think. It's sort of like being a magician. You have to set the reader up with an idea and get them comfortable, let them own it, and then you take it away and show them something they weren't expecting at all. It's very hard work, and you need to be a couple of steps ahead of them. Do you think you can do that?"

I wasn't really sure, but I knew now was not the time to bring it up. So instead I said, "Yes, sir, I think I can," and left it at that.

The ball on the roulette table made a final hop over a black number, landing on red nine. I made a fist pump and pulled back my winning stake. Maybe I'd buy Heather a new sundress to celebrate. *Girls like Heather are high maintenance, and I could never let myself forget that.*

March 4, 1943

Penny got home earlier than usual. Today was the Cape Cod Reds' grand opening at the warehouse down by the boatyard. The project had outgrown the barn on campus after several months. Today's ceremony began at 4, and she had things to do first.

"Hi, Mom, I'm home," she called, coming through the back door into the kitchen. She tossed her yellow jacket on the breakfast room table and put her books down. Hearing no response, she picked up the mail off the counter and noticed her catalog from Mt. Holyoke. She opened it and glanced quickly through it but didn't have time to do more.

Her dad owned a tool manufacturing company in Fall River, which he inherited from his father, and her mother's father was a prominent doctor. Their house overlooked the bay and sat on more than an acre. And while the house had seemed large enough before, it seemed enormous now that her two older brothers were at college.

"Hey, Tasbo," she said as the family's black lab waddled into the kitchen to greet her. "Where'd you put Mom?" she asked scratching him behind her ears.

Penny laid the catalog back down and looked at the wooden clock hanging in the hall, realizing she had only twenty-five minutes to get ready. The phone rang, and she went into the front hall to answer it.

"Hey, Kerrie, what's up?"

"Can you pick me up on the way to the warehouse?"

"Sure. I'll be there in about twelve minutes."

"Great. I don't want to be late to the ceremony."

"That's a first," Penny laughed.

She hung up the phone and raced upstairs. The hall was filled with family portraits and photos of trips and outings including her favorite, a picture of her and her father when they went to Yellowstone Park the summer she was nine. She glanced over and patted the picture, as she often did, and said, "I love you, Papa." As she entered her room, the top of the mast from their sailboat caught her eye through the window, and she wondered how long it would be before she and her brothers would be able to go out again. She spotted her work clothes laid out on her bed. "Thanks, Mom," she said to no one, before quickly changing and heading off to work.

•   •   •

Chapter 17
AN ENEMY NO MORE

Fall, 1960

When I got off the train freshman year, I didn't know what to expect. My friends were all going to schools near home. My dad's insurance agent, who had gone to St. Jerome's, was my only contact. He brought pictures by the house, and we talked about what the school was like. I wasn't really planning to go there, but they accepted me, and the idea seemed good.

The day I left home, we circled the airport for ten minutes, looking for one of those mythical parking spaces up close. Dad and I gathered my luggage and headed into the small Tampa terminal. Mom had stayed home with Cory, who was three days into a case of chicken pox.

The lobby was quiet. We headed to the Eastern Airlines counter, and I checked in. We took seats facing a tall sheet of glass with thin steel strips separating the panels and watched planes taking off and landing, without saying much. It was sunny and hot, but a storm was kicking up in the Gulf. All my life, my weather had been my parents' weather, and now I was about to go to a place of my own. Whatever storms might be brewing in Whitfield wouldn't include them. They were about to become thin voices on a phone line, growing more distant every day. It all made perfect sense and was exactly what I wanted. *Or was it?*

We talked idly about the sort of things you did when life had squeezed out all that was valuable, leaving words so cheap they sounded silly. Dad talked about the stores and one of the managers he was letting go. I nodded as if I cared. He talked about the storm and how he hoped it missed Tampa because it would be bad for business and asked what I thought about what he'd said.

"Oh, sorry, Dad, I wasn't listening."

"You want some pie?" he asked, a question that seemed funny to me, since I almost never ate pie, and he must have known that by now, but maybe not.

"Sure, Dad."

We wandered across the cool speckled tile floor to the coffee shop and sat at the empty counter on torn red vinyl-topped stools, spinning nervously from side to side.

"What can I get you?" the waitress asked, pulling a pencil from behind her ear.

More time was the answer I was looking for, but pointed to a piece of cherry pie in the pie rack as my second choice.

The pie came. I picked at it, mostly to keep busy. The imitation flavor was so strong it seemed as if it had been freshly picked from whatever trees imitation cherries were grown on. We made small talk, and I looked at my watch, twenty minutes to go. Part of me was ready and part wanted to go home and never leave again. I finished the pie. Dad paid, and we walked back across the open space without speaking.

"Well," he said, stretching out the one word containing all of our experiences, our arguments, our laughter and now our goodbyes.

"Well," I said, knowing there was no way to change or stop it. "Do you think we should call home?"

"Good idea," he said.

I went to the bank of black pay phones on the far side and dropped a dime in the first phone I came to. Mom answered on the second ring.

"Hello," she said in a voice that made me want to be six again, asking her what was for dinner.

"Hi."

"Peter, are you guys doing okay?" Her voice was faint and sad.

"Yeah, we're okay." I looked over at him, knowing we weren't fine at all.

"Is Cory any better?"

"He's fine. I'll let you speak to him."

Cory got on the phone, and we talked for a minute, and I played with the metal cord, and then Mom got back on and reminded me to call her when the plane got to New York. We had been over this at least a thousand times. *But you're really only as good of a parent as the instructions you give, and the more you give them the better they become.* She wanted to play out her role, and of course, I let her. Dad spoke to them for a minute and said goodbye.

The loud speaker announced boarding for my flight while he was still on the line, so when he hung up, my heart racing, I said, "Well, Dad, this is it." We walked back to pick up my bags and jacket. The rows of seats were empty, giving us a moment together alone.

"I'm going to leave you here, Peter," he said, not as much a statement of geography as one of recognition.

Reaching my arms out, I buried my head in his chest. He was wearing his favorite work shirt, and it filled me with the faint scent of seeds and sorrow. Then in a voice that only someone who has known you all your life could do, he said, "Peter, take care of yourself. Make us proud."

Frankly, I had packed no such plans but now felt compelled to try. So I said, in a whisper into the ear of the man who had bravely checked under my bed at night for creatures too vile to mention, who had hired me for summer work over more qualified candidates, and who had played ball with me in the fading twilight, even when I couldn't catch, "I'll try." I owed him that.

I squeezed his sides, and it was over. I picked up my bag and walked to the gate without looking back, and then turned for one last time to smile and wave. He waved back in a long slow motion that said everything would be all right. All these years later I can still see him standing there, waiting for my return. Whatever my father was, he was an enemy no more.

March 4, 1943

The mood at the warehouse was festive. Banners depicting each team's logo hung from the rafters over the work tables. People milled about the large space until Sister Margaret said, "Testing, testing," into the microphone placed on the open landing of the stairs.

Sister Margaret began, "Hello, everyone. As you know for the past three months we have worked diligently in a barn on the St. Anne's Academy campus. The cranberry project was a school project, but our success has brought the need to expand. So let me welcome you to the new home of the Cape Cod Reds. We are very pleased to be in this enormous warehouse, which has been kindly donated by Randall Caulkins. His generosity is greatly appreciated, and we hope to prove worthy of his kindness. With our larger space we are able to expand our program to include you, our community volunteers. I'd like to thank the entire community for coming to our support. We have had especially good response from several of our local businesses: Johnson's Cannery; Alden's Textile Mill; and the Marine Institute. We hope you enjoy our mission as much as those of us at St. Anne's have." After describing the program in detail, Sister Margaret said, "Each of you has been assigned to a team, and I now want to introduce your team leaders." As she called out the girls' names, each girl stepped forward from the back of the landing and gave a little wave. Sister Margaret continued, "As you will see, we have a lot of fun along with our hard work. Each group is located in the area under the appropriate banner. Thank all of you for committing yourselves to our project. Your team leaders will come to meet you now and give you further instructions."

The girls hustled down the stairs to get to their respective groups. When Penny arrived at her station, after welcoming the new Cods, she couldn't resist saying, "I want to introduce you to our happy, swimming Cod named Caleb. This design is my favorite of all the team logos, but then I admit that I am probably prejudiced. Of course, we have a healthy respect for our competition: the Whales; the Starfish; the Lobsters; and the Clams; but no one holds a candle to the Cods. No one. Our goal is to pack and send more boxes than all the other teams combined. The other students and I want you to know how much we appreciate your help." Penny then handed out instruction sheets to the new recruits and assigned each of them a student trainer who had been involved from the beginning.

Penny loved the Cape Cod Reds and the time she spent there, but the project was going to be different now. It had been much simpler in the maintenance barn at the school where they had had only five long tables, two shipping benches, and a large wooden drum that housed the dried berries. One of the girls had brought a radio from home, and the small space had always been filled with big band tunes and laughter. The students had had no real expectations about what they were doing. It was just another project Sister Margaret had dreamed up to get them all into heaven, and so in that sense they were glad to help. Now that they had moved to the warehouse, it would still be fun, but it would not be just a St. Anne's project anymore.

· · ·

Chapter 18

I COULD FEEL HER
BREATH ON MY FACE

Fall, 1960

On my way to college, I spent three days in New York. My grandmother treated me to a stay at the Biltmore Hotel, where she had stayed. I went to a Yankees game and wandered the city like a tourist, not really taking it all in. I got my picture taken at the top of the Statue of Liberty, and another one on the footpath of the Brooklyn Bridge, before leaving the next morning for Whitfield. My car was quiet, filled with only a few businessmen reading the *Wall Street Journal* and three older couples who appeared to be heading off for a vacation on the Cape. I sat on a seat by the window watching vacant buildings on the outskirts of the city roll by. The conductor came by and asked for my ticket, and a few minutes later a cute girl with short brown hair broke my train of thought.

"Is anybody sitting there?" she asked.

"No," I said.

"Great."

She threw her handbag up on the luggage rack above our heads and sat down beside me. There were plenty of empty seats, so I wasn't sure why she bothered. She brushed loose strands of short brown hair off her face and placed them neatly behind her ears. Then she opened a book from her bag.

"What are you reading?" I asked, trying to be friendly.

"Shit if I know," she replied.

"Wait. Who's it by? Because I'm pretty sure I've read that one myself."

"You're kind of funny, aren't ya?"

"Not that much. Goofy, mostly."

"Don't sell yourself short. I'm sticking with funny. Anyway it's required summer reading for this economics course, and I've got until Friday to finish. The message so far is drain the poor, buy more toys, repeat as necessary. But I am only a little ways into it, so we'll see. Maybe the poor will come out on top this time, in one of those surprise endings college textbooks are so famous for. I think the profs just give summer reading to be jerks. Those losers have no life so they want to make sure we don't either. Just because they don't have a ranch in Wyoming is no reason to cut into our fun."

"I agree," I said weakly, without really knowing. A half-empty bottle of salad dressing was as close as I'd gotten to the term "my ranch."

"Where you headed?" she asked.

"College," I said promptly without thinking and wanted to put the word back in my mouth as soon as I said it.

"No shit, you're off to college? Well, howdy, mister." Her voice trailed off.

"It sounded stupid?"

"Pretty much."

"St. Jerome's."

"Oh, that's neat. I have a couple of friends going there. It's a cool place. I stayed in one of the dorms on the Quad, last spring."

Hearing this made me feel better about what was ahead.

"How 'bout you?"

"Pembroke, the girls' part of Brown in Providence. I'm a junior."

She was very cute, and I wished I'd applied to Brown but knew my grades weren't good enough. And you probably had to be versed in all the German poets to have any shot at getting in.

"I'm majoring in economics. How 'bout you?"

"I have no idea."

"Most freshmen don't."

"Is it that obvious?"

"Well, for starters, you should cut off the name tag your mommy sewed into the back of the sweatshirt."

"Thanks, I'm pretty sure she did it in all of my stuff."

"Even your underwear, I bet. They all do. Here," she leaned over and yanked it out of my sweatshirt. "There, Mommy's all gone. I'd do your underwear, but people might stare."

"Well, maybe next time we're on the train," I said.

We talked a few minutes, and then she started to read. She was either going to have to be a very fast reader or ask for help.

"Can I ask a question?" I said a few minutes later.

"Shoot." She reached down to retie her green sneaker. She closed her book, wedging it into the seat beside us and looked into my eyes. She was sitting close and slumped over towards me. I could feel her breath on my face.

"How much harder is it than high school?"

"Some of it depends on where you're going and what you're taking. The courses aren't much worse than high school really. But it sneaks up on you at the end of the semester. The first few weeks you're meeting new people, life is good, and classes aren't demanding. You don't have to go to class, so of course you don't …. And then, wham. You walk into a midterm realizing that you're fucked, unless you have a really cute haircut."

"It's nice," I said. She couldn't possibly have known how much I knew about good hair care.

"Relax, I was kidding." But she ran her hand through it a couple of times, so I knew she was actually proud of how it looked. "But it is pretty nice, isn't it?"

"Absolutely." If she was looking for validation, she'd get no argument from me.

"You'll be fine. Everybody goes through this. It's like the great fear we have about school."

"Which one, because I have a lot of them?"

"Going to class naked. That is until you figure out, hey, wait, I like naked. So what if I'm in an enormous lecture hall without shorts. Clothes are only a temporary state on your way back to naked. Stand up and get naked for me." She tapped me on my leg.

"Right here? I couldn't." My voice was shaky.

"Naw, just jerking your chain. Call me at Pembroke if things get dull. I can take you to some great parties up on the hill."

We both laughed, and then she went back to reading. I looked out the window seeing things for the first time. The afternoon turned out sunny after the rain in New York. In New London friends of hers got on the car in front of ours and came barreling through, making a lot of racket. They seemed to be having more fun than anyone else, and they quickly became the center of attention.

"Hey, Kelly, we're going to the club car for drinks, want to come?" one of the girls asked when they reached our row.

"Sure." Kelly got up to get her bag and leaned over to me. "Remember, no nametags. You're on your own from now on, sailor."

"Thanks, I got it."

She picked up the little white tag my mother had spent so much time working on and said, "Here, Peter Dreeton, keep this. Someday you may need to remember who you are, and this will help."

Spring, 1943

Eric Ralston, twenty-seven, was a whiz kid. He always had been. He graduated a year early from high school and got a full scholarship to Boston University. He finished at the top of his class in marine biology and still had time to teach himself Icelandic. After graduation he was hired to work at the Marine Institute at Whitfield. He was assigned a number of research projects and taught biology classes at the University of St. Jerome three days a week.

One of the perks of teaching at the university was getting to use the athletic facilities, including the indoor pool and the boathouse. Eric had lost two toes in an accident when he was a teenager, which made walking or running difficult. He played squash with other researchers at the Institute, but rowing was his real passion. He took it up while in college and tried to go out for an hour or so at least three times a week. His favorite course was to Bird Island and back, but he also liked rowing out to the lighthouse.

When the Cape Cod Reds began, Eric joined earlier than most of his co-workers. He went to the first community-organizing meeting that Sister Margaret held, signed up that night, and was made a supervisor. He was assigned to the Starfish team, but like all the supervisors, he helped wherever he could.

In the spring of 1943 he received a research grant from the Audubon Society to study the habitat of migrating birds on Bird Island. He needed help collecting data and moving his equipment and wanted to hire some responsible students, so he immediately thought of his team leader Katie and her friends.

• • •

Chapter 19
OFFICE PERKS

My college days were happy times. I made varsity crew as a freshman and was captain my senior year. I enjoyed being in a fraternity and lived in the frat house the last two years. I worked harder than I did in high school and made fair grades, and to cap it off, my post-graduate position in the admissions office turned out better than I expected.

Summer, 1964

I wheeled into my spot at the back of the administration building. *I am much too strong-minded ever to complain openly about my own petty problems—far from it—or to be any kind of a burden to others—far from it—unless there is a slim chance someone is willing to listen, and then I could pretty much go all day, nonstop. But thank God for my parking permit.* Now, one of the chosen, there were no longer hours wasted assessing the risk of being towed to some obscure parking graveyard in northern Montana. My sporty rearview mirror window tag allowed for the commission of a variety of sins against humanity with zero chance of retribution. *And that's the way I like it.*

I tried not letting the power go to my head. I kept the tag in the glove box, *because outright flaunting is totally crass, unless it gets you something you need or want, in which case, all bets are off.* It was simple in design, yet complex enough to unlock all my dreams. It was my ticket to ride... anywhere, anytime, with anyone I chose. I was king of the road. I could do wheelies on the newly manicured grass in front of the administration building, tossing beer cans and delicate articles of women's clothing out the window, and all was good. The power of free parking surrounded me, and we were one.

When friends offered to drive, I would smile and say, "Oh, heavens, no, let's take mine." *Life is what you make it, and trust me, really great parking helps.*

A few students were playing touch football on the front lawn as I drove up, and a couple of small groups were studying under the shade trees lining the perimeter. I pulled into my space under the massive elm. Gathering my brown briefcase, I pushed open the door on my five-year-old green Volvo and entered the building. The buzz inside was powerful.

We were at the beginning of the summer session's drop-and-add period, which in university jargon was like sudden death: One mistake here, and the whole semester was shot. The lobby was overflowing with students trying to make the right decisions, or just any decision. When the music stopped, they were stuck with whatever courses were on their card, no questions asked, no changes made. If they had four art classes and were majoring in physics, well, too bad. At USJ we not only made the rules, we enforced them.

The three ladies behind the counter were going crazy—or maybe they already had. The oldest, Mrs. Coffee, had pulled huge chunks of her graying hair off her head. It was very sad. I've been thinking of getting her a nice scarf for Christmas or maybe one of those funny plastic cones dogs wear to keep them from scratching themselves. Anything would help at this point.

"No, checkers doesn't count toward your major, and your advisor hasn't signed this form," she said in a raised voice, tossing the papers back across the counter. "Come back when it is. Or don't come back at all. Oh, and have a nice day, won't you?" *That's the spirit, Mrs. Coffee; stand your ground.*

My office was the second best on campus. Appearance was important. The better the view, the better our chances were of reeling in good students. It included two chairs, one desk, and a long sofa underneath built-in bookcases. Above the bookcase was my oar from crew signed by all my teammates with my number five in red paint. Over the sofa, my diploma was housed in a thin wooden frame my mother bought for graduation. It was very impressive, except for the oversized Band-Aid covering the writing. A touch Naomi, my sharp-witted secretary, added to symbolize my bruised academic career. When prospective students pointed out this paradox, I laughed it off.

"Isn't my secretary funny? What a sense of humor she has. But seriously, she's embarrassed about showing off the *magna cum laude* sticker. It's under the part you can't see."

I eased myself down into my high back chair, placing my feet on the desk. A stack of phone messages several inches thick was waiting for my response. Our office generally got two kinds of calls: one from students asking questions; the other from counselors setting up appointments. The student questions were easy.

"Do I have to take another year of math? Do all the dorm rooms have private baths? Will I meet the love of my life? How many checkers are on a checkerboard?" My advice, "Keep it simple, kids. Count the red ones and double the amount."

It didn't take me long to become a "seasoned" admissions counselor. There was nothing I couldn't handle. "Can I get credit for third-year Russian taken at a college in Wisconsin during summer school?" I'd respond, "It depends on the part of the state: northern Wisconsin, yes; southern, no." If you had a question, I was one answer ahead. The questions never changed, and soon they rolled off my back without thinking. What they were doing wasn't so much asking questions; they were posing them. I tried to parse out a little extra information to make them feel at ease. I would call each of them back if need be.

Come fall I would need to make appointments at the better high schools. Naomi taught me that appointments with school counselors were set on a first-come-first-served basis. St. Jerome's mostly focused on high schools from New England, the Midwest, and the mid-Atlantic states. But without appointments at the best high schools, we would be left with the retreads, and nobody would be happy with that result. While we took a lot of average students, we were actually searching shamelessly for the gifted. The low-hanging fruit got picked first. I was already feeling edgy. I didn't want my wicker basket for cherry picking to be empty. So over the summer I practiced my spiel for getting appointments.

"Hello, Mrs. McPherson, this is Peter Dreeton from the University of St. Jerome in Whitfield, Massachusetts. I am calling about scheduling a time to meet some of your interested seniors and juniors. I am going to be in Philly on the fifth and sixth of October. Will either of those days work for you?"

Naomi explained that if I couldn't do any better, I should ask for a spot in the library. If I hit a snag, she had a ready-to-go back-up plan, a list of students the university had helped out. Naomi and I called it our "You owe me big time and don't ever forget it" list, so I could look it over to spot a winner.

"Oh, by the way, Mrs. McPherson, you remember Paul Blankenship: withered arm, pale kid. He needed a big financial aid package, and we delivered. Well, I just want to report back that he's sure been enjoying USJ, especially since we all chipped in and bought him the iron lung. What a trouper! We're so happy to have him here." I would wait to let the gravity of our generosity sink in, after which we would settle on twenty minutes out of Holy Cross's visit. "Okay, so we're all set. See you then. That's perfect."

Admissions is a dog-eat-dog world, and it doesn't pay to be the Chihuahua.

April, 1943

Eric spotted Katie at the workbench just as he was finishing up his shift. "I have a proposition for you," he said, approaching her. "I have received a research grant from the Audubon Society to study the habitat of migrating birds on Bird Island. Do you think you and the other team leaders would be interested?" he asked her. "It pays money."

"Sure, that sounds great. We're trying to save money for a trip after graduation. That is if it doesn't take too much time," Katie said, printing a label for a store in Falmouth.

"Maybe an hour or an hour and a half a week. It's on Bird Island; you'd be taking readings from some equipment and recording the results."

"I'll talk to the others. Should I call you at the Institute?"

"No, you don't need to. I'm working Dr. Weidler's shift on Friday, so I can check with you then."

"Okay. I'm pretty sure the others will all be up for it. When would you want us to start?"

"I just got the grant papers back this week, so if everyone signs on, we could start next week. I'd have to take you all out to the island and set up the monitoring stations and show you what needs to be done."

The following Tuesday all five girls showed up in dungarees and flannel work shirts. "I feel as if we're practicing dressing for our Wyoming trip next summer," Penny commented.

Eric laughed when he came into the lobby.

"What's so funny?" Kerrie asked when he walked up.

"Nothing, you ladies just look cute, that's all. And your outfits make you look as if you're in a band together. The Lady Lumberjacks, is that it?"

They all laughed, except Kerrie whose mind began churning. "You know, maybe you've got something there, Doc. With Penny's voice, Katie's looks, and my talent we could be a hit."

"Thanks, sweetheart—what's that leave for Lucy and me?" Mary inquired.

"That's easy. You can be a potted palm, and I'll be a giant redwood," Lucy responded.

"Terrific! I've always wanted a career in show business, and what better place to start than in a bucket," Mary rejoined.

"We can talk about this later," Katie suggested. "I'm sure that Dr. Ralston has better things to do than manage our music career."

"Well, it would be fun, but I have a dinner meeting back here at 6, so we'd better get going," Eric said, opening the door and holding it for the girls.

They walked down to the long wooden pier where a small powerboat was tied up.

"Will one of you be able to drive this?" he asked.

They all laughed. "We may be lumberjacks, but we know our boats, Dr. Ralston," Penny replied.

"Okay, great, let's get going." He laid his notes on the one of the seat cushions, and they all got in.

It took only five minutes to get out to the island, and he explained the project in more detail during the ride.

They spent almost an hour using his map to secure each of the twenty-five weather stations, and he showed them how to take readings. It seemed easy enough, and the girls were all looking forward not only to making a little money, but also to having a chance to get away from all the pressures of school and the warehouse.

• • •

Chapter 20

HOW BAD CAN A TURKISH NOVEL BE?

Summer, 1964

Everything I learned about admissions work I learned from Naomi. She taught me how to schmooze with the parents and kids, while appearing aloof and disinterested at the same time. Like any rookie, at first I brought too much of one skill and not enough of the other.

"Peter," she said before the start of my first interview, "the Davis family is here to see you." I popped up from my spring-loaded seat as if someone had thrown a venomous snake onto my lap.

"Bad job," she pointed out after they left. "Way too needy. That's never going to work. Relax and let them come to your space. Take deep breaths; make them feel as if they're entering a place of reverence. Act as if they've been granted an audience with the Boston Archbishop, prior to his making an important ruling on a disputed bingo call. Do you see what I'm saying?"

Soon I got the routine down. When visitors came in, my head was always buried in the second paragraph on page 86 of a carefully selected book. Naomi also marked a spot on the bookshelf opposite me, and when visitors passed in front of it, I slowly got up from behind my desk to greet them with a warm smile.

"Please," I said indicating for them to take a seat. My palms faced upward, my arms lifted in front of me, moving slowly apart, as if in the middle of some religious ceremony.

Sometimes when a single student came for an interview, I made the same gesture waiting for him to pick a chair, but as soon as he chose, I yelled out, "Not in that one. Are you crazy?" A wild expression of horror crossed my face, and of course, he'd take the other chair. You can't imagine what an icebreaker this maneuver turned out to be.

Naomi had pegged me for a loser from the first day, until I introduced my "not-in-that-fucking-chair" routine. After that, her opinion changed considerably.

"May we offer you something to drink?" Naomi asked the family as they entered the office. Generally people accepted, if only to be polite. Naomi took their drink orders and disappeared before the interview began.

I put a bookmark slowly back onto the same unread page.

We usually "read" from the same book for two or three weeks. My favorites were the foreign language books. But we hadn't gone foreign since the unfortunate incident with the Turkish family from Brooklyn.

"Oh, my, you speak Turkish?" Mr. Hasfas asked walking into my office. He had spotted the Turkish novel in my hands. Of course, I hadn't understood a single word he said because he was speaking Turkish, and there were no subtitles for me to read. The book had actually been a spontaneous purchase I had made at a garage sale two weeks earlier. I hated not buying something because it seemed rude and I thought, "For a quarter how bad can a Turkish novel be?"

"Excuse me?" I said in English. The best I could do was to explain that I was teaching myself the language, because I found the Turkish people and their customs so very interesting. Although a four-hundred-page novel about a blind avocado farmer and his family's struggles must have seemed like a far-fetched place for me to start.

"So actually it was his wife's orchard, not his brother-in-law's. Of course, that makes so much more sense, doesn't it? Thanks for clearing that up, Mr. H.," I said.

He asked why I had chosen such a difficult book to start.

"Sadly, the university's Turkish collection is quite thin at the moment," I replied and in the spirit of friendship, he offered to send a good selection of Turkish classics for all the students to enjoy.

"Geez, that's so generous. I don't know what to say," but with help from his daughter, Hanni, I thanked him in Turkish, and we moved on.

Since that episode, Naomi has retained editorial control over my reading list. "We can't afford another international fuck-up, and it's not like you're reading them anyway."

July 10, 1943

The girls were having a busy summer. Today they had called an official day off from everything else. They were going to spend the day together just relaxing and having fun.

Penny picked them all up and was taking them to the marina near her house, but first she had to go to the boatyard.

"Why are we stopping here?" Mary asked.

"Because my dad wants me to pick up a part for the other boat," Penny said. "It won't take a second." The girls all got out of the car and went inside the little office of Bellini's Boatyard.

Looking over the display rack of Cape Cod Reds, Mary noted, "Hey, look, I see my Lobsters are flying off the shelves. You girls had better get cracking if you hope to catch me in this month's totals."

Just then Mr. Bellini came through the backdoor. "Hey, ladies, it's good to see you all," he greeted them. Having overheard Mary, he continued, "We are selling a lot of boxes of cranberries, but a strange thing happened two weeks ago or so, the last time I had a case of Lobster boxes. There was one Starfish box mixed in with the Lobsters."

"That's weird," Katie responded. "We're very good about not mixing them up like that."

"My younger nephew selected that box, and when he opened it, there was no trading card inside. Instead there was a torn piece of notebook paper with a funny note on it. As I recall, some girl was asking another about her date for a dance. You must have some absentminded volunteers," Mr. Bellini joked.

"I suppose anyone can be distracted at some time or other, Mr. Bellini, but it is very curious. We do try to have good quality control," Katie replied. "What happened to the paper?"

"Oh, I threw it out."

·   ·   ·

The large white sail opened out in front of them. Penny was at the helm while Randy, her oldest brother, worked the ropes. *The Maiden Voyage,* a twenty-foot catboat, was the smaller of the Caulkinses' two boats. They used this one for day sails along the Cape. The larger boat, a sloop named *Edgar's Folly,* was used for sailing up the coast to Penny's grandparents' house in Maine or down to Newport or Block Island to visit friends. The longest trip that Penny had been on was a weeklong sail to Cape May the summer she was eleven.

Penny loved her time on the water, especially on days like today with her brother and her best friends. It was the weekend after July 4th and a scorcher. Their plan was to sail over to Bird Island and spend the afternoon gathering shells and lying on warm sand.

"I'm hot," Katie said, fanning her face. "Can't you make this boat go a little faster?"

"Yeah, a lot, but we'd need more wind," Randy replied.

"Here, have some lemonade," Penny said. "We'll be there before you finish."

Just as Penny promised, by the time Katie finished, Randy was dropping anchor off the north end of Bird Island. The water was shallow enough that they could almost walk on to land. Randy put their drinks and lunch inside a large wooden box and tied a rope onto his arm.

"Last one to the air-raid tower has to kiss Randy," Mary said jumping into the water with a big splash.

"No offense, Randy, but I hope it isn't me," Penny said.

"You're excused, Penny," Katie said jumping over the side a step behind Mary.

When Randy arrived a few minutes after them, they had ruled it a tie, and each one of the four girls gave him a kiss on his cheek.

"Just think," Lucy said as they ate lunch and chatted, "this time next year we'll all be on the train to Wyoming, ladies."

"Have you started packing yet?" Kerrie asked.

"Not yet, but maybe soon." Lucy replied.

"Oh, that reminds me. I have some really exciting news. I saw a notice in the newspaper about an audition to be held for a USO program in Newport at the end of August," Penny exclaimed. "Oh, guys, we've got to do this! We can rehearse. We'll be great."

After lunch, they collected shells, sunbathed, and swam. But by four some annoyingly dark clouds appeared in the distance over the St. Peter's church steeple.

"Come on, ladies. We'd better cut this short. It looks as if it could get nasty soon," Randy said, putting the remains of lunch back in the wooden box. Ten minutes later they were on board and heading back to the Caulkinses' dock. But heavy squall winds swept over the hull, and white caps lay ahead of them. Everyone put on life jackets, and they huddled together as Randy tried to avoid the worst of the storm. About halfway across the bay, one of the lines holding the sail came loose, and Randy told Penny to take the helm. He slipped on the wet deck as he went to fix it and grabbed the rail, but a sudden wind shift caused the boom to crack him in the head and knock him overboard.

"I'm going for Randy. You girls start bailing," Lucy said jumping off the side. She came up for air but couldn't see the orange material for which she was looking. Driving rain covered her face. She turned her head and caught a glimpse of something thirty feet to her left. Randy was being carried away by the currents, and she had to act quickly. Lucy put her head down and took long powerful strokes. She could see his head bobbing in the water and blood streaming down his face. She put her own head back down and swam hard to meet him. Getting there was only part of the problem: Lucy was tall but thin; Randy, on the other hand, was six two and weighed over two twenty.

"Randy, you okay?" she called out, not wanting to grab him until she knew the status of his injury. "You okay, Randy?" Lucy repeated her question, and Randy groaned. Lucy grabbed him under his left arm and began dragging the two of them back to *The Maiden Voyage*.

It took all the strength Lucy had in her to get them back. Sometimes they floated and sometimes she pulled, but by the time they reached the boat, the rain had almost stopped. The other girls were still bailing water, but Penny had things under control. They made it back without any other incidents, but that day changed their relationship from best friends to something more like sisters. They never talked openly about it, but they all felt the bond inside. *We are the five fireflies forever!*

. . .

Chapter 21
FLOATING ON THE WOW

Summer, 1964

"Hi, I'm Peter Dreeton. Welcome to St. Jerome's," I said in a sophisticated voice, sounding like the host of Opera News on NPR.

"Hi, we're the Petersons," a tall man with thinning hair replied. "I'm Frank, my wife Denise, our daughter Cathy, and this is our son Carl."

"Where are you from?" I asked Mr. Peterson. Of course, Naomi had already given me their personal information sheet, so I knew the side of the street they lived on and how much toothpaste they had left in the tube.

"Kansas City!" Mr. Peterson belted out.

"Wow! That's great." My lame response worked for other cities around the globe, though some were more plausible than others. I turned to Cathy and tried to get her involved.

"And where do you go to school, Cathy?" I asked.

"St. Bart's. It's a girls' school."

"Wow! That's great."

Of course, I didn't care what her answer was. I nodded in appreciation and took a moment considering what Cathy might look like naked. But then I realized this wasn't the best time for having such thoughts. Instead I moved the book back from the front of the desk and wrote down her naked score of 8.5 on the yellow tablet. Moving the book only reinforced the illusion we were trying to project. *We are a community of readers! We read for fun; we read to live; we read in the shower; we read when no one is watching. Well, not really, who does that? No one, of course, but it was kind of fun to say.* Then we moved quickly into the flow.

"In what are you interested in majoring?"

"Nursing," she answered.

"Wow, nursing, that's great. We certainly have a wonderful nursing department, Cathy Peterson." *You lucky dog!*

I had at least three minutes of worthless chatter for each major, so no matter what they asked about, whether it was nursing, business administration, or fly-fishing, it all flowed from the same stream. That would be the "Wow, that's great" Stream, which incidentally was connected to the "Wow, that's great" River before it reached fruition in the "Wow" Ocean. *The geographies of our globe, our lives, even our admissions interviews are all interconnected, and that's kind of amazing when you think about it. Therefore, in order to be a good citizen of our planet, one must understand the delicate balance between what happens on the "Wow Stream of Life" to have some idea of how things will play out in the "Wow Ocean." Capisce? We're all just little fish, swimming upstream into the big Pond of Wow.*

I explained how we had a great program with a teaching hospital in Boston. I could do this in my sleep and sometimes actually got very close to rapid eye movement. Naomi had threatened to toss her green plastic glass filled with ice water over the front of my chest if she ever heard me snoring. She would follow it up by saying to our guests, "Oh, my God, I thought Peter's necktie caught on fire again. I'm sure I smelled smoke. How many times has that happened this month? Three, maybe four times, right? That does it. I'm stopping at J.C. Penney's after work and buying you a couple of those flame retardant ties I was telling you about." Stomping to the door, she would add, "I can't remember, Peter. Do you prefer clip-ons, or the ones you tie yourself?"

"Either will be fine, Naomi. I have some of both."

I looked over at the Petersons and threw in some personal tidbits about Cathy's major to add a human touch. "I went to the nurse a few weeks back when I got this really creepy rash, and she was soooo helpful." Then pulling out an almost empty yellow tube from my desk drawer, I said, "See, it's called

Benzenheximine or something like that. Nurses provide such a useful service, don't you agree?"

Frankly, they seemed just as interested in the healing powers of nursing as I was. Then we talked about the university and some of the academic features about which I knew they would enjoy learning. "We have 2500 undergraduates, 500 grad students in 6 fields, and a faculty of over 300. We have advanced degrees in nursing, business administration, law, and religious studies."

There were two other programs that I never could remember so I just made something up. My favorite made-up degree was aircraft manufacturing. That always got a rise out of my guests. They found it hard to believe a small university would have such a specialized program, but they didn't question my authority, especially after I pulled out my brown leather aviator cap from the middle drawer and put it on my head. I began making funny airplane sounds, tilting an imaginary steering wheel left and then right, as if banking into soft white clouds in a sunlit sky.

"Whatyathink, Petersons? Have I got this baby under control? What do you say we take her up the coast and see some of the shoreline before it gets dark?" But then I would let them off the hook, explaining it was all in good fun, of course.

"Our campus is 124 acres, built by the Jesuit Fathers. We have 6 dorms, 3 off-campus residences, and 10 intercollegiate sports teams. We also have a big hot shot in our meteorology department who invented clouds."

"Peter, you can't be 'cirrus'," Mr. Peterson answered. "Nobody invented clouds."

Apparently the Petersons were pretty much up on their cloud trivia, and I liked to see that. Smart parents meant smart kids, and we were always on the prowl for some of them. *Let's face it; in some ways I should've been paying the university for this job. I was having so much fun. And no, of course, I wasn't "cirrus" either. I needed the money too much. Beer doesn't grow on trees you know.*

Naomi returned with their drinks and Cathy's transcripts.

"Wow, look at these grades. Very impressive, Cathy. I know someone who's been working hard."

She timidly said, "Thank you." She looked really cute with her big smile and dimples so I moved her naked score up to 9.0.

I looked over at the elder Petersons on the sofa, giving them a nod, which translated to "Good job, Peterson parents. You guys are the best!! What's your secret?"

After another good chuckle, they launched into a lengthy serenade about how they had always tried to instill a good work ethic into their kids, and to teach good family values. I had to be careful, because often during one of these long-winded conversations my tie would catch on fire. In order to stay alert, I began counting backwards from twenty-seven.

Fortunately they came on a spectacular day, and both of my double windows were opened wide. From her seat Cathy could see out to the water.

"I love you guys. We'd really love to have Cathy apply. With her grades and test scores; she'll certainly qualify for a hefty academic scholarship. How does that sound, Mr. P.?"

"Naomi," I called out, although she was actually standing just outside the doorway watching the whole scene take place. "Please, come in when you get a chance."

Usually she waited an appropriate amount of time before making her dramatic entrance. Sometimes she began a countdown with her fingers before entering. She counted them off without saying any of the numbers out loud. With each number she ticked off, she pulled her arm back to her side before shooting it up again. Sometimes when she was jerking my chain, she left a number out or bugged her eyes out with a weird expression that said: "Oops, what the hell happened to three?"

She smiled back at me and said, "Yes," turning her head away from the door to make her response seem far away and busy.

Everyone smiled back, and we moved a step closer to sealing the deal.

"Unless I am wrong here, Cathy's going to be a Crusader," I said looking at Naomi when she entered the room.

Cathy nodded in approval. The deal done; she was toast. The Petersons' heads bobbing on the sofa were also toast. This job was exhausting, so actually, I was toast as well. The five of us had become stacks of wheat toast sitting along the buttery banks of the Wow River and nothing more.

August 28, 1943

The USO canteen in Newport was held at the Naval War College a week before Labor Day, to entertain troops getting ready to go overseas and to raise money to open canteens in other cities. The girls had no delays getting to Newport, other than being held up at the start by Kerrie looking for her wallet, but that time cost them being stuck behind a long line of cars leading into the Naval War College.

"How long's this going to take?" Penny asked the man directing traffic at the entrance gate.

"From here, I'd say maybe a half hour," he responded and waved them to turn into the far parking lot. Katie looked at her watch. It was almost 2:45, and the auditions were supposed to stop at 3:30.

"Come on. We need to hurry," Kerrie said jumping out of the backseat.

"Oh, really? Well, you heard Kerrie. Let's go, girls," Mary replied sarcastically.

The registration table was under a large white tent sitting in the middle of a grassy field overlooking Narragansett Bay. Lucy was the first to get there, and she asked for the appropriate forms. One of the three women working the booth handed her the applications but said, "Don't get your hopes up. They're shutting down the tryouts soon, and whoever is left in the line is out of luck."

Once in the queue they decided to take turns. "Let's do shifts," Katie suggested. "Mary and I will start. Lucy and Penny, you be back here in ten minutes."

"Hey, what about Kerrie?" Mary asked.

"I think she went to the bathroom, but who knows?" Penny volunteered.

The line moved quickly and by 3:25 they were within ten feet of the making the cut. But a few minutes later, one of the Navy officers came out and gave the bad news.

"Sorry, folks. Thanks for trying, but we've got a full show for this evening. I hope you'll stay and enjoy the entertainment and better luck next time. If you're interested, there's another canteen next month in Boston."

Penny threw her hands in the air. "Where's Kerrie? I'm going to choke her."

"Not till I finish," Mary added.

"Say, where is she?" Katie asked. "She's been AWOL for quite some time." Just then Kerrie came walking up to the group with a big smile on her face. "You might want to wipe that grin off your face. We're about to read you your last rites," Katie warned.

"For what? Saving the day?" Kerrie answered.

"What are you talking about?" Penny questioned.

"Come on. You'll see. I sweet-talked one of the members of the Shore Patrol into getting us in the "back door," so to speak. He said they never lock the back door to the stage for fire safety reasons. He even got us costumes to wear so we won't be noticed."

"Costumes? Why would that matter?" Lucy asked.

"Well, it's actually sort of a restricted area, but let's not quibble over details. We've got a show to put on. Right, girls?"

"Is anyone else nervous about this?" Lucy questioned.

"I'm sure it will be all right. Won't it, Kerrie?" Katie responded.

"Relax. It'll be fine. Let me tell you about it," Kerrie assured them.

At ten minutes to five they walked up to a security gate. Kerrie introduced the other girls to the guard, Tom, who gave them instructions about where to change and how to tie a sailor's knot. Ten minutes later the Navy's five newest recruits marched out on the grass beside the barracks.

"Remember, we have to salute if an officer goes by," Kerrie advised. "Tom told me just to hang out here behind this building until we hear the music stop. Then we are supposed to race up those metal stairs, push on that door, and go on to the stage."

A few minutes later they heard the music coming to an end, and Kerrie said, "Come on, girls. This is our big chance. Break a leg." And she climbed the black metal steps to the stage door and pushed. It didn't budge.

"So much for that hare-brained idea, Kerrie," Mary said.

"Don't be such a pessimist. Let's all try it at once. Maybe it's just stuck."

They all said in unison, "One, two, three, push." In one display of brute force, the doors both swung open, and they tumbled out onto the stage on the last note of *Somewhere over the Rainbow*. Confused, the singer looked around, and the stage manager came from across the stage to get them off. Kerrie, who was first out, tripped over her long white sailor pants, falling face down into the lap of a trumpet player. She righted herself, rolled up her pants legs, and without missing a beat, tap-danced back to the other girls who were now standing beside the microphone in the middle of the stage. The master of ceremonies shook his head and told the girls they had to leave. But the sailors in the front rows were enjoying the girls' spunk and began yelling to let them sing. The master of ceremonies gave in, and the girls curtsied to the audience.

Penny stepped to the microphone. "Hi, there. I'm Penny, and we're part of the Cape Cod Reds. I guess you've all heard about the dried cranberries we sell to support the troops." A loud cheer went up from the audience. "This is Katie the Starfish, Mary the Lobster, Lucy the Whale, and Kerrie the Ham—I mean *Clam*—and I'm Penny the Cod, and we'd like to do a song for you."

They broke out into Cole Porter's "Anything Goes." After the song, they bowed, blew kisses, and started walking off stage, but the sailors called for an encore. The girls looked over to the master of ceremonies, and he reluctantly nodded his approval. They were huddled up deciding what to do next, when Lucy said, "Let's have Penny do her favorite song, Gershwin's "They Can't Take That Away From Me," and we'll back her up." This performance was greeted with even more applause. The girls waved to their adoring fans and went out the same door they came in.

On their way out Kerrie stopped to thank their talent agent who had got them in the back door. She wrapped her arms around the young recruit and gave him a wet kiss on the cheek.

"She's not always like this," Katie said to him, trying to defend Kerrie's honor.

Mary jumped in, "No—sometimes she's worse."

They changed back into their civilian clothes and spent the rest of the evening dancing with sailors and accepting their newfound fame as entertainers.

• • •

Chapter 22

CUFFED TO A URINAL IN
THE GIRLS' BATHROOM

Summer, 1964

I started my tour with the Petersons at the nursing department so Dr. Canfield could walk Cathy into a couple of classes, to give her the flavor of college life. Then we headed off to one of the nearby classroom buildings. I picked the building closest to us, even though it needed a little repair. The rails on the stairwells were bad, and it looked sort of worn, but it didn't faze them. Mrs. P. called it charming, which I thought was overdoing it. We took a short tour of two of the dorms before stopping at the bookstore. I chatted with Robert, the bookstore manager, while the Petersons bought T-shirts and caps. Robert had a theory that if you counted the USJ Scotty dog vest sales, you could tell your admission winners. So far he'd been right. Robert even placed four stuffed Scotties in the vests by the checkout stand to track his theory. It made sense but the other day I noticed that some student had placed two of the Scotties in what can most politely be called a rear end collision. I thought it was funny but wanted to say "Hey, grow up, people. This is college, not elementary school." But I have to admit it did seem funny. The Petersons finished up in the bookstore, and we ended the tour in the cafeteria. I had brought along a food chip and put it in Mr. Peterson's hand.

"Please, sir, have lunch here on us."

He seemed appreciative, but embarrassed.

"Oh that's not necessary, Peter."

"No, no, we insist. A full creamed pie for each of you."

If he played his cards right, there were well over twenty-four thousand calories buried in this one chip. "And just for fun, you've got to try the chef's surprise: chipped beef on toast. It's a memory waiting to happen."

We all smiled again and said our goodbyes. I looked at my watch; even though it had only been forty-eight minutes, I stopped at the counter to buy Naomi a Snickers. It was always a good idea to build up a reserve for later. Plus, a pair of identical twins from Albuquerque was coming in at three, and for certain they'd take up the rest of my afternoon.

Campus tours took anywhere from twenty minutes if just hitting the highlights... "Yeah, yeah... the gym is over that way ... bounce balls, shoot hoops, you got it; classroom buildings are down there on your left; you got it; great, call me; and don't be a stranger, stranger"... to over an hour, if I was fully engaged.

Generally, they had to be really cute and appreciate my dry sense of humor to get the full hour deluxe tour. The current record stood at one hour and thirty-five minutes with a former "Miss Ovaltine finalist" and was worth every minute. My time is way too valuable to be wasting it on "Miss Runner-up" or "Miss Sews-her-own-clothes" for heaven's sakes. To those contestants, I simply say, "Thanks for dropping by, ladies. Have you two been friends long? Yup, that is Van Zandt Gym way over there beyond the brown building: bounce balls; shoot hoops. Don't forget your room deposit is due on the twelfth, and don't be a stranger, stranger."

After an hour, Naomi said it was officially loafing, violation 136B in the school's criminal code, and she'd call campus security to have me rounded up. You can't imagine the humiliation of being stuffed in the back of their golf cart, with my left hand cuffed to the dark metal support frame. Then just to rub it in, the school's rent-a-cops would turn on their blinking red light, indicating another dangerous felon had been brought to his knees. *Whoopee, great police work, fellas.*

"What's the offense this time, poor use of a sand wedge?" Let me just say for the record that if my job involved driving a golf cart with a caution light on top, I wouldn't go around acting as if I was Mr. Big Shot. But face it, not everyone is as humble as I am.

When we got back to the office, they bragged to Naomi, like two small boys catching their first fish.

"Great police work, fellows," Naomi said, feeding their already inflated senses of accomplishment.

"Miss Ovaltine and I were sitting under a shade tree sharing our favorite Walt Whitman poems," I responded.

Just then Father Myers passed us in the hall outside my office and asked about the handcuffs.

"Oh, another fraternity prank: A couple of the Kappa Sig's cuffed me to one of the urinals in the girls' bathroom." But Naomi, who was leaning against the doorframe simply frowned and said, "That's ridiculous, Peter. They don't have urinals in girls' bathrooms."

"Yeah, that's what I thought, but boy, was I wrong."

"An hour and thirty-five minutes. No, really, Peter. What took you so long?" she questioned.

"Father Didmanano stopped us on the way over, and you know how much he loves to talk." It always worked better for me if I could drop the name of a priest who just happened to be wandering around campus while I was out. But she always seemed skeptical when the priest didn't work at the school or worse yet if he'd recently died.

"He did? Are you sure? I ate lunch with him last Thursday."

"Yes, Peter. I sang at his funeral, open casket." She left me empty-handed. I shook my head, throwing my hands in the air.

"Well, we're certainly all going to miss him. What a dear friend and mentor he's been." I bowed my head for a moment of silence. After that screw-up, I always checked the school paper to see if my alibis were still on the "active" squad.

Or I tried the famous celebrity routine. "No, I'm not kidding; Frankie Avalon in front of our library. I said, 'Frankie, no way, man. This is crazy. What the hell are you doing at USJ?' And look, Naomi, he autographed this for you." Then I tossed her a napkin, on which I had scribbled, "To Naomi, all my love, Frankie." I kept a handful of similar autographs in my jacket pocket, for just this type of occasion.

She was hungry and tired of playing games. "What did you bring me?" she asked.

I tossed a Snickers bar on her desk. "Just make sure the bosses upstairs don't know how long I was gone."

"No, of course not. Do you think I'm some sort of a snitch?"

"No, of course not." We were both lying through our teeth, but hers showed delicate chunks of creamy caramel goodness.

September 17, 1943

Penny's house was the only one large enough for sleepovers, and every year the girls gathered there for a back-to-school night. Her mother made lasagna, and they sat at the dining room table and talked about their teachers and boys. Mrs. Caulkins ate with the girls and peppered them with too many questions for Penny's taste, but she let her mother have fun. Penny's dad had gone to visit her older brothers at Yale and then on to New York for a business meeting. After dinner the girls helped to clear and do the dishes and then left for the movies. Mrs. Caulkins asked if they were meeting boys; Katie explained this was their girls-only evening at the movies. They thanked Penny's mom for a wonderful dinner and drove to the 7:15 showing of Alfred Hitchcock's *Shadow of a Doubt.*

The Majestic was a small movie theatre built in the late thirties. It sat on the corner of Center and Daniel Streets. Out front an art deco spire with five neon lights rose into the nighttime sky, and in large lettering the word "Majestic" wrapped around the circular base. Two enclosed boxes featured posters of the upcoming attractions: *Girl Crazy* with Judy Garland and Mickey Rooney and *Stage Door Canteen* with lots of stars doing cameos. Kerrie said she was dying to see Judy's latest release. While they were buying tickets, Robin and Vicky, two other girls from their class, showed up, and the group of seven went in together. They handed their tickets to Robin's younger brother, who had just started working there the week before.

"Nice threads," Kerrie said admiring his short gold jacket and black tuxedo pants.

"Lay off, Kerrie. He looks good to me," Lucy said shoving Kerrie in the shoulder.

"Thanks, Joel," Katie said handing him her ticket and eyeing the concession stand. The lobby was half-full, and there was short line waiting at the candy counter. A fresh bucket of corn was crackling over the top of the pan, and the aroma was overwhelming. They walked across the ornate red carpet and bought three bags of popcorn, four sodas, and a box of Mary Jane candies.

As they walked into the theatre, Mary suggested sitting in the small balcony, but Katie liked sitting in the middle of the theatre and pointed out that the balcony's rows were closer together. The Majestic had two main aisles and featured ceiling art of two Greek goddesses in long flowing togas meeting in the center. Kerrie had named the two figures Betty Grable and Hedy Lamarr, and Mary always had to ask her which one was which. "Honestly, Mary, Betty Grable has blond hair. We've been over that before; don't you remember?" Kerrie replied digging her hand deep into the bag of popcorn, just as the lights went down. After several previews, a Woody Woodpecker cartoon was followed by the

MovieTone News feature. The announcer reported stories on a new tank project being built in St. Louis and the latest comings and goings of Hollywood movie stars, and then it switched to the shouts of sailors at a canteen in Newport, calling out, "Let them sing! Let them sing!" The announcer recounted how five high school girls from Whitfield, Massachusetts had crashed the party without an invitation but then had stopped the show with their energetic performance.

"Oh, my God," Kerrie jumped up and began screaming. "Hey, people, that's us. We're famous."

Other moviegoers around the girls looked over to see what the commotion was about, and Kerrie obliged by pointing to the screen and repeating, "That's us. We're famous." Kerrie began blowing kisses to the crowd, until Mary pulled her back down into the seat.

·   ·   ·

Chapter 23
I DIDN'T SEE THAT COMING

September 17, 1964

On my first big road trip, I didn't know what to expect. Naomi had me running from one school to another, and on the second night, there was a college night program at the coliseum. Joking aside, I loved my job and put in lots of hours for which I wasn't paid. I'd come back sometimes a couple of nights a week to check up on people who had sent in their applications. I'd talk to their folks, help the students with their science homework, and give them dating advice; whatever it took to make them feel as if they were part of the team.

At this program they mixed schools in a random fashion. Tonight my booth buddies were Betts Vocational and Technical, a local trade school, and Duke. On this occasion Betts was featuring TV repair, though they offered a whole host of similar job opportunities, including backhoe operator, which sounded intriguing as well. The rep was setting up his demo television set when I walked up.

"Hi, I'm Peter Dreeton, your new neighbor."

He looked over while plugging in the big black box and introduced himself. "Harold Vines," he answered.

"Will we be catching the Cubs game or *Bonanza*? I'm dying to see who Little Joe takes to the hoedown."

"'Fraid not, this is only a demonstration TV. It doesn't pick up live shows."

"Really? That sounds a lot like my set....No Cubs then?"

"No Cubs." He coughed a deep smoker's cough, leaving a glob of something yellow on the floor near the plug. I could tell we were headed for a long night of wheezing, hacking, and watching tiny vertical lines flipping over and over on the face of the set. *The thought made me nervous. Repetitive activities can freak me out, especially the ones that keep happening over and over again.*

"Are you going to fix that thing, soon?" I asked, feeling my hands starting to sweat.

"Sure, not to worry." He pulled the moving line down to a slow roll, and I started feeling better right away.

"Where are you from?" he asked, lighting a cigarette.

"Boston—well actually Cape Cod, but it's easier to say Boston. What about you?"

"Right here, south side of the city, over near the ballpark."

"You guys do pretty well here?"

"Yeah, we do okay, and your place?"

"This is my first time here. I think it's sort of hit or miss, but we'll see."

"Well, good luck."

"Thanks, same to you."

There were several TV questions I wanted to clear up but didn't want to seem pushy. I jotted down, "Ask Harold about my vertical hold button and where snow comes from."

As visual aids, I placed two large posters on the wall divider behind me. Just as I finished hanging the second one, the Duke rep walked up carrying a large black luggage bag and two posters under her other arm. She was my age and full of energy.

"Hi, I'm Susan Williams," she said with a big smile.

"Hi, Peter Dreeton with St. Jerome's."

Harold went with a pithy one-word answer, "Harold." Then he burst out in another round of hacking sounds.

"Did you go to Duke?" I asked.

"Yeah, I graduated last year in sociology and am going to grad school at Penn next year. How 'bout you?"

"Me? Well, no real plans yet. This is my first year, but eventually I'd like to work in advertising in New York."

"Really? That sounds neat. Did you major in it?"

"No. I majored in beer actually, but I'd like to be a writer or at least creative, and I'm pretty good with origami."

"Well, that should help."

"Thanks. I hope so, and good luck to you."

I decided to make a stop at concessions before hearing confession and gave into my desires for a package of peanut butter crackers. When I returned, Susan had all of her materials displayed in a neat fashion. Even the response cards were divided into stacks by major. Her small give-away banners were lined up in perfect rows. I realized I needed to turn my own motivation up a notch. But, not wanting to peak too soon, I threw down four course catalogs, a stack of reply cards, and a copy of *Sporting News* with Roger Maris's picture on the cover. Then I pulled out a deck of playing cards, in case things got really slow. Harold dialed up a snow scene on his demo set, and we were ready for takeoff. The opening chimes went off, and from the front came a wave of students. I rocked back and forth in my brown steel folding chair, wishing I'd brought my transistor radio and a fishing pole. During the first hour Susan never took a full breath, while my heart rate slowed to three beats a minute. At one point I almost fell over backwards but caught the back edge of the table.

"Whoa. That was close."

"You okay?" Susan asked, looking over between three girls, all of whom were hanging breathlessly on her every word.

"Sure. I'm fine," I answered back. "Just practicing my meditation exercises, that's all."

Harold's business was steady, and he seemed to be having good luck with the ones who were stopping by.

I talked to eight students the first hour, which didn't sound too bad, but two of them just wanted directions, and a third needed a light for his cigarette. I wanted to say to him, "Cool people don't smoke," but I just shook my head and pointed toward the concessions area. *So our*

score at halftime read: Duke 49, Betts 14, and St. Jerome's 5.
Then six girls from St. Michael's Academy stopped by for a
visit, and we had some good laughs about some skin care
products that had just come on the market. They were only
sophomores and couldn't have cared less about what school
I worked for or even if I was employed. Nevertheless Cynthia
shared an amazing story about a new acne treatment, which
in her words "cleared Jennifer Simon's face overnight."

"As if she needed it!" one of the girls added.

"That's crazy, don't you think?' another girl asked me.

"Absolutely, Lauren," I replied. "I'll keep it in mind the
next time I'm passing through puberty." They all giggled.

They were fun, and it's always nice to give the illusion of
being busy. With about a half hour left, we hit a lull. There were
a few more bursts, but by nine the place had thinned to a crawl,
so Harold began dismantling his booth. I still had a number
of important television questions to ask, but he explained he
couldn't help with crummy programming decisions.

"We can't make the shows better, just clearer," he
volunteered, chuckling to himself. It was probably a line he
used a lot when making his presentations, and I wondered
what funny comments he had about backhoeing. I nodded
and helped him load his bulky equipment onto one of the
steel carts which the exhibit hall provided.

Susan finished packing up stuff and wished me good
luck. Then she and Harold left together. "Whoa! I didn't see
that coming!" I said to no one in particular.

September 17, 1943

After the movie Kerrie wanted to stand outside and sign autographs for the other moviegoers, but the rest of the group wouldn't go along with her plan. "Maybe we should hire an agent," Kerrie proposed. "I can call Judy Garland and see who she uses."

"That sounds good. When you get a hold of Judy, let us know," Mary chuckled sarcastically.

They said goodbye to Vicky and Robin and headed back to Penny's house, where they shared their exciting news with Mrs. Caulkins, who was in the living room listening to the radio. They chatted there until a little after 10:00 and then went up to Penny's room. Laughter came periodically out from under the door, as a boy's name would be called out and a response would follow. Around 10:30, Mrs. Caulkins came to Penny's door and said good night. She told them not to be up too late. She noticed they had already changed into pajamas, which she saw as a good sign. She congratulated them for their moment on the big screen and walked down the hall to the master bedroom with Tasbo following behind.

The girls patiently waited until 11:00 before changing into beach clothes and sneaking carefully past Penny's parents' room and down the staircase. Josh and some other boys were waiting at the end of the drive. They piled into Josh's parents' car and headed out to the far end of Whitfield's beach. As long as they didn't cause any problems or make too much noise, they could be there all night and not be noticed. Two of the boys made a fire near a summer cottage that was already shuttered for the winter, and they all shared beer that one of the boys had taken from his garage. A boy named Joe jokingly asked Mary to marry him. Mary said yes but only if she didn't have to do his laundry, pick up his clothes, or sleep with him, and he promptly withdrew his offer. Katie and Josh walked together along the beach, almost to the lighthouse and back. Josh talked about tomorrow's game, and Katie bragged about their big news of being celebrities.

Around 12:30 the beer ran out and so had their time. The boys dropped the girls back at Penny's house, and a little after 1, all the girls were fast asleep.

·   ·   ·

Chapter 24
WE DID MAKE A CUTE COUPLE

September 19, 1964

We met at a fraternity party three months after I got hired to work in admissions. Julie Mathers was sitting alone on the back steps drinking a beer.

"Hi, I'm Peter." I said, sitting on the same back step. She assumed I was a student.

"Not really, I work at the university."

"Oh, my God, You're Peter Kowolski, the university president, aren't you?"

"Correct. *El Presidente* at your service, but please call me El, won't you? My close friends do," I responded, continuing her joke.

"You have friends?"

"Does that surprise you?"

"Pretty much, but isn't El a girl's name, Mr. President?"

"It can be, *señorita*, but that one has a different spelling."

"So, seriously, what's your last name?" she asked.

"It's Dreeton, Peter Dreeton."

"That shouldn't be hard to remember, you know, in case I need to file charges. I mean how many Peter Dreetons can there be in a town like Whitfield?"

"Currently there are eleven of us. We meet on Tuesday's up at the Harbor Inn for dinner and drinks, and sometimes we have a guest speaker. You're welcome to join us. Just ask for Peter, or Petey or Pedro. It's all good."

"You're kind of funny, aren't you?" she said finishing her beer.

"No, goofy mostly. Say, do you want another one of those?" I asked. She nodded, and I headed off to the keg for refills.

When the evening was over, I offered to walk her home, but she wanted the time to herself. I watched her walk to the end of that block and then the next. Standing under a streetlight, she turned and gave the faintest waves of goodbye. It made me happy, and I waved back perhaps a little too vigorously for a first encounter. Later when I reminded her about the incident, she laughed saying she hadn't been waving, only scratching a sweaty armpit. And I said, "Yeah, me, too," trying to save face.

September 26, 1964

"Here, these are for you," I said.

"Wow, I don't know what to say," Julie replied standing in her doorway before our first date. "What a surprise. No one's ever brought me cranberries before, and certainly not this many. There must be at least a pound here. Very impressive."

"It's two actually, and I picked them up at the farmers' market."

"I see that. Very sweet."

"Well, do you like them?" I asked.

"Yes, Peter, I do." And with those words I time traveled two thousand days into the future, to our imaginary wedding in the National Cathedral in Washington.

Julie halted the ceremony after completing her vows. Raising her hand, she turned to the overflow crowd and spoke in a soft voice. A restless hush fell over the church.

"Peter Dreeton is the sweetest boy I've ever met. I have loved him from the first time I saw him and in all the days since, through college and med school, while he was still a struggling writer, unsure where his beautiful words would lead him."

"No," I interrupted, "it is Julie who has made my life rich and full. All the characters that you have read about in my best selling books and movies are from times we shared together. When she was awarded the grant to cure scurvy from the Congo, I went along to teach the beautiful children in the village the correct use of a dangling participle. I will love Julie until the end of time and then some. Yes, I brought her cranberries on that first date, but she made the sauce."

The crowd erupted in joyous applause. *Let's face it we did make a cute couple.*

Once the two of us were in the car, I told her I had another surprise for her. "So," she asked, "is your surprise better than cranberries?"

"No, it's not really better than cranberries, just different."

Suddenly she started sniffing around her. "Does it have anything to do with fried chicken?"

"You are astute," I responded. My original idea had been to take her to Angelo's, a favorite hangout for faculty and students. Their food was good, and it was an easy place to talk, but on the ride over to her place a different plan with unexpected consequences had popped into my brain. I had pulled into a local diner and ordered a large bucket of fried chicken with two sides. "But there is more to my surprise than fried chicken," I added.

We drove for ten minutes, passing small farms and houses with broken tractors decorating the front yards. I could tell she was starting to get nervous.

"Where are you taking me?"

"To the cave to join the others."

"I should have known this wouldn't end well."

"Yes, that was probably your first mistake, but you need to put on your blindfold before we get there."

Just then we turned into the Cape Cod Golf and Tennis Club driveway, and her mood brightened.

"This is it? You joined a country club just for me? You must be the president after all. My prince has come, and he has a PhD in something, right?"

"Of course: beer with a minor in wine coolers."

"That's great, I love beer, but what are we doing here?"

"Picnic on number four."

"They won't care?"

"Not really, I used to work with the summer tennis program, and I've caddied a little."

We pulled into the parking lot and parked in a space in front of a long row of shrubs facing the lot and separating the hole behind them. We walked halfway up the fairway, a four hundred twenty-five yard par four dogleg to the left. I pointed to a series of three traps sitting two hundred yards from the green and said, "Pick one."

She made the typical rookie mistake going for the first one she saw.

"Please, Julie. Are you fucking nuts? If this is the best you can do, you can forget about getting one of the coveted invitations to my newcomers' topless brunch and whipped cream extravaganza next Sunday."

"Please, Mr. President, give me a second chance," she said, and after some consideration she chose the second trap.

"There, that's what I'm talking about. Better sand, better view, what's not to like?"

At this time of evening, we had the golf course to ourselves. Well, almost. Two seagulls set down a few feet away, hoping for treats. Julie tossed little pieces of chicken and ends of two dinner rolls in their direction. One of them moved close enough to take it from her hand, and both birds made low squawking sounds of pleasure. I pitched them a clump of potato salad, which they rejected completely. *What a pisser.* It hurt my feelings, of course, but I was way too mature to show it.

The gulls stayed for a few minutes by the edge of the trap and then flew off in search of other treats. The sprinklers went off near the green sending a high spray of water into the air. The sun had settled deep in the trees behind the green and spray rose above their tops creating a tiny rainbow.

Julie started telling me about her sister Marion, her mom and dad, about high school, and going to the University of Chicago her first two years. She was a pre-med student who dreamed of being a doctor like her father.

"Do you want to work with your dad when you finish med school?"

"No, I want to start a women's clinic. I'm a free spirit, of sorts."

"Yeah, me, too."

"Which one, a free spirit? Or you want to work in a women's clinic?"

"Well, both, I guess, because university president is not something I want to be stuck in forever," I said. "Confidentially, being a pirate has been my lifelong ambition."

She rubbed her hand across my leg, indicating her inquisition was taking a recess. She wanted to hear about my family, but first she had to go pee. I started to get up, but she put her hand down on my shoulder.

"Relax, I can do this by myself," she said, patting me lightly on my head. She began retracing her steps and ducked in between three small trees a hundred yards behind us.

I was nervous now. The clock was running, and she had given me a list of questions to answer. I could only hope that she had a full bladder and that her zipper got stuck because I didn't have much to say. It wasn't as if our family had been on the cover of any magazines, or I'd swum the English Channel in under eight hours. My life hadn't been littered with a long string of accomplishments, and other than my senior yearbook award, "Most likely to receive an eviction notice," there was almost nothing to set me apart from the crowd. I ran through a series of possible scenarios before deciding on one I hoped would work.

October 2, 1943

Lucy moved into the clear and received the pass. The white ball settled on her field hockey stick, and she eyed the defensive player a few feet ahead. She dipped her left shoulder indicating a turn to the center of the field, and the girl from St. Cecilia's moved to cut her off. Lucy pushed the ball off her stick in the direction of the girl, but a few feet later reversed direction toward the sideline. Lucy's height gave her good vision of the field, and she was very fast and had great hand-eye coordination. Her move left her open with no defenders between her and the goalie. She took three more steps and shot. The ball rose a few inches off the ground and flew past the goalie, landing in the back of the net. She probably should have taken a few more steps and gotten closer, and she knew her coach would bring that up when she got back to the sidelines, but taking a riskier shot was more of a challenge, and with a four goal lead and only a minute left to play, the shot seemed worth it, even necessary.

Lucy loved sports. Years before, her father had taught her to play golf. On Saturday mornings he would take her to the driving range at the public course and let her hit a bucket of balls, and then she would walk the course with him. She loved those mornings she got to spend quietly with her father and wanted them back again. Golf was her best and favorite sport, but she liked field hockey and basketball almost as much.

A loud cheer went up from the sidelines. Mary, standing behind the goal with her camera, looked up from taking the picture and shouted, "Nice shot." Lucy smiled and waved her stick in the air behind her. She didn't want a fuss being made over her, but the team mobbed her at the center line after the St. Cecilia coach called a time-out. With so little time left in the game, her coach pulled her out of the game and put in Deb O'Reilly, the sophomore version of Lucy. The two clicked sticks as Lucy came off the field. Deb smiled and said, "Fabulous job, Luce."

"Thanks," Lucy said. She got water and leaned on her stick watching her replacement try to work the same magic. She could tell her team would be in good hands next year with Deb playing her position.

"You did it again, Lucy. That move of yours fools them every time. Say, does anyone have a car here?" Kerrie asked. "I would love a ride home. I don't feel like taking the bus or walking."

"Sorry, I biked here," Lucy explained.

"I can take you. You'll just have to squeeze in around my tripod and other gear," Mary volunteered.

Lucy picked up her stick and headed home. Her family lived only a half mile from campus in a small two-story house, which was settled back in a thick stand of pine and elm trees, near the water, on a quiet street. She liked the fact it was close to town and school. When she biked up, her younger brother Roscoe was out front playing catch with Malcolm, a kid from the neighborhood.

"Hey, I thought you said you were coming to my game," she groused, not really hurt by his absence.

"You always win," he said letting the ball fly across the yard.

"Not always, but today we did. So what did you get me for my birthday?"

"Nothing," he answered.

"Same as last year, Roscoe. That's not good."

"Sorry, better luck next year," he said indifferently as the ball missed his glove and rolled into the trees.

"See, that's what happens when you don't look after your sister," she quipped, and Malcolm laughed at her answer.

Lucy's birthday dinner began when her dad got home at 6, followed by cake, and the opening of her presents: a book and two new dresses she had already hinted to her mother that she wanted. The meal was capped off by Roscoe's big surprise: a photo Mary had shot during the second game of the season. Lucy gave the twelve-year-old a big slobbery kiss and said, "I thought you said you got me nothing." He shook his head and said, "That was last year." She smiled and gave him a second kiss, which he promptly wiped clean. Kyle, her boyfriend, who had come for dinner, laughed at the unwanted affection Roscoe was receiving, and Lucy's mother, trying to save the day, suggested it was time to go because it wouldn't be good to be late to her own party.

"Thank you, Mom and Dad. I love the dresses and the book," she said as she gave them each a big hug, and her mother added, "Well, remember, we got the green dress because of Mike. That's his favorite color."

Lucy teared up, remembering her brother in better days. "I know, Momma, I know." Lucy's older brother, a sailor, had been badly wounded on board a ship in the Pacific and was now recovering in a Navy hospital in San Diego.

Kyle picked up their jackets and headed for the door. "Luce, we'd better go," and she followed him out the door.

There was already a crowd at the Rockin' Robin Roller Rink when they got there. Lucy looked down at her watch. It was 7:15 on the beautiful fall night of her seventeenth birthday, with her party about to begin. She wrapped her arm around Kyle's waist and smiled. "My life couldn't be better," she thought, "except for my brother not being home."

. . .

Chapter 25
MY MOTHER IS THE ACTING GOVERNOR

September 26, 1964

"Okay, I'm back," Julie said, settling back into the sand trap. "What's your answer? Let's hear it."

"Well, my dad runs a chain of stores in Tampa, I have one brother named Cory, who's five years younger, and my mother is the lieutenant governor of Florida."

I wanted to end with a strong finish and figured it would take at least a week for her to verify such an obscure fact.

"No shit, that's amazing. So what you're telling me is your mother is Robert Hedgeworth, the lieutenant governor of Florida?"

"Yeah, kind of crazy, isn't it?" I replied trying to cover the lie but was completely caught off guard by her knowledge of Florida political trivia. "Peter Dreeton has two daddies, who knew? Of course, there are drawbacks, but I always have someone to play catch with, and we get to leave the toilet seat up, so it has its plusses, as well."

"I can imagine, but has it been hard at school? Did you get teased a lot?"

"Yes, but we're a strong family, so we get by." She took in my response without question. I thought about waiting her out, but she didn't budge. Finally I gave in.

"Okay, how could you possibly know who the lieutenant governor of Florida is?"

"My dad operated on his knee a month ago, and I met him. Small world, isn't it?"

"Yes, it is," I replied.

"But the good news is your second daddy is nice and really hot," she added.

"Really, you think so? Because everyone tells me that I favor his side of the family."

"I can see the resemblance now that you mention it, especially around the nose and eyes."

"I should have gone with the lieutenant governor of New Mexico instead."

"Wait. Did you say New Mexico?"

"Yeah, why?" I nodded taking a long swig of beer.

"Oh, so your mother is actually Steven Wilcox, lieutenant governor of New Mexico?"

"Jesus, Mary, and Joseph, do Montana for me. That's always been my favorite, and then Oregon after that. And when you've finished, you can name all the state birds and corsages. This is nothing to be proud about, Julie."

"No, it's not like that at all. Steven Wilcox just happened to be on *Meet the Press the other day*, talking about a new dam project they're building in the state, even though it's going to be bad for the environment. That's the only reason I know his name." She patted my knee. "Listen this hasn't gone well for you, and I'm partly responsible. Let's start over. Your mom can be governor of any state you want—even a territory, like Guam. You pick it, and I'll act completely dumbfounded. How's that sound, Peter?"

"You promise?" I asked, looking longingly into her soft brown eyes but not totally convinced I could trust her. "Listen Julie, what good is making up stuff, if people call you out on it?"

"I see your point, but we'll get through this together." She nudged me again. "Go ahead, Peter, don't give the truth a second thought."

"Okay, my dad runs a chain of stores, my younger brother plays on the high school soccer team, and my mother's the acting director of the Nevada Department of Mines." *I have to admit it just felt better getting away from elected offices altogether.*

"Really? That's very impressive, Peter. What's her name?"

"Ginny Dreeton." I held my breath wondering if Barbara Niebauer or perhaps Betty Johnson's name was about to be tossed back in my face, but when it didn't come, I continued.

"My mom keeps a second house in Reno for work, near the State Capitol. Do you know Reno at all?"

"No, never been there."

"Oh, I see. It's quite nice. I should take you there some time. We can go spelunking with her if you're willing. Anyway she flies out there twice a month to descend hundreds of feet into very dark caves with only a single flashlight and a peanut butter and jelly sandwich."

"Creamy or crunchy?" she asked.

"Creamy, mostly, with grape jelly. Sometimes she's underground for six or seven days at a time, sometimes more. She's quite brave. Her other department heads stand up on top of the cave holding a megaphone and a couple of extra sandwiches. Every few hours they holler down into the black hole, "Everything okay down there, Director Dreeton?" and she flashes her light back up at them.

"You've got to be very proud of her."

"Are you kidding, the acting director of mines? I'm very proud."

"That's great. Is there anyone else you want to tell me about?"

"Well, there's an aunt in Vermont," I said, hoping to get in at least one more lick. My voice trailed off, waiting for some sign of encouragement, but Julie dashed my hopes.

"Careful, Peter, you're pushing your luck here. The fun stops in Reno; you must know that."

October 2, 1943

The Rockin' Robin Roller Rink on Route 6 was originally built as a produce center in the 20s. The current owners bought the building in '38 and removed the individual stalls, added a wooden skate floor, and converted one end into an office, private party room, and a snack bar. There wasn't much money for other upgrades, but they did install a mirrored ball over the center of the floor and a sound system. A wooden rail separated the skating floor from the viewing area and a long line of bench seating had been built against the walls. On the outside wall near the entrance a "Drink Coca Cola" mural showed two skaters enjoying a beverage.

Kyle pulled the door back for Lucy, and Frank Sinatra's voice tumbled out into the parking lot along with the sounds of many skates moving on the wooden floor. They waited in line to get skates and then headed into the dark cavern of sounds and flashing light. Katie waved a greeting as she whizzed past them.

They found the group, put on their skates, and joined in. Lucy's spotlight dance, she had been told, was for 8:30, followed by a half-hour use of the party room. Katie and Mary had already brought the cake and ice cream in and given it to the owners to store in the office refrigerator. Just before her spotlight dance, Kyle gave her a small chain necklace with a gold heart. All the girls gushed, including Lucy, who wasn't used to being fussed over, and when they went on the dance floor, she couldn't stop blushing. She had picked out "Someone to Watch Over Me" as her song, and the full skirt of her yellow dress moved to the music. Kyle whispered a small joke, and she finished by giving a curtsey.

On the way home Kyle stopped for a few minutes at their favorite spot on the beach. They looked at the lights of two fishing boats moving slowly across the horizon, and by 11:30 Lucy's magical birthday tour was over.

• • •

Chapter 26
THE BROKEN COKE BOTTLE

September 26, 1964

A small flame shot up through the trees on the fairway ahead of Julie and me. At first we couldn't tell what it was, and then I realized that it was coming from a barbeque pit at one of the houses lining the left side of the green.

"What is that?" she asked.

"It's a ritual involving the burning of meat," I replied. She smiled at my simple response.

We saw men standing by the fire talking and small children playing on the patio. They were faceless figures with tiny red cinders dancing in the air above them. We sat quietly drinking and listening to the sound of far-off voices muffled and uncertain and then lost in the evening sky. We heard laughter as older kids came out to play on the patio and then silence. A few minutes later we smelled the aroma of hamburgers cooking on the grill as the flames drew down from our sight. Then noises again and then quiet as they all went inside. A string of lights outlining the trees was turned on from inside the house, framing the patio with soft light. I told Julie how interesting it was to watch something from a distance and then see it disappear. For whatever reason she found my insight important and told me that it was sweet.

"Maybe you should be a writer, instead of a pirate."

I laughed and promised to find one of my tales for her to read. By then it had become dark, and the pink was lost from the sky. We were quiet, and she moved close to me in the trap. It was cooler now, and she started rubbing the bottom of my foot. When she came on the long indenture at the base of my right heel where a deep cut had been, she stopped.

"How did you get this?" she asked rubbing her fingers over the spot.

"In the war."

"One or two?"

"Crimean," I said, nodding my head and remembering the heat of battle.

"Really? I didn't realize we fought that one."

"Oh, certainly, I was a proud member of the second mounted cavalry under Colonel Robert Hedgeworth the fourth. What a fine officer and gentleman he was. You've heard of him, no doubt?"

"Not specifically, but I know the Hedgeworths come from a long line of public servants. He must have been very brave."

"Yes, his grandson is in politics now somewhere in the south."

"No, it's Arizona actually. He's the director of mines," she teased.

"Interesting, but not surprising really that you'd know that."

She kept running her finger over the scar and then stopped.

"So when did it happen?"

"In a pickup basketball game in tenth grade. I was barefoot, and this kid dropped a full Coke bottle on the pavement, and the glass shot right up into my heel."

"That must have hurt," she said and began rubbing the injured spot again, almost by reflex.

"You bet. Right as it was falling, I heard him say, 'Hey, Peter, look I got one from New Mexico, from Santa....' But after he said, 'Santa,' the rest was kinda blurry. I'd been looking for a bottle from Santa Fe and was going to trade him an extra one I had from Baltimore when the pain took over. I went running off the court, my bloody footprints tracking all the way home. Mom was in the bathtub when I busted in the door, and seeing her soaking in all her glory was upsetting to both of us, but she was still my mother. The split had gotten much wider during my run and was now gushing blood at a heavy rate, squirting it up on the commode, into the tub, and on top of her fluffy white bedroom slippers. While she was bending over to wrap one of the towels around my foot, her right breast flopped out right on top of my face. But by the time she got me to the emergency room the white towel encircling my foot had turned rusty red. Dr. Wyman got the long sliver out and sewed me up, but it hurt for weeks after that, and I never found another bottle from Santa Fe."

"I'm sorry. That's a sad story, especially the part about the boob in your face."

"Well, it wouldn't have been so bad—" I began, but she cut me off.

"I know. I know: If it hadn't been your mother's boob."

"Exactly," I replied.

She put her finger to her mouth and kissed it and then touched the scar. A shooting star flew overhead.

"Look. It's a sign."

"It is, but I've got to pee. But when I get back, I have a surprise to share with you."

She was gone for a minute or so and when she got back, she stood over me on the sand, her legs straddling mine. She slowly pulled her soft green tank top off and unhooked her bra. Then she dropped her green shorts and her white underpants after that. She ran her foot over my right leg and said, "Come on, Mr. President. It's time to hit the putting green."

"Without clubs?"

"Don't worry. We'll think of something."

Finally my most basic prayers had been answered: finding someone to watch over me.

October 8, 1943

The drum roll moved from the back of the warehouse through the crowd to the front of building. Sister Margaret stood in front of a hundred workers and raised her hands above her head. The smell of dried fruit filled the room.

"Thank you for coming. We've been blessed with another great month. I'm pleased to report that our sales this month exceeded our expectations by almost a thousand boxes." A loud cheer went up, lasting for some time.

"But," she said, "before I announce this month's winner, I have two important things to say. First, today is Tom Crawford's sixty-third birthday." A single hand went up from the middle of the crowd. "Tom has worked tirelessly as a shift leader since we moved to this building. Sister Marie has baked a cake in his honor, and as soon as we are finished here, everyone, please stay for a slice of good cheer. Now, some other very exciting news." She paused letting the anticipation build. "*Life* magazine is doing a story on us, so each one of you is invited to come and be famous."

Noise filled the converted warehouse, rising up to the open balcony above her and out the large utility windows to the streets nearby. It was early autumn, and the leaves still stubbornly held most of their green. Outside along DeCarlo Street a twenty-foot hand-painted cloth banner flapped restlessly in the warm night air. The banner read: "Home of the Cape Cod Reds."

The cheering lasted several minutes. Sister Margaret let it go on. It was good for morale. Finally, she raised her hand again. "Enough for now; our next shift starts in ten minutes. We still have a job to do and cake to eat. But do plan to join us for the photo shoot this month. It's a great honor. When I get *Life's* confirmation, I'll post the date and time. Remember; wear work clothes, not fancy dresses. We don't want to give the impression we're not dedicated. Just bring a big smile. Now, ladies, please come join me."

She motioned to the girls with her left hand. From inside the crowd Penny, Lucy, Mary, Katie, and Kerrie worked their way up onto the temporary stage. As they passed the workbenches, outstretched arms patted their backs and people wished them good luck. Another long drum roll from two sophomore girls built up suspense for Sister Margaret's announcement. The five stood beside her. She turned to look at each of them, proud of their hard work, before turning back to face the crowd. She opened the envelope in her hand and read the results.

"So without further delay the September winners are... the Lobsters."

. . .

Chapter 27
THE GIANT CHICKEN CLAIMS HER NEXT VICTIM

Fall, 1964 - Spring, 1966

Julie loved to play miniature golf. Our third date we spent at Del's Putt Putt World next to the Surf Restaurant.

"Let's see," she smugly replied putting the stubby pencil to her tongue. "You had a forty-one—no wait, sorry, it was forty-two actually, and I had a thirty-seven." Julie gave me a gentle pat and laid her green putter on Del's counter.

"You kids have fun?" the white-haired owner inquired.

"Sure, lots of fun. We'll be back," she replied confidently. I smiled and placed my yellow putter on the same counter. Julie turned heading for the car, but Del, sensing my frustration, offered consolation: "You'll get her next time."

"That's very doubtful, Del, but thanks," I answered.

On the way home Julie listened to the radio and asked if anything was wrong. Humiliated, I choked out, "No everything's great." In hindsight my decision on twelve not to take the bank shot off the concrete toadstool proved to be a bad one. And then, of course, there was the giant chicken, her beady eyes tempting me to come into her coop. The safe play would have been to go up the worn green felt ramp and down to the hen house, but needing to make up ground, I tried to squeeze one in between her skinny chicken legs. Every five seconds the giant chicken laid one of her hard plastic eggs, knocking anything in its path into the wire basket below, resulting in a two-stroke penalty. The trick was making sure the ball was released as soon as she finished clucking. Hearing a passing car honking on Lime Street, I hesitated, and my ball arrived too late for a safe passage. Julie gave me a soft kiss on my cheek.

"Better luck next time," she complimented my courage, before pointing out the statistically small chance of ever completing such a maneuver.

Soon we became regulars on Del's golfing circuit. The only good part was getting signed up for Del's customer rewards program, under which every thirteenth game was free. The card read "Del's Putt Putt World: Home of the Giant Chicken," and it had a row of punch holes running down the side. Sometimes she pulled the card out of her wallet while we were eating a burger at Kaman's or heading back from the beach, and asked, "Whatchya think? Only three more games, and we get one free." Sometimes I gave into her craven needs, and other times I came up with a lame excuse. "Not today, sweetie, I have a headache."

Del's was a dumpy little hole in the wall, a small wood-framed building with two long benches out in front and a snack bar featuring six flavors of snow cones and a pink cotton candy machine. A massive oak shaded holes six through twelve during the middle of the day. There was usually a sea breeze, and on warm nights, the string of white twinkle lights gave the feeling of stepping into a small Mexican fishing village.

Julie sometimes brought friends to play putt putt, and after we finished, the four of us would go back to my place to cook burgers on the deck and play charades late into the night. In many ways those were the best times we had together, even if *To Kill a Mockingbird* or *Little Women* showed up in almost every game of charades we played. One of the upsides of our golfing adventures: Julie always spent the night at my place afterwards. I would come back up the stairs after walking our company out to their car and find Julie in some state of romantic undress. Maybe she'd be slipping into one of my crew shirts or brushing her teeth in front of the sink, her hair pulled back off of her face. There seemed to be no good reason our lives couldn't go on like this forever, and I wanted to blurt out, "Marry me," but never did.

October 8, 1943

Cheering from the Lobster section filled the warehouse after Sister Margaret's announcement. Mary stepped forward making her now famous Lobster-claw gesture. When the energy had subsided and the other girls had left the stage, Sister Margaret pulled the head Lobster aside and quietly said, "Mary, I would like you to be the tour guide for the *Life* photographer when he comes. Will you do it?"

"Oh, yes, Sister Margaret. I'd be happy to show him around," Mary said excitedly. Mary thought back to the time she got her first camera.

Mary got a Baby Brownie camera for her thirteenth birthday, a gift from her grandfather in Ohio. Paw Paw worked as a news reporter for the *Cleveland Plain Dealer,* and he had dreams of his granddaughter following the same career path. Mary wasn't sure she wanted to be a journalist, but she definitely wanted a job where she could take pictures. Her secret hope was to work in films, but she had only shared that hope with Katie.

That first year Mary took hundreds of pictures of life in Whitfield and put them together in a book she titled *A Year in Whitfield.* She took pictures of the first snow, ice hanging off trees, Christmas decorations, spring flowers, and fishing boats. In June she went to visit her cousins in North Carolina. During her two-week stay, her older cousin Chris took her and his younger brother Nick to a traveling air show in Raleigh. Mary took pictures of mothers with small babies and food vendors. She shot pictures of both cousins clowning around, and she started taking a series of rapid shots of two bi-planes performing in the air. Suddenly the planes clipped wings. One burst into a fiery ball, and the other spun slowly to the ground at the far end of the field. She caught it all on film, as well as pictures of the crowd's reaction to the tragedy. Her cousins thought she should turn the photos over to the local paper since there was not a reporter on the scene. But Mary couldn't do it. She thought to herself that the people's pain was too private, and she didn't want to expose their hurt to strangers. Instead she took the photos back home with her. She only looked at them occasionally. These pictures made her realize how much she had to be thankful for.

She finished her yearlong journal with shots of fall in Whitfield and then, on her fourteenth birthday, sent the album to Paw Paw.

Mary was glad she was a photographer and looked forward to meeting the professional photographer from *Life*. Maybe he could give her some tips.

• • •

Chapter 28
THE RED BIKE GUY

Fall, 1964

I had a wonderful life during those years in Whitfield. Most days found me biking the mile and a half stretch from home to the university. The air was cool and clean, the ocean's blue water off to my right; it made me think everyone should only live in towns like Whitfield.

My bike was red, my favorite color for a bike because it told the world you were serious about the sport. You weren't just some guy peddling to the store to buy a pair of nail clippers or a quart of motor oil. No, sir—on a red bike you were a speeding fast guy on a mission. You might even have a Tour de France jersey stuffed somewhere inside your pants.

"Look, kids: there goes red bike guy," a father on Route 1 said to his sons, as I breezed by them at warp speed. Naturally they lowered their heads in respect. I passed pretty coeds and waved at people on the streets. They waved back.

I loved my job, my friends, my red bike, and mostly my girlfriend, Julie Mathers.

Julie was a girl of great talents who came to Whitfield to answer every dark lonely prayer I could imagine. For the record, my walk-in closet was chock-full of dark lonely prayers.

Julie was my life. We rode bikes together, (hers was green), went to dinner at little sidewalk cafes, and generally made the world a better place with our deeply intellectual insights. Like all people in their early twenties, we went about the complex business of unraveling the great mysteries of the universe, with the same easy pleasure that one gets when opening a bag of Doritos. *Yum!*

"How 'bout no more war?" she suggested one night while sitting on top of my bed, her legs Indian style, wearing only a blue USJ crew team jersey and a pair of red socks. She took a long swig from her beer and pulled the hair back off her face.

"Yes, brilliant, Julie, and how 'bout food for everyone?" I inquired while stuffing another fistful of toasted corn goodness into my mouth. *I know firsthand how good everybody feels when their stomachs are full.*

"Hugs and kisses, Peter?" she queried.

"Absolutely, Julie! I'm buying!"

It made us both wonder why the world hadn't dealt with these important social concerns sooner.

"Good job. We're so smart. We deserve more beers!"

"Absolutely, sweetie. I'm buying," she replied.

I loved Julie's smile, her steadiness, her willingness to be daring. I loved the loose hours she spent curling the wild hairs back over my ears or thanklessly removing the small bits of fluff caught inside my belly button. *Oops, I've gone too far again, haven't I? I've been told it has something to do with boundary issues.*

October 14, 1943

Katie finished her final station reading on the north end of Bird Island and entered the information, as she always did, into the brown leather logbook. Having finished early, she sat down on one of the dunes and looked out to the ocean. Her days were so busy now what with school, college applications, the Cape Cod Reds, and this job for Eric. Any time off was welcomed.

Her mom had been more stressed because the fighting in Europe had moved closer to the navy medical unit where her dad was stationed. There were daily broadcasts of heavy casualties, and it was a roller coaster ride for all of them. Katie tried not thinking about it and to help out at home as much as she could, but there was only so much she could do, and all of her wishes couldn't bring her dad home for now.

The wind turned from the north, and the waves kicked up small clouds of white dust across the tops of the water. It would be much colder soon, and their work would stop for the winter. She wondered where she'd be this time next year; if Josh would get into Notre Dame or join the navy, and if he'd still care about her. She wanted to go to Vassar, but without some sort of scholarship there was no chance. Josh was a sweet boy, and she could see herself marrying him after he finished engineering school.

Last week they had gone to Kaman's for ice cream sodas, and while they were sitting there, Josh had asked Mrs. Kaman if he could carve a small starfish into the counter. He had been expecting to hear a "no," but she had said sure. Josh had been surprised and thanked her, taking out his pocketknife. He'd cut tiny little grooves deep into the wood and smoothed them over with his fingers.

"Are you finished?" the voice behind her broke Katie's thoughts in two. She turned and saw Mary standing over her.

"Yeah, my readings didn't change much from last week, so that was easy. How 'bout yours?" Katie asked, putting both hands under her knees to keep them warm.

"Some did, and some didn't, but mostly it was moving the stations. That always takes a while. But one thing for sure, we still have time to kill. Kerrie takes forever. So I'm going to take pictures."

Mary pulled her brown box camera out of her tote bag and began checking on the focus. She took rolls of film whenever she could afford it and sometimes even when she couldn't. Her bedroom walls were covered with shots of friends, of bicycles leaning up against the sides of a Cape Cod cottage, and of seagulls feeding in the marshes.

Eric had seen Mary's work, and he put her in charge of taking pictures of the island's bird population. She was happy to comply. The program had money to buy extra rolls of film; so as long as she turned in six or eight good shots per week, she could use the rest of the film as she chose.

"Hey, Mary, it's only a few more days until the *Life* photographer's visit. I'm so jealous that you get to take him around," Katie said.

"Yea, I'm really excited. I'll introduce you, if you like," Mary replied.

Without telling her, Mary turned her camera on Katie and took several shots before Katie realized what she was doing.

"Hey, no fair," she blushed.

Katie was beautiful. Everyone in town knew it, but she didn't like being the center of attention.

"Come on, you look great as always. Anyway you can give them to Josh."

"Okay, I guess."

Mary shot a few more stills before saying, "Ham it up."

Katie jumped to her feet pretending to be a fashion model, putting on a serious pout and moving her arms around in the open air. Mary laughed and finished the roll.

"Oh, by the way, I love what Josh did for you at Kaman Drugs."

"You mean the starfish he carved for me?" Katie asked picking up her notes.

"Yes. That was really sweet, Katie. I hope you know that."

"I do, Mary. Thanks."

"Say, let me ask you something," Mary said as she began putting her camera back in its case. "Do you want to stay here after college or do you still want to move out west? Remember? You used to talk about that when we were little."

"Oh, I still want to move to San Francisco. But I guess that could change if something happens with Josh and me. Who knows when the war will be over. What about you, Mary?"

"I guess I'm like Kerrie and her Broadway dreams. I want to work for a newspaper or magazine in New York. So I guess the only two of us that will be left are Penny, who will never leave, and Luce, who doesn't know what she wants."

"That's true," Katie said. "Come on, we should get going. They're probably through by now, and we don't want to keep the other three fireflies waiting. Besides, we're having that stupid math test tomorrow. Not to mention, I've got tons of Spanish homework," Katie said to her. "*Que lastima.*"

"*Que lastima,*" Mary answered, as they started walking back to the boat.

· · ·

Chapter 29

BOLIVIA IS A COUNTRY, NOT AN ANSWER

Spring, 1965

On nights when Julie stayed at my place, the two of us fixed dinner and listened to music. She studied while I did dishes and some work for school, and then we lay on the bed under the whir of the ceiling fan. Julie talked about medical school, and all the big things she wanted to do with her life…. blah, blah, blah…Big, Big, Big. *What's your hurry, sweetie? Slow down; let the world catch up with us. Let's not make any major moves until after we finish the case of beer in the fridge.*

Frankly, it was sort of disgusting. I wasn't sure my small room could hold all her goals, except my own dreams were so tiny they fit nicely into a cardboard box marked "odds and ends." When it was my turn to talk, I rattled on about things with a shelf life of under a week: sports; politics; or a good movie we'd seen together. Then she'd clear her throat and ask, "Peter, so what do you want to be when you grow up?"

"Be with you, Julie," I replied. It was a good answer, true and simple. She exhaled, completely unsatisfied with my flimsy plans.

"No, seriously, Peter, what do you want to be?"

"Fireman," I offered.

She shook her head again disapprovingly.

I thought for a moment. "Well, okay, my other big dream is someday to roll a bundle of yellow yarn into a fluffy ball."

"That's perfect, Peter," she answered, half-choking on the hairball shed from another of my worthless ideas. Generally, it went better for us when we stuck to drinking beer and solving global problems. Those were much easier to get my arms around.

"I'm getting another beer. Do you want one?" My brain starts shutting down after a certain point, and I need a rest. Aunt Helen blamed herself for my disability, the result of an accidental drop on the head when I was three months old.

"Sure, get me one," Julie replied. I padded across the darkened floor, still warm from the heat of the day. Opening the refrigerator door wide let out coolness and light into the room. I stood there long enough for the air to spill down to cool my feet. I looked back at Julie, her legs draped loosely over the top of the sheet with one arm on top of her knee, smiling, in a lazy late night manner. Looking into the darkness beyond her, I knew I didn't want any of this ever to change. Then I closed the door, came back with two cold bottles and the hope that my dark lonely prayers had no expiration date.

"Peter," she said, "what's your answer?"

"Bolivia," I replied confidently, having scored three points with that exact answer during a ninth grade geography bee, entitled "Latin America, our friends to the South."

"No, Peter, Bolivia is a country, not an answer!" Julie yelled, her teeth grinding in disgust. "How about law school? You'd make a wonderful public defender. Or how 'bout the Peace Corps?"

I let out a "maybe." *I did like the idea of helping people, but I wasn't sure if that was for me, especially since I still needed a lot of fixing myself.* Over time Julie's job list expanded to pretty much anything I had a shot at getting. Court reporter, dental hygienist, Sherpa guide, game show host, and crossing guard, all dropped by my apartment for a look-see. I liked the guide idea a whole lot, because I like to yak, but then I'm not good in cold weather, and heights scare me, so that wasn't going to work after all. Julie left no stone unturned, no job applications incomplete.

Julie and I almost never fought, except when she was trying to resurrect my career or start a new one for me. We had a two-week falling out when she uncovered my law school application still buried in my desk next to the left side of a grilled cheese sandwich, an application I promised had been mailed weeks before.

"Damn, that's bad luck."

She held it up to my face, but I was pretty sure she didn't believe my regrets. I offered her the rest of the sandwich as a consolation prize, but she remained inconsolable. Other than occasional scuffles like this, we got along, and she kept her quiet nervousness about my bleak future in check. But when she did get on my case, it sometimes felt as if she'd morphed into some kind of quasi-third parent, the one with whom it was okay to have sex.

"I am what I am," I told her one night lying on my bed, and for the most part, she accepted those limitations.

Julie never gave up on me or what she wanted me to become. I was to her a mixed-up puzzle with many essential pieces missing. But that complexity just made her task more appealing, and for a time, in a strange way, I became more appealing as well. It was like the perfect storm; the more dysfunctional I became, the more she believed having wild jungle sex might make me whole again. *Of course it didn't work, but we had fun trying.*

October 14, 1943

Eric looked over the results the girls left on his desk. There would be only two more trips before the season ended, and he would need to send the data to the wildlife society with his report. He had so much else to do, but he had a fondness for the island, the girls, and, of course, the migrating birds. He pulled the clear plastic overlay out from his top drawer along with the map, which contained one hundred small dots representing potential weather stations. Every couple of weeks he moved at least some of them around the island to get different readings. He transcribed all of the readings, finishing with Katie's findings for station 22 at the north end of the island.

Eric picked up his leather-strapped briefcase and slung it over his arm. He walked down the narrow corridor with a series of windows on the south side. Late afternoon sun poured in, warming the space. He liked the heat and was sorry to see it come to an end. The faint blue sky had only a little sunlight left, and he wanted to take advantage of it. He went through security and unlocked his bike from the bike rack for his twenty-minute ride. Loose gravel crunched under his feet. He passed only a few cars going back into town and stopped for a minute as the road bent back to the water and looked at a lone sailboat coming back into the harbor. He started up again and made it to Kingsley's Market at a few minutes before five. The store was empty except for two older ladies at the meat counter. He recognized one of them from church and waved. He picked up a small container of homemade potato soup and a loaf of grain bread. One of the ladies was trying to reach something off the top shelf, and he went over to help. At six-four, he could easily reach it.

"Here, let me. It's Mrs. Roswell, right?" he asked handing her the can of coffee.

"Yes, that's right. You go to eight o'clock as well," she replied.

He laughed and confessed, "Yes, if I'm not playing hooky. Some Sundays I take one of the sculls out for exercise, especially when the weather's like this."

"It has been a beautiful fall, hasn't it? Well, thank you for your help, and I guess we'll see you at the fall bazaar in two weeks?"

"Oh, yes, Father Mike already has me signed up to work."

He remembered then that he was supposed to call his mother that night. It was his parents' anniversary, and he knew she'd want him to remember. The store was three blocks from his apartment.

When he biked up the driveway, his landlady who lived in the downstairs unit was bringing in clothes off the line. Trailing close behind her was Eric's wiry-haired mutt with an old worn sock clenched in his jaw.

"Plankton, have you been helping Mrs. Venzenna with the laundry?" Eric inquired. The dog dropped his treasure, yipped his response, and wagged his tail briskly at seeing his roommate come home.

Mrs. Venzenna laughed, "Oh, yes, Plankton always keeps me company when you're away."

"Can I give you a hand?" he asked, getting off his bike.

She shook her head and said, "No thanks." They talked about cutting back the privet before the frost came, and he offered to do it over the weekend. It was a two-man job. Mrs. Venzenna was a short plump Italian with a thick accent. She couldn't maneuver the eight-foot ladder, and he needed someone to hold it steady while he reached over to trim it back below the McKelvey's white fence. Last year she had forgotten to remind him of this chore, and Eric skinned up both forearms reaching over the half frozen sticks. Her yard was important to her, and Eric was happy to help. He threw his briefcase over his shoulder, picked up the small bag of groceries and held the door as she worked her way up the three gray wooden steps to the front door.

"So it's a date. I'll see you Saturday around 8 AM?"

She nodded, saying, "Thanks, you're sweet," and patted him on his arm.

· · ·

Chapter 30

SLEEPING ON A BED OF WILD RICE

March 16-19, 1965

Over Julie's spring break that first year I had to make a trip to Chicago to visit some high schools. I stayed for several days at her house and met her family.

I picked up my rent car from Avis, an avocado green Corvair, got directions from the counter agent and headed out the expressway to Lake Forest. The homes were beautifully manicured, and I felt out of place in my green rent-a-bomb. At 23 Remington Circle I pulled into the drive. The sound of my engine brought Rosie, from around the side of the house. She barked wildly but not as if she were mad. Perhaps the car was troubling her inner sense of being.

I put my hand out, and we'd become friends by the time the front door opened. Julie came running out and gave me a big wet kiss. Her mother was right behind her. I stuck my hand out, licking the last of Julie's kiss off my mouth.

"Hi, I'm Peter."

"Hi, Peter. Nancy Mathers."

The Irish setter put her two front paws up on my waist.

"Down, Rosie," Mrs. Mathers admonished her. "Down, girl."

"She's okay," I said, putting my arms around her head.

"Come in," Mrs. Mathers said, and we entered a long open foyer with large rooms on either side. Mrs. Mathers pointed to her left and said, "Let's sit in the sunroom." It was March and still very cool, so the idea seemed good. Several overstuffed sofas sat in the large open space with tasteful art on the walls. Julie sat on the first sofa and patted her hand on the cushion for me to join her. She moved a needlepoint that

Mrs. Mathers was working on for her own mother, a chateau scene in the South of France.

"It's nice," I said, moving it to the other cushion, and wondered how my mom's two dots in the snow were getting along.

"Thanks," Julie said.

"This room is amazing." Small blue-and-white flowered pillows sat on a soft, off-white sofa, beautifully weathered red oriental rugs lay at our feet, and a mixture of original artwork surrounded us. Unlike the Dreeton house, there were no dust bunnies running wildly around on the floor, no remnants of a Cheetos salad, or cans of spilled soda beside them. Through the picture windows their backyard had a view broken only by the pool and the bathhouse. At our house Cory and I played whiffle ball on our broken concrete patio and could easily knock a double off the rotting back fence twenty feet away. At Julie's house a well-struck five iron wouldn't make the woods nestled behind the pool. Mrs. Mathers asked what we wanted to drink and got up from the sofa.

"Iced tea, water, whatever, will be fine," I said to her.

"Julie, can I bring you something?" she asked.

"No thanks, Momma," she said. We had a moment together, and she asked about my flight and whispered parts of a dream she'd had about me the night before. I was going to ask what it was about, when the tea came back. So I dropped it because if it was really good, she'd show me later.

Mrs. Mathers asked me about school and where I was from. The slum was the correct response, but I went with Florida instead.

"Oh, really? How nice! Julie's uncle has a wonderful place in Boca Raton, and we love going for a visit."

"Yes, those houses on the water are beautiful, aren't they?"

After a little while, Mrs. Mathers said that we had better take the bags up to my room if we were going to pick up

Marion from soccer practice. We went up the grand stairway to the second floor landing. We passed a number of rooms until coming to my room. I put my bag up on the bed. Julie gave me another kiss, running her hand over the back of my head, and then we went downstairs to leave.

"Shall we go in the green crusader?" I asked.

She smiled, not taking me seriously. "No, let's take my car."

Her father had given her a silver Mustang, with a big engine.

"He really got this for himself, but he doesn't want to admit it," Julie said.

She slumped into the dark blue leather driver's seat, and I got in beside her. The aroma of new leather surrounded us.

Marion's school, Deerpath Country Day, was about ten minutes away. The school sat on a rolling hill with dark green cedar trees shading old red brick buildings. One of the athletic fields was right off the main driveway. We got there in time to watch the last few minutes of Marion's practice. We sat on soft green winter grass watching blond girls in ponytails run up and back on the field. Her team was good, well-coached and well-heeled. So far life hadn't thrown them the kind of sweaty jerseys we wore at Woolly Mammoth High with the school slogan written proudly across the front "You're in for an ass-whipping." *At Woolly we took territorial issues seriously.*

I met all of Marion's giggling chums, and we went back home. When we pulled into their driveway, Marion said, "My God, whose car is that?" in a manner that made Republicans everywhere look bad. Julie said, "It's Peter's."

I smiled sheepishly and asked, "Do you like it? It's new."

"Oh, it's nice," she said trying to be polite until Julie said, "Marion, it's a rental car."

"Well, thank God," Marion exhaled. The thought of an avocado green Corvair successfully invading their air space was frankly a concept too unpleasant for them to get their arms around. What was coming next, people from different races or cultures moving into their lily-white neighborhood? *Get serious, this was the sixties. Nothing like that was about to happen.* But still the fear was out there and growing more real every day.

In Julie's defense, she was not overly concerned with possessions, but she didn't mind slathering herself with all the good things her daddy's money could buy. We went in the kitchen, and Marion left to take a shower. Around six her dad roared in, driving a sleek, black Mercedes, parking it behind the Corvair.

"Whose car is that?" he asked in an annoyed tone, closing the front door.

Julie answered the question of the day, "It's Peter's, Dad."

Dr. Mathers said, "Oh, that's nice."

He kissed Mrs. Mathers, who was just coming back down the stairs, and gave a kiss to Julie before turning to me.

"Hi, Carl Mathers." His eyes looked me over as if I were a racehorse he might buy.

"Hi, Peter Dreeton," I said, glad we'd gotten the opening ceremony behind us.

He sized me up, but that's probably something any dad does when he has an old-enough-to-be-having-sex daughter. I tried to smile and look harmless.

He gave me a jolly pat on the back and fixed himself a stiff drink. We all moved into the family room and visited until he announced our dinner reservations at the club were for six-thirty, and so we should be going. *By all means, Carl, we wouldn't want to keep the people at the club waiting any longer than we had to.*

When we got outside, I said offhandedly, "We can go in mine if you like?" and that seemed to break the ice. *Crappy car humor is always a winner.* It came as no surprise they turned me down.

Julie said several times on the way to the club how funny and sweet I was. At first I was embarrassed by all of the attention before realizing that she was making some good points. Frankly, if she went on much further, I might fall into a diabetic coma from her sugary description. I tried changing the subject, but my complaints just made her gush more. *Finally it hit me. I was pretty special, once you got past all the average parts.*

In their club Mercedes was the minimum opening bid for valet parking, and we had plenty of company. We planned to eat in the main dining room, but the wallpaper was being redone, so we slummed it in the men's grill. The grill looked out over the tenth tee, with the huge swimming pool off to the side.

"Oh, neat," I said as we sat down at the oversized table with an expensive white tablecloth. "An in-ground pool. I've never seen one before, at least not this close."

Julie explained that I was kidding, of course, and I tried to reassure them.

"Sure, there's a public pool three blocks from my house, and it's well below ground. In fact, after heavy rains, water moccasins often turn up in the deep end, and that gets dicey if the water is cloudy."

But I could tell this wasn't the kind of story they were enjoying, so we ordered dinner. When it was my turn, I ordered the grilled chicken Lake Forest, served on a bed of wild rice with vegetable medley on the side. I followed it up by asking how they'd feel about actually sleeping on a bed of wild rice?

"How 'bout you, Mrs. M.? Wouldn't those little grains bother you, especially if you got some up your nose?"

She nodded meekly but didn't respond.

"Me, too," I said and quickly changed my side order to mashed potatoes with butter. Carl asked several times what I was going to do with my life. *I guess he wrongly assumed I'd been making plans.*

"That's kind of hard to say at this point, Doctor. The future is a long way off."

I wished I'd had better answers, but Julie hadn't prepped me. I could tell he was definitely looking for more of a response than "No fucking clue, sir. Do you have any good suggestions?" followed by a nervous giggle sounding like a broken whistle. But that was the best I could come up with on an empty stomach. He looked at Mrs. Mathers, giving her a slight frown. It was only a fleeting glance, but it seemed unmistakable.

I stayed at Julie's for three days and went into the city each morning to make calls at various high schools. We made out one night in the library, or maybe the den; who knew? Frankly I needed a map. *In our house if the room didn't have a bed in it, you knew where you were. My folks left nothing to chance.*

It snowed hard that night, and we sat on the sofa watching the flakes fill the backyard, a small fire lighting up the darkened room. Julie talked about growing up and her friends from high school. Around midnight she slipped her bra off without taking off her top. Afraid someone from upstairs might come down and find us, she stuffed it in her purse, and we sat in the dark watching the snow fall.

October 19, 1943

The *Life* magazine photographer's name was Will Harris. He was twenty-four, tall, thin, and now ten minutes late. He had on khaki pants, a short brown leather bomber jacket that was badly worn on the sleeves, and was carrying a dark blue duffel bag over his right arm.

Mary was standing beside the front desk in the lobby of St. Anne's when he arrived.

"He's cute," said Sylvia, who was working as the front desk senior monitor.

"No kidding. I wish he had been on time," Mary whispered back as he walked up the long hall.

He put down his bag and said, "Hi, I'm Will."

Mary only had thirty-five minutes before staring down another impossible chemistry test in Mrs. Carpenter's class. But now chemistry was the last thing on her mind. She was especially glad she had been given the assignment.

"Hi, I'm Mary, the Lobster."

"Exactly what I was looking for: a Lobster named Mary. And you're the first one I've met."

"You're just not traveling in the right circles, I guess. You're from *Life* magazine?"

"Yes, indeed. That's me."

He took his camera off his shoulder and took a picture of the school's main hall.

"This one won't get used, but I take a lot of shots just in case, and it's good for background for the story." The flash went off lighting up the hall. "This is a nice looking school. You like it?"

"Yeah, it's okay for high school," she replied without enthusiasm.

"I know the feeling, but don't rush it," Will commiserated. "I understand you're going to show me around."

"Sure, let's go. It won't take long."

She waved to Sylvia, and then they headed out. The buildings were all run down, but no one really noticed or cared. The complete tour, including the athletic field, took only a couple of minutes. The leaves had started changing and a small handful of them covered the entrance in front of the barn.

"I'd forgotten how pretty it is out here on the Cape," Will observed.

"I guess so. I never really think about it."

"Trust me. After living in the city, any green space is welcome."

Mary wished she were out of high school and living in New York. Trying to refocus on the purpose of Will's visit, she asked, "So what do you want to see?"

"Well, I'm going to need a shot of where the project started."

"Sure, it's in here."

.   .   .

Chapter 31
MAN CANNOT LIVE ON
WATER CHESTNUTS ALONE

June, 1965

I lived my last year and two months in Whitfield in the garage apartment of a house at the corner of Chestnut and Water Streets. For fun, I told friends I lived on Water Chestnuts. Sometimes they didn't get my simple joke, and I repeated it as much for my benefit as theirs. The house was light gray with wooden shingles and dark green shutters. My apartment was tucked back in at the end of the wide driveway.

In early June of '65, coming back from the beach, I saw the sign stuck in a front lawn: "Garage Apartment, $125.00 per month, utilities included." That was more than I wanted to spend, but the house looked nice, and the apartment seemed big. A boy was coming around from the backyard. I got off my bike and asked if his parents were home.

"Mm..mm..my my father is in the ga...ga... garage," he said, painfully spitting out the words. I waited patiently for him to finish.

"Thanks," I said and smiled back, trying to overlook his pain. My brother used to stutter, and I knew how hard it could be.

A man, fresh from putting the lawnmower up, came out brushing wet grass from his jeans. He introduced the boy as his son Nate, and showed me the apartment. My current lease didn't run out for another month, but an assistant Spanish professor had been hounding me about wanting to take it over, so I dove in. I biked home, changed clothes, called Eduardo, and said, "*Hola, mi amigo. Mi casa es su casa.*"

A little after three, I took over the first month's rent. Julie came along to meet my new landlords, Dave and Caroline Pendleton. Caroline was unloading Casey, their two-year-old, from the backseat. Julie loved Casey's fat round face. Dave called Casey "Miss Moon," a tag that stuck with all of us. We all got along, and they invited us to stay for burgers in the backyard. Nate told us about living in Washington. Caroline spoke about how excited she was to be moving back to the Cape, and Casey made faces for Julie and me. Dave, who had a law degree from Harvard and an engineering degree from Penn, talked about his next project: selecting the location for the new power plant. Julie discussed her med school plans, and then they looked at me. Not wanting to disappoint, I gave my opinion on the chances of the Red Sox making the World Series. The party lasted until 9 when the excited Miss Moon cratered in her father's arms, and Julie and I went back to her apartment.

My new apartment came furnished with an almost new double bed, a large brown sofa, a wing-backed chair, and two standing lamps. At one end was a galley kitchen and behind that a tiny bath with a large claw-footed tub. At the other end were three crank windows opening out towards the water a block away. The view was blocked partially by trees and houses, but I could still see pieces of blue between the green. At the top of the stairs was a small deck of weathered white wood, large enough on which to string a hammock.

On Sunday I moved boxes of clothes, and Nate helped. Later in the day the two of us biked to the hardware store to get a new window crank.

Julie had her own apartment across town, but sometimes on the weekends she would stay with me. When I was issuing the invitation, I would say, "Julie, man cannot live on water chestnuts alone. He needs a buddy." She laughed at how sad my joke seemed.

Things were going well for me then. I liked my job in the admissions office. After a full year there, I had learned how to get a lot done without breaking a sweat. I loved still being in the college environment without the bother of unnecessary papers or midterms, or their "oh, so judgmental" grading system. Soon the history department's exhibit on the Cape Cod Reds would open, but for now Nate, Julie, Caroline, Casey, and I had a tree house to build and a travel magazine to write.

October 19, 1943

Mary pulled back the squeaking doors to the maintenance barn. The room had been restored to its former purpose of housing an old tractor, tools, a school truck, and office equipment. Will got out his camera and took a series of shots from inside the barn. Shining in the sunlight, the bumper of the school truck read: "Buy War Bonds."

"This must have been tight, working in here."

"Yeah, but we weren't here that long. Right from the start there was a big demand for the berries; of course, it doesn't hurt any that all the profits are going to a good cause."

"No, it doesn't. So what did it look like?" Will asked.

"Well, we had about six or seven tables over here and a large bin in which to keep the cranberries. The nuns did all the shipping invoices at night while we were doing school work. But not anymore: We've grown to multiple shifts, six days a week, working from noon until nine or ten at night, with over a hundred volunteers per shift, sometimes more. We had only student workers here in the barn, but at the warehouse we also have a lot of volunteers from the community. You'll see when you go to the new building."

"This is really an amazing homegrown success, isn't it?"

"Well, we think so, and in fact *Life* magazine is doing an article on us," she said smiling at him, squinching up her eyes.

He smiled and played along, "Really, no kidding? When?"

"Very soon, maybe later today."

"You're funny for a Lobster. So what are your plans for next year?"

"Either U Mass or URI, but it's going to depend on how much help I get from either one. I may not be able to go at all. Maybe I'll just apprentice with a photographer," she said, looking to see if he caught the hint.

"I wish you luck. I know it's tough right now," he said, adjusting the strap on his camera. "So tell me about the Cape Cod Reds, from your perspective."

"It's been great. The town has really pulled together to make it work, and we've become friends with people we wouldn't have otherwise known. Of course, we want to do whatever we can to support the families of the troops. There are five of us who head our own teams. I'm the Lobsters. Katie's the Starfish, Kerrie's the Clams, Penny is the Cods, and sweet Lucy took the Whales. We kid her about that since she's a bean pole. Wait till you meet her. Oh, and I was supposed to give you this."

Mary pulled one of each of the boxes out of her purse and gave them to him.

"Thanks. These are neat. Who did the graphics?"

"Each team designed its own logo. Let's be honest, the cranberries are great, but the boxes make them special. It's kind of funny how that works, don't you think?"

"Yes and no," he said leaning against the school's old blue tractor. "I guess what motivates most people is how things look. It's stupid in a way, but we're all the same." He kicked his foot against the snow blade on the tractor.

"Anyway, each team leader puts in about ten hours a week, but we're all involved in other things: sports; student government; photography; music; and drama; so it's tough getting it all in. We also work for this scientist over at the Institute a couple of hours a week collecting data from Bird Island. So we stay busy."

"That is a busy schedule. You girls are amazing. Are you close?"

"Yes, very. I am really going to miss them next year. For one last fling of togetherness we're planning a trip to a dude ranch in Wyoming after graduation. It's hard to believe we're seniors. It got here so quickly."

"Just wait. It gets worse when you're out of college."

"I bet. How long have you been out?"

"Only a couple of years. I went to NYU in journalism and got hired right out of school."

"You must like it?"

"I do. It's a lot of work and long hours but nothing like the guys overseas. The only reason I'm not there is a punctured eardrum from an accident when I was twelve. But I get to go a lot of places, so that's good. Next week they're sending me to a munitions factory in Georgia."

They started walking back to the administration building. Mary opened the back door and said, "Well, here we are. Sister Margaret's office is down on your left. I hope you enjoyed the tour."

"Thank you. I did. I've had some good tours in my time, but this is my best Lobster tour by far."

"Thanks. That means a lot," she said, putting her fingers together in Lobster-claw fashion.

By lunch the word was all over school that Will was cute, so all the students were planning on arriving early for the photo shoot.

• • •

Chapter 32
I LOVE MY WEDGIE

Summer, 1965

Shortly after the Pendletons moved into Chestnut, Dave promised Nate that they would build a tree house together. But things came up at his work, and Dave had to cancel their plans. Julie thought it would be fun for us to give it a try. I had my reservations. The saw is not my friend, and that goes double for the hammer and nails.

"No, you'll be fine, and anyway I'll be there to help," Julie said reassuringly. We lay on the bed the afternoon she hatched the idea. She rolled her chin on top of my chest and made big eyes which she knew I couldn't resist. Her voice exuded a quiet confidence. "Anyway, what could go wrong?" Her words came back to bite me in the ass.

A few days later Nate, Julie, and I sat around the kitchen table, trying to come up with a simple design. We lingered over the details as long as Caroline's freshly baked chocolate chip cookies lasted.

Somehow the construction went better than I anticipated except for several badly bruised appendages.

"What's he done this time?" Julie asked while coming out the back door, carrying a pitcher of lemonade and a box of Band-Aids.

"Whacked his finger again," Nate replied indifferently.

"Oh, man, is that seven already?"

"Yup. Number seven."

"I didn't think it was even possible, but two more, Nate, and you win," she said, shaking her head.

"Win what? Have you people got some sick betting pool involving my injuries?" They both denied it, but too weakly for my taste.

Nate loved the tree house and spent many happy hours up in its perch during the rest of the summer.

• • •

The public television station in the summer of 1965 ran a series of travelogue specials with a jolly, overweight Englishman named Reginald Firth as the host. The program was called *Traveling with Reggie*. I only understood a little of what he said and nothing after one of his many jokes with himself, his belly jiggling like half-done Jell-o. The series started in mid-June and finished at the end of July. Caroline asked me to pick up a book from the university library, and I was dropping it off when the first show was about to begin. Caroline, Casey, and Nate were slumped on the sofa and invited me to watch with them.

"Come on. Join us," Caroline requested, patting the brown cushion on the sofa. I was supposed to meet friends at a bar, but figured I could be a few minutes late.

After that first week, we were all hooked. Wherever Reggie headed, we went along for the ride. Caroline had gone to Europe with her three college roommates after graduation, and she chimed in when one of her memories flashed across the screen.

"Oh, my God, I've been there," she'd say loudly, leaping off the sofa, as if the last of her six lottery numbers had been called. The rest of us would shrug our shoulders and go back to watching Reggie work his way through a farmer's market on the Greek coast. Reggie dropped by a lot of places that Caroline had been, but he also went down alleys she hadn't seen. I was never sure if she really cared what he was saying, or if she was only biding her time for the chance to throw out her favorite line: "I've been there!"

"Look out, kids," I said to my sofa-mates as Reggie's car began circling the Arc de Triomphe. "I have a really bad feeling about this one." They covered their ears on my command.

But some of her outbursts seemed totally random. Who knew she'd gone into some dusty old bookstore in London, until boom "OH, MY GOD! Mrs. Prattelbee's! Can you believe it?" she cried out.

We had differing opinions about which places we liked the best and why. We all agreed that Rome, Paris, and London seemed neat, but we broke up into little subgroups about other spots. We were prepared to sell our allegiances if all would concede that Luxembourg looked interesting and that Amsterdam smelled. Soon secret messages were being passed under the coffee table hoping to build new alliances.

"Meet me in the foyer in ten minutes, and don't let anyone see you leave," the curt instructions read. It seemed simple enough, but with only four bodies in the room, the removal of half of us could hardly go unnoticed, not to mention that three of us had no idea what a foyer was. But that's what happens when you're desperate for power. These alliances were shaky at best. Would the Spanish have to learn Dutch after our coup? Would El Cordobés, the famous matador, have to take on a charging bull in wooden clogs? The entire world order awaited our instructions. Mostly we never agreed on anything. Alliances were formed and broken before we finished the bowl of popcorn Caroline had made at the start of each show.

I liked the Scandinavian countries. Nate favored France and Spain. Caroline was into England and the whole British Isles, and Casey was just a hopeless Reggie groupie ready to go wherever he led. Dave usually worked late on Tuesdays, so he missed most of the series, but he was home to see the one about the British Isles. Every time Caroline let out with one of her "I've been there" squeals, he'd look at her funny and then over at us, but we'd just roll our eyes.

The week Reggie was doing the southern coast of Spain, *The Boston Globe* TV section had his picture on the cover. Casey saw it and said, "Wedgie. I love my Wedgie."

Caroline laughed and said, "Sweetie, his name is pronounced Reggie, RRRReggie."

About halfway through the series, we came up with the idea of doing a travel guide about the best places to visit in Whitfield. It seemed like a good way for the Pendletons to learn about their new town, and my schedule at work wasn't busy. Once we'd agreed on the plan, we swung into action. Caroline packed sandwiches, loaned me Dave's bike with the baby seat, and the four of us went exploring. We checked out all the high and low spots Whitfield had to offer, making notes about the pros and cons of everything we saw. We decided to call our publication *Biking in Whitfield.*

Nate reminisced about friends from Washington and how much he hadn't wanted to leave the city, and we tried getting him to look forward rather than back, but it wasn't easy. And on one of our outings, when Nate was showing Casey the proper technique for bug eating, Caroline asked if I had any thoughts about how to help Nate make friends. I said that friends would come easily once Nate started school in the fall. Caroline said, "I hope so. Nate is pretty shy and is nervous about starting at a new school. His stuttering only makes the matter worse. Do you have any suggestions?"

I didn't really have a good answer but told her I'd give it some thought. Then Casey spotted a bird, and we all got sidelined sharing the discovery with her. It took us twelve days to get around to all the possible locations we needed to inspect. Dave's bike had an odometer attached to the handlebars, so we kept a record of the miles we covered, which was just short of thirty-six. Sometimes we went out for the whole morning, and sometimes it got too hot, or Casey would have to have herself a big poop, and our plans got cut short. One afternoon the chain came off Dave's bike out near the bluffs, but after a little work, we got it back on and made it home. Most of our trips lasted two hours.

The day we finished our information gathering Caroline made a chocolate cake, which we ate in their kitchen, and then the hard work began. We couldn't afford photos so Caroline agreed to do drawings. She had taken art classes at Smith and was pretty good. She drew the masthead for the front page and other smaller drawings of a starfish and whales, which she placed throughout. The final edition totaled eight pages stapled together. Dave printed them at his office, and we sold copies for a quarter at stores around town. All the profits went to the Cape Cod Preservation Society. We sold four ads to: the Whale Inn; the A&P; First City Bank; and Mike's Bikes. They each paid twenty-five dollars to be included. The guide wasn't worth much, certainly not the quarter we were charging, but we sold over four hundred copies. People saw it as going to a good cause, and some of the information was actually pretty helpful. We included a list of important city services: ferry schedules, boat charters, hotel and restaurant phone numbers, and the mayor's hotline. There was also a section entitled "Festivals & More" with information about all the major events on the Cape.

When *Biking in Whitfield* was finished, Caroline invited Julie and me to dinner. Dave cooked hamburgers out in the backyard. Caroline made homemade peach ice cream and brownies, and we ate dessert in Nate's newly-built tree house.

The paper also featured artwork by both Casey and Nate and one drawing of sailboats I contributed. There was a small segment Caroline included entitled "About the Authors." I didn't really see the point of it, but it did take up some unused space and displayed Caroline's wry sense of humor.

"Casey Pendleton, age 2, likes long walks on the beach with her dad, finger food, and her dog Sam. Nate Pendleton, age 9, likes reading adventure stories, biking, and going to the movies. Peter Dreeton, age 23, works in the admissions office at USJ—at least until his writing improves—and is considering an unwelcome career opportunity from Impervious Life and Casualty. Caroline Pendleton, age 34, a Smith graduate, is parent of two of the editors and house mother to the third.

She likes long walks on the beach with her family, their dog Sam, and something she almost never gets...naps."

The feature article was "The Five Best Places to Bike in Whitfield," and it covered almost four pages. Our favorite pick was the top of St. Peter's Episcopal Church tower. I wrote: "A dusty old climb up eighty-eight steps with more creaky noises than an old time radio drama, but worth the effort, a must-see."

The writing was shaky, but we wanted to catch the reader's attention with our flare for the dramatic.

"After finishing the climb, you'll be treated to one of the best views on the Cape. A narrow catwalk allows for three hundred and sixty degrees of eye-popping views. Bring a camera and a friend. Look off to the west and see Buzzard's Bay, look north and enjoy the University of St. Jerome's beautiful campus, then look east all the way to China! That's not the country, of course, but the China Farms cranberry bogs, one of the state's largest producers. If you bring binoculars you can see a Chinese symbol painted on the side of the barn. We've been told by the owners that it means peace. St. Peter's was constructed in 1842 by Thomas Hancock, a prominent Boston architect. You can find out more information by stopping in its gift shop, open daily."

The photo on the cover of the university catalog was taken from this lookout. Shot during the first changing of the leaves with every color captured inside the zoom lens, it looked down through trees to white colonial clapboard buildings and dark green grass. Leading up to campus, you could see buildings and shops on Front Street, the wharf, and a small cove. Behind were residential areas, city hall, and the high school.

The lady who ran the gift shop lived down the street from the Pendletons, and she let us make as many trips as we wanted at no charge. The only restriction was that we not come at the same time as paying customers. I suggested that we have press badges printed, but Caroline thought that was pushing our luck.

On one of our visits to the tower, a bus tour was coming through from Hartford, so we spent most of the morning wandering around the small graveyard next to the church.

"Just think," I said to Nate, "someday we'll all end up in here, and our tombstones will read: 'Here rests an editor of *Biking in Whitfield.*'" Nate thought it unlikely our work would bring that kind of fame.

Our second favorite spot was the lighthouse at the far end of town. "The ride out along the shoreline is hard to beat, unless you go on a windy day, and then you spend half the time fighting the headwinds. A working lighthouse damaged by a hurricane in the late eighteen hundreds, it was repaired in 1903. Like the church tower it's open for visitors and offers amazing views of the bay."

Our third location was McKinley's, an upscale boat accessory shop in town, located next to the main pier. They sold fishing and marine equipment as well as a full line of clothing and gifts. In the middle of their showroom was an old white rowboat with fishing gear inside. When we dropped by, Caroline put Casey in every silly hat combination and shot a whole roll of film with her inside the boat. Caroline's favorite outfit was a yellow rain slicker and hat, but I liked the little sailor suit as well.

We propped her up holding an oar, a brass lantern, a plastic swordfish... too many combinations to go into here. Caroline had two of her favorite photos enlarged for Dave's birthday gift.

"The neat thing about McKinley's," I wrote, "is all of the tall fishing tales you hear. Plus it is right next to the boardwalk, and that's fun in itself."

The fourth pick was the university football stadium. "Even in the middle of summer, it is a great place to visit. Located in a residential part of town with towering oak trees rising over the top of the stadium, it's a great place to spend a summer afternoon. Discover our neighborhood charm or read a book. Sit on the bleachers or get some exercise. All summer high school and college athletes chase balls up and down the field, and players run the stairs during the heat of the day. The west gate opens daily at nine, and admission is free. It's a great way to scout the upcoming Crusader season."

Our last recommendation was the visitor's center across from Amy's Ice Cream. "Here you can learn every interesting fact about the town and pick up travel information about island cruises and more. Then walk across the street and treat yourself to a scoop of your favorite homemade flavor. Amy's is great place to meet people. The editors suggest homemade chocolate chunks with sprinkles on a waffle cone."

October 19, 1943

Sister Margaret had worked hard to make the warehouse presentable. She asked several ladies to plant mums in the six window boxes in front of the building and got students to haul trash around to the back.

Will was staying at the Wayfarer Inn, and Mrs. Neumann, the librarian, was acting as his chauffeur. Katie saw them first as the car turned the corner, and she called out to the crowd gathered outside, "He's here."

Will was genuinely surprised by all the fuss. He was neither a celebrity nor a war hero. But he was from New York and worked for *Life*.

As soon as he got out of the car, the local high school band started playing the "Stars and Stripes," and a greeting committee presented him with gifts. Mayor Wilson gave him a whale tie clasp; one of the ladies presented him with a copy of the *Cape Cod Reds Cookbook*; and a nun gave him twenty-five boxes of their cranberries. He thanked them all and wondered how long it would take to consume that many cranberries. Small children released a handful of colorful balloons, which sailed above the three-story building. Sister Margaret invited the delegation to move inside, and they all followed.

She made a few announcements and explained that it would take a few minutes for Will to get his camera set up and asked everyone to please get to their stations and be patient. The actual shoot took longer than Will had expected, but he wanted to get human interest shots as well as wide-angle ones. When they were done, an Italian feast was waiting for everyone, and the party lasted until after 10. Twenty tables with red-and-white-checkered cloths were set up in the open part of the warehouse, and for dessert Mrs. Hartwell had made her famous cranberry cheesecake, found in the cookbook. Will sat at the head table with Sister Margaret, several of the nuns, and Mayor Wilson and his wife. Around 9 he excused himself and moved over to have cheesecake with the five girls.

The lead photo, taken from the second-story balcony, looked down on all the workers. They were looking up at him waving flags and signs. The other photos included two nuns looking over a shipping order, a small gathering of workers by the benches, and a shot of the five leaders in aprons holding up boxes, all smiling together.

•   •   •

Chapter 33
CAN I HAVE HIS LIVER?

My last fall on the Cape was part joy and part challenge. It began with a bike ride after work in the middle of September. Nate had begun his new school, Julie was sending off for med school applications, and I was busy getting ready for the fall push in the admissions office and the opening of the Cape Cod Reds exhibit.

September 16, 1965

A long line of cars pulling boats were lined up at Charlie's Quick Stop to buy gas. These were end-of-season tourists hoping to enjoy the last warm days before the weather turned. I usually stopped on my rides after work for water but decided today to wait until I reached the boathouse. I avoided a large pothole in the asphalt and turned off the main road. Thick trees and heavy brush closed in tight around me, holding in both heat and dust. Ahead was the steepest hill on my course. I licked my bottom lip and tried to think about finishing, but at the top of the last hill my front tire spun out on loose gravel. I was close to the edge and in danger of a precarious ride down a steep ravine. I hit the brakes hard. The back wheel of the bike rose over my head, trying to decide whether to drop me back to the ground or toss me over the handlebars. Neither seemed a good idea. I held on tightly trying to get ready for whatever was next. My arms twisted out of place, I went flying, and my face cracked down on a piece of broken concrete.

I spent the next three days in a hospital bed. The "Marquis De Sade Clinic for Recuperative Health Sciences and Bondage" was also known as the Cape Cod Medical Center. It was far enough removed from the milling crowds that their nasty little secrets went unnoticed from the authorities. Once they had unloaded me from the school's station wagon, they wheeled me in for what seemed like hours of fun—the way biology experiments can be really fun, as long as you're not the frog.

"Ouch," I shouted when they poked a sore spot.

"Does that hurt?" the doctor asked. He followed it with, "How about now?"

"Are you fucking crazy, Doc? If this is how you treat the infirmed, remind me never to come back when I'm feeling better."

"Here, I'm giving you something to relieve the pain," the doctor said while injecting me with some instant-acting potion.

"Terrific," I replied as the world around me became fuzzy.

"We've worked him over well enough for tonight. We'll take another crack at him tomorrow," the doctor said routinely as if rebuilding a car engine in a friend's garage.

"Hell, yes, Doctor! Shall we say four-thirty, my place? Bring tweezers. I'll sleep like a baby knowing there's more of this coming."

"Can I have his liver if he doesn't make it?" the nurse standing over me asked. I figured she had to be joking, but then maybe not.

"I guess so," the doctor said. "But remember, Carla, if the coroner stops by, tell him housekeeping misplaced it. We can't afford another medical inquiry about missing body parts."

"No problem, Doctor. I'll throw what I don't need in the dumpster," Carla casually responded. *Ah yes, the perfect ending to Peter Dreeton, as I knew him to be.*

They put me in a long ward on the second floor with beds for eight, but the only other patient was Andy McPherson, a man in his late sixties recovering from hip surgery. Chet, the orderly, unloaded me in bed six next to Andy's. Of course my preference was bed five, my favorite hospital bed number, but it was late, and getting Andy to switch seemed like more trouble than it was worth.

"What happened to him?" Andy asked Chet, who then rolled me off the cart.

"Not sure," Chet answered indifferently.

"How ya feeling, big fella?" Andy asked.

"Not good, but I can't really talk now." I wanted to be friendly, but it felt as if all my words had "suches" added on the end of them.

"Okay, get some rest, partner." He went back to watching the late movie on the overhead TV. And soon enough, I rolled over onto warm sand and was gone.

. . .

Julie started applying coconut oil to my back. It felt good with the sun beating down. Seagulls floated quietly above. I moaned every once in a while, depending on where she applied the oil, or if my body hit a painful spot on the sand.

"How did we get here?" I asked.

"The same as we always do: horseback."

"Horseback?" I said in disbelief.

"Yeah," Julie waved behind her to the hitching post, where two horses, one brown, the other painted, were tied together. "You came on Pistol, and I came on Whiskers."

I was going to ask which was which but decided to wait until we left. Then, after she mounted Whiskers, I'd call the other one Pistol. There were only two horses so if she took one away…well frankly, my odds couldn't be any better. Another math challenge conquered by Peter Dreeton, PhD.

"One, two, three, four, five," I said and was just getting started… "Six, seven, eight." *Hell, yes, the sky's the limit. There were whole numbers for as far as the eye could see, and I could name them all.* At this point, I must have shouted some of them too loudly because one of the night nurses came over, shaking me gently back onto the beach.

I was about to ask Julie where we kept the horses, when the orchestra started playing. She tapped me lightly on the arm; turning me back around. In front of us a large rink filled with an ice show about to perform. There were leading ladies with long blond hair in pink costumes, gracefully skating animals, and clowns to make us laugh. *Really it was all of the gala and pageantry one expects from a small-time traveling extravaganza, and more!* It was one of those ice shows heavy on themed characters and light on plot line. You know the kind I'm talking about... beautiful girl meets oversized cuddly animal, they fall in love, and their children come out hairy, not looking like either of them.

"What is this?" I asked.

"Shush, just watch. You'll like it," Julie replied.

I watched intently for a while wondering how one ice skates on sand. It was puzzling really. Yet another of life's riddles I couldn't solve: that would be riddle number 9416 if memory serves.

Finally, I got completely bored and looked over my shoulder. Shaking my head, I turned to Julie and said, "Hey, look. The horses are gone."

She looked at me funny and asked, "What horses?"

. . .

For breakfast the next morning one of the ice skaters from the show brought me pancakes, juice, and bacon.

"Did you sleep well?" the nurse asked, a warm smile crossing her face.

"Like a baby with colic," I answered. I wanted to ask how she liked playing Spurlina, a buxom blond from an unnamed eastern bloc country, and Princess Trudy's best friend in the ice show, but I decided against it.

"How did I get here?" I asked uncertain about the past events.

"You had a bike accident. Two students found you unconscious in front of the boathouse, and the school station wagon brought you here," she said.

"Really?" I smiled. She smiled back, and unable to contain myself any longer, I motioned for her to lean down close so no one else could hear. "Well, I have to tell you something. You were really great last night, the best in fact."

She seemed perplexed at my comment and didn't respond at first. Then she let out, "Excuse me?"

I said, "No really, the best!"

"Good. That's nice to know," she answered, deciding to leave this conversation where she found it and went back to the nurses' station.

I spent the next three days lapping up pain medication whenever they gave it out and listening to Andy complain about his hip. On the second night, Andy watched a World War II spy movie, and I drifted off and dreamed of a magical fruit: the cranberry.

September 19, 1965

Julie brought me home from the hospital. I was still woozy from my medication, and she was telling me a long story about how two of her lab rats, Ramona and Candy, were not getting along. At the moment I was just so glad to be out of the body shop and not in a body bag. We passed an old house with a dark green sign reading: "Brooks Realty: Ask about our vacation rentals."

"Say, I used to have French lab in there!" I said, pointing at the house.

"In a real estate office?

"Well, the building used to belong to the school, and every Tuesday and Thursday, right after lunch, we spent ninety minutes in a mind-numbing review of the uninteresting.

French lab was a bullet shot through the temporal lobe of our afternoon. We curled up in the cubicles, and in a space that depressing anything was possible. Confessions came as cheaply as promises on a first date."

"Say, are you talking about our first date?" Julie asked, making a face.

"No, of course not. I loved your confessions, especially the one about how cute you thought I was."

"Apparently your medication hasn't worn off yet. But what was so bad about French lab?"

"We followed the adventures of a young boy named Gustave, his sister Angelique, and their dog Sophie. We made trips to the car repair shop, a bookstore and my personal favorite, the supermarket. We learned a lot of interesting expressions like how to say 'Who moved the baking soda to aisle one?' and 'May I touch your asparagus?'"

"That sounds fun," Julie said, pulling up to the light on Elm.

"Oh, it was, and then there was the time Gustave put his socks on the wrong feet, and of course we all got a big belly laugh out of that one."

"You have to give the French credit. They do have a wacky sense of humor."

"I suppose so, but I found it a waste of time. Say can we stop for some candy on the way home. I need a sugar rush?" I asked as we passed the A&P.

"Not now. I have a class to get to in twenty minutes. Anyway you need to rest. If you're a good boy, I'll bring you some tomorrow." Julie pulled up into the Pendletons' driveway and turned off the engine.

"Say, can you help me with the door?"

"Of course." She assisted me up the stairs and unloaded supplies. "When are the Pendletons getting back?"

"Tonight, but I'm not sure when. Before you go, let me ask you a question."

"Sure," she smiled while fixing the covers at the foot of my bed. "What do you need?"

"Can I touch your asparagus?"

"No, not now sweetie, and don't think about leaving this room for twenty-four hours. Got it?" she added.

"Don't worry. I won't." Drool had already formed on the top of my pillow, and I drifted off to sleep.

October 21, 1943

Dr. Schneider would wait until lunch for an office to be empty, and then he would slip in to photograph documents, to copy a formula on a piece of paper, or to make a drawing. Always he prepared an excuse. Always he had a reason to be in Dr. So-and-so's drawer or to be rifling through the file cabinet. Dr. Schneider was never a suspect, only a co-worker looking for a pen or rubber bands or whatever he needed at the moment.

Today Dr. Mitchell's office was the target of Dr. Schneider's espionage. Since Dr. Mitchell had planned a trip to his physician to see about a nagging sore throat, this was a perfect time to check on things. Dr. Mitchell was the Institute's official contact with the Navy, and he had general information which would be of interest to German counter-intelligence: Everything from dates of merchant ships crossing the Atlantic and the routes they would take to documents on new weapons technology. The downside to this visit was the location of Dr. Mitchell's office next to that of the director. Plus the two scientists shared a secretary, Mrs. Crosby, whose desk faced Dr. Mitchell's door. Mrs. Crosby's daughter was halfway through her first pregnancy, and Dr. Schneider knew that she liked to drive over to her daughter's house to have lunch together. The director was in Boston for a meeting, so this wing of the building became empty when Mrs. Crosby breezed by his own office. They traded pleasantries, and he asked how "junior" was doing.

"Oh, we don't know if it's a boy yet, Dr. Schneider," Mrs. Crosby pointed out, and he responded that she was absolutely correct. Mrs. Crosby waved her white-gloved hand and headed out of sight. Dr. Schneider finished smoking the last few draws from his pipe and laid it down on his desk. He picked up a handful of unnecessary papers and headed off to his mission. These papers would serve as his cover should anyone walk in on him during his visit. During the next half hour he moved undisturbed between file cabinet and desk drawers pulling out and copying bits of useful information. By the time Mrs. Crosby returned from her corned beef sandwich on rye bread, he was back at his own desk with the information safely in hand.

"Any change yet?" he asked as she passed back by.

"No, but I'm hoping for a boy as well." She smiled back at him.

Dr. Schneider gave her a thumbs-up and picked up his phone to make a call.

·   ·   ·

Chapter 34
LIFE'S BETTER WHEN A NAKED PERSON IS RIDING SHOTGUN

September 19-20, 1965

When I awoke, rain was pulling in off the ocean. My room, hot at first, had turned cooler. I looked down into the backyard. A Little Lulu coloring book was soaked through, and a plastic beach ball, that Casey had spent the summer trying to swallow whole, rose off the ground. Its yellow and white colors blended into one. I started counting raindrops and stopped at forty something. I fell fast asleep again. Around eleven I woke up with a start, having realized my office keys were still at the boathouse. The knowledge became an uncontrollable itch, a train wreck I couldn't take my eyes off. The keys didn't matter—or did they? I had to have my keys *right then*. It was still raining, but that didn't matter. I was still in pain, but that didn't matter. I put on an old pair of jeans and a T-shirt. I grabbed my crutches and hobbled down to the car.

I swung my body into the worn leather seats of the Volvo and backed down the drive without turning on the lights. At Charlie's Quick Stop, the town's only all night drive-in market, I pulled in for a treat. The lot was empty except for the night manager's car and an old Ford with our fraternity's sticker on the back window. The store, set back on a small lot next to Dunbar's Boatyard, stayed full during the day with boat workers and craftsmen talking about their work, and after 5 the benches filled with men drinking cold beer. But after 11 on a warm rainy night, Charlie's was just a place to buy something cold to drink or salty to eat.

A soft bell tinkled my arrival. "Avon calling," I said, noticing the cooler door open. Felix, the night manager, was restocking the beer shelves. He looked up and waved with oversized blue cooler mitts.

"Cool mittens, Felix," I called out, while picking a Coke bottle from the bottom of the iced tubs and shaking the loose bits of ice off my hand.

"Hey, Peter," a voice behind the news rack said, and I turned.

"Hey, George, what's happening?" I said to my fraternity brother.

"Not much. What happened to you?"

"Don't ask," I said.

George was deeply involved in Miss October's outfit, or lack of one. In one hand he held the magazine open, and in the other a half-eaten creamed cake with the residue coating the edges of his mouth.

"Feeding several fantasies at once?"

"I'm taking this one to meet the family."

"Which one?" I asked unclear if he meant the sponge cake or the girl.

"Here, look at these." He turned the magazine around for me to see. I blushed, but felt compelled to say something. "Nice boobs" was the best I could come up with on short notice.

He pulled out the bottom half of his shirt, wiping food particles on it, and revealing huge portions of a sagging stomach, now completely defeated from too many dessert bombs. His shirt provocatively asked, "Who wants seconds?" a question that his 285-pound frame had long since answered.

"Say, what are you doing out in this weather?"

"Going to the boathouse to get some lost keys. Want to come?"

"No, thanks, I've got better things to do."

"I bet."

. . .

The phone was ringing as I climbed the stairs a little after midnight. I kicked the door open with my good foot, threw my crutches on the bed, and picked it up in mid-ring.

"Where have you been?" Julie began her inquisition without me. "I've been calling since 11! You weren't supposed to leave, remember?"

I told her about my trip to the boathouse, finding my keys, and how wet and tired I was. But Julie was on a mission, and she wasn't listening.

I gave her an occasional "yes, sweetie," and tossed in a "you make a good point" every now and then, while stripping to my underwear.

"Let me get this straight: You got out of bed and drove yourself to the boathouse to look for your office keys. Is that it?"

I was cold, wet, and looking for any escape from her tiresome questions. She ended her summation to the twelve sympathetic jurors sitting on the edge of my bed, "Ladies and gentlemen of the jury, I rest my case. He's nuts."

My father, who was serving as jury foreman, and the other eleven members all nodded, confirming their acceptance of her argument.

"Peter, driving out there was a waste of time."

"Really? Why?"

"You could have sent one of the student aides to pick them up. Peter, how you use your time matters."

"So what did you have in mind?" I asked, climbing in bed.

"I don't know. Come up with something. Write a book for God's sake."

"Okay. Maybe I already am."

"Yeah, great, you never take me seriously. Anyway, I was just calling because I was worried."

"I know, sweetie. That means a lot." It was late, and I knew I would have a busy day of work ahead, so I said goodnight and hung up.

•   •   •

"Peter, are you up?" Caroline's voice called out the next morning.

"Hey, sure, come on in." I was pulling a green and white striped tie out of the top drawer.

"I wanted to check on you. We got back last night about 8, but when I came up you were fast asleep. You still don't look great, but better than when we saw you in the hospital."

"Yeah, I was pretty out of it with all the painkillers. How was your trip?" I asked.

"Good, the kids had fun." She was holding a tall glass of orange juice and a blueberry muffin and set them down on the coffee table. "These are for you."

"Thanks. I could use an energy boost right now."

"Guess what? Nate got some great news on Friday afternoon. Miss Mayfield chose him to be one of the team captains for the cranberry project with the university."

"That's wonderful. Miss Mayfield and I have worked on a planning committee together. She's a great teacher. Tell Nate I'm proud."

"I will. Miss Mayfield said the leaders will be coming to your office for a meeting."

"Yeah, in a few days I'm giving them a tour of the exhibit, and Naomi has been hatching some surprises of her own. It should be fun."

"Thanks, Peter."

"Hey, I'm just happy he got the gig. I know he'll do well."

After finishing the glass of juice and eating my muffin, I hobbled to the door. She pulled the door shut and waited while I carefully shuffled down each step.

October 21, 1943

Dr. Schneider put the drawings and notes in his briefcase and headed to the security gate. "Hello, Eddie," he said and got a nod back in return. Eddie was somewhere near sixty, out of shape, not very attentive, but always friendly. Dr. Schneider smiled at Eddie and put his briefcase up on the wooden counter, before letting out a loud yawn.

"You look tired tonight, Doc," Eddie noted.

"Just a little. They have me working on too many things again. Same as always, work follows you around like an unwelcome friend."

"You're right about that one," Eddie said moving his evening paper to the other side of the long green table and opening up the briefcase for a quick inspection. But Eddie wasn't really looking for anything, and he found nothing unusual. He moved papers around and put them back together as disorganized as he had found them.

"Say, Eddie, do you know when they are supposed to finish the roof repairs on my wing?" Dr. Schneider asked, in an effort to distract the security guard.

"The foreman was in here just a few minutes ago and said they are hoping to finish by the beginning of the week."

"I certainly hope so. They've been stomping around up there for days, and it's been hard to get any work done," he groused.

Eddie looked up and smiled. "There you go," he said, closing the briefcase. "Get some rest."

"I'll try," Dr. Schneider answered. He went to the glass double doors and pulled one ajar, much colder air blasting through the slight opening. He quickly let the door close again. "Wow," he said. "Colder than lunch, huh? Especially after the warm fall we've been having."

"Cold front coming in, Doc. They say we may get a hard freeze tonight," Eddie commented.

"Kind of early for that, don't you think? I hope it doesn't impede the progress on the roof."

"I know what you mean."

He buttoned the top of his light-colored coat. Just as he was about the pull the door open again, Eddie called out to him, "Wait, Doc. Not so fast."

For one quick moment Dr. Schneider feared what he always feared: being caught. And the worst part was being caught by a half-asleep security guard. "What's up?" he asked as casually as he could.

"Don't forget this. You're like me. Men of our age and hairline can use all the help we can get in this weather," Eddie said as he rubbed his own balding head.

"Thanks, Eddie. You're right."

•   •   •

Chapter 35
I'VE ALWAYS WANTED TO BE POCOHANTAS

September 20, 1965

"Don't you look great? Does mummy need his mommy?" Naomi chuckled as I maneuvered myself and my crutches into the outer office.

"Your concern is overwhelming. Is it too late to switch departments?" I asked. Naomi held open the door separating our office from the rest of the first floor.

"Don't get your hopes up. By the way, I've never seen so much tape on one person. I must say it's a good look for you. Not everyone can carry it off."

"Thanks, I tried on several rolls before picking this one. But seriously, be honest; does it make my butt look big?"

"No more than usual," she smiled.

Naomi helped me back into my office where I gave her a blow-by-blow account of my accident. At noon Naomi went to Otto's and brought back turkey sandwiches to eat. Over lunch she went into her plan for the elementary school visits.

"So what do you think?" she asked as she finished up.

"It's cute, Naomi. Call theatre arts and see if they can help us out."

September 23, 1965

"You're late. They're going to be here any minute," Naomi said, as I came back from a meeting with financial aid.

"Has the box arrived?"

"Yeah, they dropped it off about an hour ago. It's on your desk."

"Okay, give me a couple of minutes."

The first in the room was Gloria Travers, a tall, big-boned girl with wild red hair. She stopped dead in her tracks seeing a fully dressed pirate on crutches waving a sword over his head.

"Avast, me hearties, Captain Peter Dreeton welcomes you aboard."

She gave an uncertain stare but moved cautiously into the room. She was followed closely by a thin, dark-haired girl, named Angela Carlucci, with small eyes. Angela smirked but didn't make a comment. Nate, looking embarrassed, was next, followed by Dennis Wilson who started laughing, and finally a much bigger boy, Toby Simmons. Naomi, deadpan as always, urged them all to take a seat.

Gloria, Angela, and Dennis settled comfortably onto the couch across from my desk. Nate took a chair beside them, and Toby helped himself to one of the two seats up by my desk. .

"What?" I said looking at Naomi. "Have none of you ever been on a college admission interview before?"

"Apparently not," Naomi replied.

"Listen, this is what history is all about: bringing the past to life. When you make presentations on the Cape Cod Reds or sell boxes of berries, you need to be in the spirit. History is made up of real people just like you and me. Sure, a lot of them made some really bad fashion choices, but we can't hold that against them. Today we're all going to wear costumes to get into the spirit. So are there any questions?"

"Is the candy for anyone?" Gloria asked, eyeing the bowl on the table and giving a whimsical smile.

"Why, yes, sweetheart, for anyone named Gloria," Naomi replied.

Gloria looked perplexed, but Angela instructed her to take a piece and pass the bowl down, which she did without hesitation. I could tell that Gloria and Angela were joined at the hip, but the three boys didn't seem to have any connection to each other.

"Is this really your office?" Angela asked.

"No, of course not, Angela, I just borrow it for important occasions, like interviewing fourth graders. Why do you ask?"

"Because it's pretty big, and you don't seem that special."

"He's not," Naomi chuckled, "but how do you know so much about big offices?"

"My father has one."

"Oh, really? What does he do?"

"He's president of First City Bank, which my grandfather started," she said routinely, as if this was information we should already possess

"Well, that's great, but this is the office they gave me. So maybe it proves that if you stay in school long enough, good things happen."

"Maybe," Angela replied while sucking on a peppermint stick, not seeming to accept my explanation.

I looked at Nate squirming in his seat and could see that he wasn't happy about having a pirate for a neighbor.

"Well, we need to get started. Miss Mayfield picked you to be class leaders of the Cape Cod Reds. You will be responsible for running group presentations and helping out with the berry sale. This project made a real contribution to the community, and it's important to honor all those who worked on it. We're going over to the exhibit hall to meet the curator, Dr. Wallace, who will give you even more information."

Toby asked what a curator was, and I explained that it was a job with a fancy title and a big office.

"All right, kids, it's time to find outfits for us," Naomi directed them. She started pulling costumes out of the box, before finding one she liked. "Oh, wow, look, my favorite. I've always wanted to be Pocahontas," she said picking up the headdress, beaded necklace, and moccasins. "And look, there's even an ear of plastic corn. I must say theatre arts thought of everything. I love plastic corn. Well, chop, chop, kiddoes, we can't leave until everyone finds a costume."

Dennis took the conquistador helmet and sword. Nate went for the cowboy gear. Toby put on the Abraham Lincoln beard and stovepipe hat. Gloria mulled over a couple of different choices on the table before seizing the Queen Victoria crown and scepter.

"Hey, I want that one," Angela complained and made a face.

"Too bad, sweetheart," Naomi said. "Pick something else. There are lots of the other good choices," Grudgingly, Angela put on the black shawl, white collar, and pilgrim hat, looked in the mirror, and seemed pleased with her decision.

"All right, kids, we need to have a picture taken before we go," Naomi said. As if on cue, Mrs. Coffee from the registrar's office came in, picked up the camera, and asked us to pose. Then she took our picture, commemorating the beginning of the kids' Cape Cod Reds adventure.

Then we piled into two golf carts for the ride over to the exhibit. At first they seemed restrained, but by the time we arrived they were all getting into the spirit, especially Gloria, who was waving her scepter at every passing student and professor.

Like most of the community, Dr. Schneider put in several hours a week at the warehouse volunteering, packing, and filling orders for delivery. It was just enough time to appear to be working. He was officially a Lobster, but he also had been assigned to be a supervisory floater, giving help wherever it was needed. He was able to move seamlessly between tasks at the cranberry project with nothing more than a welcoming nod.

Today Dr. Schneider made a quick trip to the market to pick up a few essentials. After dropping off his groceries and letting the cat out into the backyard, Dr. Schneider took off his tie and sat down to transcribe his notes from Dr. Mitchell's office onto a scrap of notebook paper. For the finishing touch, he scrawled in red pen on the backside, "Hey Mary, did I tell you I'm on a diet to lose ten pounds? Lucy," making sure the lettering looked as girlish as he could make it. He folded the note and put it in his pocket. Then he headed out the door.

At the warehouse the Lobsters' workbenches were closest to the shipping office, giving him more opportunities to pop in and have a smoke. While he was there, he would look over the week's shipping schedule. As support for the project and as a promotional for the stores, each Saturday the *Cape Cod Courier* listed five local stores that sold the boxes. If someone saw him looking at the list, he would just comment on how many good outlets were stocking the product, but tonight no one was watching. He simply looked at the first location. It was the only one that mattered. Next to the name of each store was one of the five designs, indicating the type of boxes being shipped to that location that week. Next to Wallace Market was a drawing of a cod. There was nothing complicated about his scheme. There was no risk-taking. It was simply a matter of reading what had already been decided by someone else unconnected to his cause and then of directing his information there.

After Dr. Schneider finished his smoke, he stopped to chat with the ladies at the Clam table and listened to stories about their husbands or sons and wished them all well. He casually palmed one of their boxes with the Clam design and put it in his pocket. He went into the bathroom, where in the privacy of a stall he loaded the box with his note containing information from the Institute and slipped the box back inside his coat pocket. Then Dr. Schneider headed over to the Cod table and told Corinne, the student assistant in charge, that he would give her a break. She was happy to comply. After she had gone, he printed the label for Wallace Market, 125 Old Harbor Rd., Chatham, with a thick point pen. Then he loaded a case of Cod boxes for delivery. On the bottom row he placed a single Clam box. His job was done. The box would be delivered on Friday, and on Saturday the contact would drop by the store to pick it up. The mule would glance over the new case before selecting the Clam box from among the Cods. That box would be taken to Boston and dropped off at a coffee shop near the wharf. The job was completed. No contact ever occurred between either of them, and neither knew the other's name, so if the deliveryman were caught, he had no secrets to tell. All that he had ever been told to do was read the paper, buy the random box and deliver it. He had memorized a phone number to call in case of emergencies, but that was his only connection. An envelope was sent to his apartment once a week with the payment for his work.

Dr. Schneider finished his shift and said goodnight to Corinne.

"Thanks for your help," she said. "Were you here for the photo session?"

"Oh, yes, I wouldn't have missed it. I can't wait for the magazine to come out."

They both smiled, and then he went home to have dinner with his cat.

· · ·

Chapter 36
ALUMNI DAYS

October 16, 1965

The alumni crew boat passed the quarter mile point two boat lengths behind the varsity's first boat. In the seat ahead of me Roger Dawson, class of '63, was already struggling. "Hey, Pete, how much farther?" he asked, short of breath, pulling the oar back up to his chest.

"Don't think about it," I responded, my body bent forward in a half-curl finishing the same stroke. The coxswain picked up our rotation trying to make up the distance.

There was something peaceful about hearing the sounds of oars digging into the water with the same motion, of air being sucked out of lungs and then reloaded, and of brass grommets squeaking in their tiny wooden holes with every rotation, as our boat slid quietly toward the finish. We entered a steady rhythm. It was all muscle memory, back and forth, high to low, one rotation leading into another and another after that. It was always best not to think during races but only to breathe. We pulled almost even with the first boat, only for a moment. As if they were teasing us, the varsity surged forward again. They crossed the finish line two lengths ahead. The first boat cheered as we passed under the flapping red flags a few seconds later

"Good job," an insincere voice called out from the varsity boat.

"Right, Tommy," I responded sarcastically, as we glided slowly to a stop.

"Hey, don't be a sore loser. Anyway, you came close, especially for old guys. Better luck next year."

"There is no next year," I replied. I wouldn't be coming back for lobster dinners with the couple from Chapel Hill or for tours of the new science building when it opened. Wherever I was going, it wouldn't be here.

Julie and a large crowd of spectators were standing near the beer station. "Good job, sweetie," Julie said, clapping her hands without spilling a single drop of beer from her cup. I grabbed a beer and joined her. We finished our beers and visited with some of the other alumni crew and then biked back to town. On Main Street we rode underneath a banner reading, "Berry Power: Whitfield salutes her brave past, the Cape Cod Reds. October '65 – May '66 at Kirsch Library."

"So how has the attendance been at the Reds so far?" Julie asked.

"Great, even better than Dr. Tiller expected. They had a dozen school tours during the week and great crowds on the weekends."

"Peter, it's nice of you to have volunteered all the time that you have. I know Dr. Tiller really appreciates your help."

"Hey, she got me through all the tough courses. I still owe her big time."

We pulled up in front of Kaman's. The two bike racks were both full except for one space on the end. I carefully slid Julie's bike into place, locked it up, and then chained mine to hers.

I stopped here most days to buy a Boston paper and catch up on local gossip. I grabbed the "Serving Sunbeam buns" advertisement, a faded sign painted on the door's metal handle, worn thin from twenty years of service, and we went inside.

Two white ceiling fans moved slowly overhead and sounds of dirty dishes banging into each other tumbled towards us from the back of the soda fountain. The imposing oak counter extended out from the back wall with fourteen seats facing a mirror. Above it, a black-and-white menu board offered daily favorites and breakfast specials.

Sitting in the first stool was Mr. Wilson, the former mayor. A white-haired jovial man, in his early seventies, Mr. Wilson was a widower who ate at least two of his three meals a day at Kaman's. On top of his now occupied seat cushion Mr. Kaman had taped a sign reading "This space reserved exclusively for Mayor Wilson. Use only in case of emergency." It was perhaps a little too oblique drugstore humor for some, but I found it endearing. And today it certainly applied. Every seat at the counter was taken and all of the five booths. A family of four was finishing lunch, and as the mother got up, I grabbed two of the stools.

It was "Pick Your Own Banana" weekend. A large bowl of perhaps twenty bananas sat on the shelf below the mirrored wall by the "Pick, peel, and pay" sign.

Abby, one of the waitresses, put down a small glass of ice water and wiped the counter clean with her wet rag. Little drops of water from the bottom of the glass filled up a tiny starfish carved into the counter. I liked this seat best because I was curious about the carving. I ran my hand over it, wondering how long it had been there.

"Hey, guys, what'll it be?" she asked, pulling a pencil out from behind her right ear.

"I'll have the tuna salad on wheat and an iced tea," Julie responded.

"And I'll take a burger, fries, and a Coke." Then I asked, "How long is the banana split sale going on?"

"Until the bananas run out, I'd say tonight or tomorrow noon at the latest."

"You talked me into it. Pick me out a good one." Abby left to place our orders.

Julie talked about all that she had to do after lunch, and I announced that I was going home to nap. "It's disgusting that you're going to spend Saturday afternoon in the library," I commented.

"It must be nice not having any work to do," she said.

"Not bad, you should try it some time."

"It's not that simple," she replied.

Our meals came. I devoured my burger and fries, and then watched Abby pile pieces of pineapple topping over a mound of vanilla ice cream. Julie ate most of the chocolate and a fair portion of the strawberry and left the rest for me. The price sticker remained folded on the counter until we put down our spoons. When I finally opened it, the price was forty-four cents, a cheap extravagance.

On the way to leave I bought a can of shaving cream and a football magazine, and we left the warmth of the store behind.

Light filtered down through the trees overhead, and we began a mostly shady ride. Julie noticed Nate's class getting set up for a presentation in the town square. "Hey, I haven't seen Nate's performance yet. Let's stop to see it," Julie suggested.

A crowd of perhaps fifty people closed in around the front of the temporary stage. A wooden frame in the front held a large hand-painted banner, "Home of the Cape Cod Reds."

Miss Mayfield, standing by the side of the stage, was helping a student with her costume, and several others were arranging props. I gave a wave, and we worked our way to the front of the crowd, ending up next to a young mother with two small children.

"Do you have one in this?" I asked the woman, uncertain if she was a fourth-grade parent.

"No, these two are it, and they're a handful. How 'bout you?" she asked looking at Julie and me.

"Nope, I live in the garage apartment behind the house of the kid in the green shirt," I said. And then for no good reason volunteered, "She's my girlfriend." I pointed to Julie, as if this information would somehow validate me.

"That's nice," the woman chuckled.

Julie laughed at my unnecessary response and curtseyed.

Angela stepped to the microphone, cleared her throat loudly to silence the crowd, pulled her hair over her ears, and said, "Good afternoon. Today Miss Mayfield's fourth grade class will be reenacting a part of the Cape Cod Reds history. Other classes from our school will be doing their own presentations on this stage on other days. Today we take you back to Saturday, September 12, 1943. We are in the warehouse where we package boxes of dried cranberries to raise money for needy families in our area, especially those affected by the war. My name is Angela, and I am one of the leaders of the Cape Cod Reds. We offer five different boxes: the Lobsters; the Cods; the Starfish; the Whales; and the Clams. We sell them in stores throughout New England. Over the last year we have sold thousands of cases of delicious berries for five cents a box. Each month we compete to see which team can package and sell the most. It's a friendly but spirited contest. Now some of my fellow classmates will demonstrate how we do our jobs."

Angela stepped back, and another student came up and gave an explanation of how the berries were received and how the boxing and shipping process was handled. Nate, Dennis, and two girls did the demonstration.

Gloria took the stage and spoke about the *Cape Cod Reds Cookbook* that St. Anne's school had sold in conjunction with the project. It contained cranberry recipes of all descriptions. Gloria brought her stirring demonstration to life by wolfing down a large piece of cranberry upside-down cake in two bites. Toby came to the microphone, thanked the audience for coming, and ended by encouraging the spectators to visit the exhibit at the university.

Miss Mayfield's students had become old hands by now, and they all seemed to be enjoying the chance to be celebrities. The program had been a good thing for both the school and Nate's class. We said hello to Miss Mayfield and congratulated Nate and the others. Julie left for the library, and I headed home to nap. The beer man lay heavy on my shoulders.

October 21, 1943

After dinner, Dr. Schneider turned to his cat. "You know, Strudel, things are better now, not like the unfortunate incident last February. I'm glad I don't have to move the information that way anymore." He leaned back, deep in thought, while gently stroking his contented tabby.

On a business trip to Boston, Dr. Schneider went to his favorite restaurant on the wharf. He hung his long black coat neatly on the rack by the door. Two pegs down, Dr. Schneider eyed his contact's dark brown herringbone coat with a navy scarf wrapped around the collar. The monogram R.O.T. was clearly visible. Just as he was carefully slipping an envelope into the coat's right pocket, he was bumped slightly from behind.

"Oh, pardon me," the businessman said. "Crowded today," he added, trying to be friendly.

Dr. Schneider hoped the man hadn't noticed what he was doing and considered saying something but decided against it. It wasn't necessary. This was just some banker or lawyer in a hurry to get a table and nothing more. Instead Dr. Schneider smiled back and said, "Yes, it is."

"Their Tuesday special always draws a crowd," the man replied.

"It is good. I eat here whenever I'm in town," Dr. Schneider added and then turned to the hostess.

"How many?" she asked.

"Just one," Dr. Schneider responded.

"Do you mind sitting at the bar?" she asked.

"No, that's fine," he replied as he followed her. He noticed his contact sitting with a younger woman at a table on the opposite side of the room. The man looked up from his menu, glanced over in Dr. Schneider's direction, but gave him no acknowledgment.

Dr. Schneider ordered a drink and looked over the dinner menu. Two men at the far end were engaged in a loud discussion over politics. "That's it, Reggie, no matter what you say," the older man said slamming his drink on the bar. Both men appeared to have been over-served.

Dr. Schneider made a quick trip to the restroom, and when he came out, he saw that the brown coat was gone from the coat rack. He thought it seemed strange that his contact would have left so soon. Dr. Schneider knew someone else must have taken the topcoat by mistake. Quickly he turned and ran out of the restaurant without getting his own coat. The street was crowded with evening traffic. He looked in all directions. Out on the wharf he spied one of the men from the bar wearing the missing coat. The man stumbled badly, falling face first towards a baby carriage. The mother swerved the stroller, and the stranger landed on the snow-covered wooden pier. Two police officers came running over and got the man up on his feet.

"Let's take him to the drunk tank to dry out," the older officer said.

Dr. Schneider knew he was in trouble. Thinking fast, he yelled to the drunk, "Reggie, I told you to wait for me on the corner." To the officers, he added, "Sorry, fellas, he's had too many, but I can take him home."

"You can?" the drunk man questioned.

The two officers hesitated but then released the confused man into Dr. Schneider's care. Dr. Schneider took a deep breath as he helped the man back to the restaurant to get coffee and something to eat. More importantly, he returned the coat to its place on the coat rack.

With the Cape Cod Reds Dr. Schneider's involvement was more oblique. Even if the information ended up in the wrong hands, people would assume at a glance that it was simply a note being passed by a high school girl. "Yes, Strudel, this current plan is so much safer, especially for me."

.   .   .

Chapter 37

TRY LISTING DECEASED ON YOUR NEXT JOB APPLICATION

October 22-23, 1965

"Whitfield's biggest event of the year takes place this weekend: Back to the Bogs, a celebration of the Cape's favorite fruit. The festival, which was started in 1927 by the local growers' association, has grown over the years to be one of the Cape's premier fall events. In addition to walking tours of the bogs, enjoy a wonderful parade with marching bands led by the Amazing Dancing Cranberries. These 'berries,' a costumed group of six and seven-year-olds, are a must-see. Try your luck at games of chance, carnival rides and much more. Learn all about the famous fruit in a short lecture given at the town library, and this year there is the added bonus of viewing the Cape Cod Reds retrospective exhibit in the annex of the Kirsch Library at the University of St. Jerome. Enter your favorite cranberry recipe in the bake-off. Every year the festival selects a special theme, and this year's, *A Salute to Sleepy Hollow*, sounds more spectacular than ever. The show begins nightly at 10:40 p.m. So grab your favorite cranberry-lover, and come experience small town living at its best."

Most of the year Shelley Clausen, the *Boston Globe*'s Cape Cod reporter, got stuck trying to salvage cabbage cook-offs in Cohasset, too boring to read about, much less attend, but here she had a story to sink her teeth into, and she did.

"Treat yourself to a stick of corn on the cob, a roasted turkey leg, hot dogs, clam chowder, or lobster tails dripping in cups of real drawn butter."

"Stop it, Shelley, stop it now," I shouted back at the Boston paper while reading her article from my sofa. "You're killing me, girl."

But, of course, she didn't stop, nor did I really want her to. This was merely a little dance Shelley and I did together every fall, like two birds about to mate for the first time on the hot desert floor, scratching up small clouds of dust behind us. I wanted this moment to go on forever. In fact, I really wanted to go back to the part about the corn on the cob while we were close by.

Her article moved on to "homemade pies, frozen treats, slices of Boston Cream pie." Now we were getting somewhere. *If this gets much worse, I might have to ask you to step out of the room for a few minutes to give Shelley and me a little privacy, at least until the dust settles.*

I put my fingers in my ears, waiting for her description to pass, all the while thinking about the delicious land mines waiting inside the fridge. *Can you excuse me for one minute while I go check? Officially, I was now a dead man walking toward a large yellow bowl of golden vanilla ice cream swimming in a warm sea of Hershey's chocolate. Oh, my God, don't stop me now. I was on a humanitarian mission to rid the world of forty thousand calories. And when I'm dead and gone, please bury me inside a two-hundred-pound bag of Hershey's Kisses. I wanted the feeling to last as long as possible.*

"Every year there are two pirate boats to take riders to Bird Island's Dungeon of Horror, where the dead walk freely through the night," she continued. Markle Brothers Fishing donated two boats, which the fraternities transformed into pirate ships, right down to store-bought yellow parrots hanging off the yardarms. One of the ships was named the *Jolly Dead Man* and the other the *Ship of Fools*. Down at the docks the barkers stirred up business. "Many go over to the Island of the Dead... but only a few come back."

The whole island adventure could easily be done in thirty minutes unless our "lost souls" were on one of their mandatory rest breaks. Two years ago, with no prior warning, union bosses drove down from Boston and organized them into Local 138 of the Dead Entertainment Workers of America. With their slick union package, these dead workers were enjoying all sorts of goodies, including mandatory breaks every two hours. I hadn't seen the entire list of benefits, but apparently it was quite extensive. For example, one of the old geezers told me he'd been saving a bundle on his car insurance under the new agreement. Apparently, no one had yet broken the sad news about his current condition – dead – and frankly, I felt uneasy being a messenger of gloom. Who could blame the dead for wanting a little extra cash to sock away for those endless retirement years? *And if you think I'm kidding, try listing deceased on your next job application and see how many calls you get back. My guess is not many.*

The last paragraph of Shelley's article described Ichabod's Last Ride, the premier event of the festival. Not wanting to spoil things, she didn't reveal much: "If you want to see what happens, you'll have to attend," she teased us. For the six years that I've read Shelley's witty banter, I've quietly tried imagining my own. *I guess the sad truth is whenever I read a newspaper article, I wonder how I would have written it, if the stupid paper had hired me instead, but the point is, nobody's offered me a job.*

"Thanks, for the memories, Shelley. It's been real," I said, putting the Boston paper back on the coffee table.

.   .   .

The Pendletons invited Julie and me to dinner on the opening night. Caroline and Julie fixed an early supper, and we ate around the Pendletons' kitchen table. They made Reubens, my favorite sandwich, and homemade potato salad. Julie was working at the pumpkin patch, and I was serving at the kissing booth. Caroline asked Julie if I was really qualified. Julie shook her head and said, "Not exactly."

It was a warm evening for this time of year, and we ate with the windows open. We heard sounds of trucks unloading last minute supplies at the booths, and the excited voices of festival workers. Just as we were clearing our places, the doorbell rang. I opened it to find Angela and Gloria.

"What are you doing here?" Angela asked, surprised to see me.

"Hey, it's good to see you, too, Angela. The school's remodeling my office to make it even bigger, so the Pendletons invited me to dinner to celebrate."

"Really?" she responded.

"No, not really. I live in the apartment in the back. You guys come on in."

"Thanks," Gloria said stepping inside. She carefully inspected where Nathan lived. "We were wondering if Nate wanted to come with us. We're meeting Dennis, Kirk, and Sylvie."

Nate said, "Sure," and Dave handed him money to buy tickets, and they headed off.

. . .

By 6:30 the streets along the festival were overflowing. The rides were filling up with screaming kids, and tiny colored lights twinkled in the early evening sky. Small children had already been lost, then found, and lost again. By 7 the specialty events were open on the lawn in front of the elementary school, with bake sales, quilting shows and fortune-tellers.

We were busy all evening. Around 9, Julie finished up at the pumpkin patch and joined me at my booth.

"Having fun?" she asked, as she walked up holding the shallow remains of a pink cotton candy.

"Yeah. It's pretty exhausting work, but Dr. Lips can't reveal more. It's professional ethics, you understand. I never kiss and tell."

"Well, Peter, if it makes you feel better, I'm sure none of them do either."

Julie helped me close up the booth, and there still was time to take in some of the attractions before the main event. She made me ride the Ferris wheel. I kept my eyes closed on the scary parts. I threw baseballs and almost won a ragdoll for Casey. Then a few minutes before the main event, we squeezed into a small opening along the rope lines in front of the post office.

The Ichabod show was everything Shelley promised and more. Ichabod came out of his tiny school house and began chatting with kids lined up two deep along the rope lanes. He mounted his horse. A crack of thunder went off, and Headless entered at the far end of the village. The rider was actually a Pi Phi sorority member in a costume designed by the theatre arts department. Her eyes peered through the buttonholes of Headless's massive shirt which extended another foot above the top of her head.

"Which way did he go?" Headless asked the audience in a gruff voice. The crowd loved it, their emotions driven to a fever pitch. We smelled testosterone in the air. The crowd began shouting, "We want blood. We want gore. We want teachers who won't make us snore." *Let that be a lesson, teachers of America. Students want to be entertained, not informed.*

Headless's horse rose on her back legs, taking off at full speed. Crane's horse limped slowly into the darkness of the covered bridge. Julie leaned over and asked, "Do you think this act of violence serves as a metaphor for what we all will find on the other side of life's dark bridge?"

"Quite possibly, but no matter what, we all owe a huge debt of gratitude to Boston Local 138 for lower insurance rates when we get there," I replied.

After a blood-curdling scream, Crane's rider-less horse came out from the covered bridge clomping slowly down the street. Several minutes passed. The suspense mounted. Another crack of thunder exploded, and out from the bridge

Headless flew with Ichabod's waxed head engulfed in flames. Julie squeezed my arm. Headless rode the entire course waving the blazing head before tossing the fiery ball off the end of the pier. You could smell little bits of burning hair and see one of the eyeballs melting away. Headless's scream sent shivers down our spines.

"That was great, Peter, but I'm sad that neither of us will be in Whitfield next fall for the cranberry festival, this is my favorite time of year." Julie reached up and gave me a kiss.

"Me, too," I agreed.

It took several minutes to work our way through the excited crowd. At the main pier Julie spotted Nate and his group. We raced to catch up with them.

"What did you guys think of the show?" Julie asked.

"Amazing, the best one ever," Gloria gushed.

"My father's bank sponsored the Sleepy Hollow performance," Angela added, making sure we fully appreciated his benevolence.

"It was really great. Tell him thanks from all of us."

Then Julie led the group in a chant, "We want blood. We want gore. We want teachers that don't make us snore."

Looking back on it now, those cranberry days were the sweet spot of my last year in Whitfield. Julie would be graduating, but there was still time for us. I hadn't found a career, but there was still hope, and Nate had settled in with a nice group of kids, and Washington was becoming only a memory for him….Life in Whitfield couldn't have been better.

October 21, 1943

It wasn't until after Katie got back from the library that she realized Colleen hadn't returned her Spanish book and notes, which she had lent to her at the warehouse. Katie had taken her sister Angie to the library to work on a report, and that took longer than expected. When they got home shortly before 9, her mother was getting ready to leave for the hospital. Katie asked her mother if Colleen had come by, and her mother said, "No."

"I knew that was a mistake," Katie said in an angry voice to herself. Colleen was a nice girl and a friend, but she almost never followed up on things. "Hey, Mom, I've got to go get them. We're having a test tomorrow."

"Katie, I've told you I don't like leaving Angie here by herself at night, and I'm late for work as it is."

"It wasn't my fault, and she can come with me. We'll only be gone a few minutes."

"I guess we don't have a choice. You can drop me off at the hospital on your way."

"Okay, let's go," Katie said.

Katie grabbed her purse and headed out the front door. In the car her mother said, "I'll call in thirty minutes to check if you've made it back home."

"Make it twenty. All I'm doing is picking up the book. I just wish you trusted me more," she complained.

"It's not that I don't trust you. I just worry about you being out at night," Mrs. Welch responded.

At the hospital Katie pulled under the covered driveway. One doctor and two nurses were leaving, and they waved to Mrs. Welch.

"I'm sorry. I know it wasn't your fault that you have to go back to the warehouse, but please don't be long, okay?" Katie's mom said.

"I won't, Mom. Trust me. I have loads of work to do when I get back." They smiled at each other, and when her mother got to the door, she turned and waved goodbye to her two daughters.

The last shift was just finishing when Katie and Angie got to the warehouse. She found a space up close, and they raced inside, passing friends coming out. Katie waved but didn't stop to talk. At her work station, she found her Spanish book on the floor, just where Colleen had left it. As they were leaving, Angie accidentally knocked over a carton of boxes ready for shipment. The boxes slid across the brick floor, and a few broke open.

"Gosh, I'm sorry, Katie," Angie said sadly.

"That's okay. It won't take a minute to pick it up," Katie replied. She really didn't have time for this and considered leaving the mess for the next day's crew but knew that wouldn't be fair. She put her book down on top of the table and started picking the boxes up and putting them back in the shipping box marked, "Wallace Market, Chatham, Mass." One of the last ones was a damaged Clam box, and she wondered what it was doing inside a case of Cods. The box was bent and didn't close properly. She started to toss it in the trash container but decided that was a waste of good cranberries, so she poured the dried berries into an empty Cod box. Just as she was about to toss the damaged one, she noticed something taped to the inside cover. She used her nail to pull off the tape and unfolded a piece of lined paper. The writing seemed to be formulas for something, but she couldn't tell what. She was sure they weren't anything she'd worked on in chemistry class. She turned the paper over and in red pen at the top was a notation, "Hey, Mary, did I tell you I'm on a diet to lose ten pounds?" It was signed Lucy. Knowing Lucy, Katie knew immediately this note was not real.

"Oh, my God," she said in a soft whisper, realizing what she'd found. They had seen newsreels at the movies about being on the alert for espionage, and now she was looking at it. In the back of the building Mr. Jenkins, the custodian, began turning off the banks of overhead lights. With every section a loud popping noise went off. He was just about to turn off Katie's section when he noticed the two girls standing there.

"Sorry, Katie, I didn't see you there. Will you be long?" he asked.

"No, Mr. Jenkins, We're leaving now," she answered, trying to figure out what her discovery meant and what to do about it. Her hands shaking, she stuffed the notebook paper inside her Spanish book and headed for the door. When she got home, she called Mary to determine what to do with the unwelcomed information.

• • •

Chapter 38
THE CRANBERRY FLAG

October 29, 1965 – November 1, 1965

The week after the Cranberry Fest, Nate's class finished its outdoor presentations and stopped selling the boxes of berries. His class alone raised over eight hundred dollars, which was enough to buy some new playground equipment for the school.

On Friday the fourth grade went on a field trip in the afternoon to China Farms to watch the cranberry harvesting. I took off early from work and picked up Julie at the library. We rode on the school bus to join in the fun. There were several large fields on the farm covered in deep blue water with a sea of red berries floating on top. Many of the kids who grew up on the Cape had seen this before, but for Nate, Julie, and me it was a wonderful outing. We spent a good hour on the tour, watching the water paddles stir up the berries, seeing the workers pull them into an ever tighter circle, before sucking them off the top of the water and loading them into large trucks. After the event, the farmers set up snack tables where the students sat and ate cranberry treats, while Mrs. Tilson, the manager's wife, explained every fact, great and small, about America's favorite fruit.

The fun didn't end there. The next day was a trip to Bird Island that Miss Mayfield had organized as a thank you to her class and a last chance to see the air-raid tower before it was torn down.

Bird Island consisted of a few scrub trees, ten-foot sand dunes, wild vegetation, and one badly worn air-raid tower with a couple of Maidenform bras hanging off the side. Sometimes when I was on crew, we'd stop there after practice to drink beer before heading back to the boat barn, or we'd play a little football as sort of a cool down.

Legend had it that Bird Island got her name from early settlers who thought it looked something like a plump bird with a long neck. Twice a year, snow geese from Canada used it for an overnight landing strip. During those times, the island turned into a sea of white feathers moving in the still warm breezes off the water and was closed to outside visitors. The rest of the year she waited patiently, like the rest of us, for the work week to end and another Friday night to come along. *Let's face it; some islands just know how to party, and Bird could party with the best of them.*

Recently the city council approved the plan to build a nature sanctuary, and construction signs went up notifying Whitfield residents that the island would be closed for three to six months. The council agreed to have the old World War II air-raid tower torn down as part of the beautification program. Mayor Martinez told the council members, "This eyesore needs to go. Fraternity boys climb up it, drink beer, and hang their dates' underwear off the edge in some kind of sick mating ritual. Do we really want to promote this kind of juvenile activity in Whitfield?"

He was met with a round of solid applause, *but for my money, sick mating rituals are the highest and best use of Friday nights. Without them, fraternities have no reason to exist; none, nada, zilch.* Honestly, however, what probably settled the mayor's vote was learning that Erica, his seventeen-year-old daughter, had gone on her own jungle cruise with one of my fraternity brothers the weekend before his speech.

Early Saturday morning eight large rowboats left for Bird Island from the boathouse. After we landed on the island, we raced to the highest dunes. Dave planted a red and white cranberry flag that Caroline had sewn. She had decorated it with all five of the team symbols. Dave proclaimed Bird Island free at last: free to grow wild berries wherever it wanted.

Around noon we had a picnic on the dunes. Julie and I sat with Miss Mayfield. She talked about how much the students had learned about teamwork and the town's history. Afterwards the kids played touch football and other games Miss Mayfield organized. We spent the rest of a sunny afternoon enjoying the last warm weather until spring. Later, when we had dessert, Gloria asked if she could have a second piece of cake, and Angela gave her blessing.

Julie and I played volleyball for over an hour. We were on opposite teams, with Gloria, Dave, and Miss Mayfield on my side, and we won every game. Shortly after the last game finished, Caroline gave me a kiss on the cheek.

"What was that for?" I asked.

"Miss Mayfield told me you were responsible for getting Nate picked to be a captain. That was very sweet. This has been so good for him."

"Well, thanks, but it was nothing personal. I picked him because I knew he'd be great."

"Anyway, Peter, thank you. It's really helped."

As everyone was getting ready to leave, Dave, Nate, Julie, and I climbed the air-raid tower to take a quick look before the old gray lady was brought down. Dave and I unhooked the last remaining bra hanging off the rail, and set it free. It tumbled softly to the top of a low bush.

This was the end of our cranberry adventures. Construction began as scheduled on Monday. With stormy weather pulling in off the Cape, we watched from afar as machinery undid whatever mysteries were hidden there. During the dismantling of the tower, a construction worker from McLeay Demolition saw something shiny in the bottom of one of the narrow shafts inside the structure. He lowered himself down on a rope, and pulled up several curious items including two left shoes, a bag of hand tools, and the dog tags from a Boston Navy man missing since 1943.

We stood during those days in Whitfield on sandy dunes with tall sea grasses blowing at our feet. We looked out to the white caps dancing across rough water beyond the horizon, each of us seeing something different. Our life together was good. Change was in the wind. Pirates were spotted off the coast. Sometimes in life you get what you want and sometimes what you need. But in the end, one is not better than the other. They're just different.

October 22, 1943

The Institute parking lot was almost empty at 4:30 PM when the girls pulled in. They barely spoke to Eddie, the security guard. They knew that they could trust Eric and that he would know what to do with this unfortunate information.

Eric's office was at the far end of the north hallway. They moved like flying geese down the long hall with Katie leading the point. The usually busy hallways were quiet, as most of the scientists had left for the day or were attending a conference in Boston. Through the half-glass partition, Katie could see Eric sitting at his desk. He looked up just as they arrived and waved them in.

"Well, ladies, to what do I owe this pleasure?" he asked, figuring this was either a social call or one to ask for a raise.

"This," Katie said, "and there's nothing pleasurable about it. I don't know whether this stuff has to do with the Institute, but I can tell you for sure Lucy doesn't need to lose two ounces, and she didn't write this note."

Eric read the note and agreed, "No, you're right. Where did you find it?"

"Last night at the warehouse, I accidentally knocked a carton over, and this was in the only Clam box with a bunch of Cods going to the Wallace Market in Chatham."

"It's just like what Mr. Bellini from the boathouse told us this summer. He had an odd box in one of his shipments, and it had weird message written on notebook paper in it instead of a trading card. We didn't think much about it at the time," Kerrie added.

"What do you think it means, and who put it there?" Katie asked.

Eric shook his head and leaned over the front of his desk.

"Listen, girls, I may be wrong, but there's been talk about information leaks out of the Institute, and this could have something to do with it. If you're willing to help, we might find out what's going on."

"Sure," Mary said, and the others agreed unanimously.

"Okay. First I need to make a new note with some changes to these drawings. Penny, do you have a blank sheet of notebook paper in that notebook?" Penny ripped out a blank page from her notebook and gave it to him. Eric transcribed most of what was on the originals but altered the formulas and information enough to make them worthless. He copied the red ink message exactly. Then he put the note that Katie had given him in his pocket. The girls watched, not sure what he was doing. He folded the new note up and handed it back to Katie.

"What time does the shipment go out?" he asked.

"At 6 PM, why?"

"Take this back to the warehouse and put it in a Clam box, just the way it was. Send it out with that group of Cods to Chatham, and let's see if we can catch ourselves a fish. The information is worthless now, and my guess is that someone will pick it up tomorrow when the store opens. We'll need a couple of you to drive over and see who does. I have a shift at the warehouse tomorrow morning, or I'd do it."

"Are you sure they're getting it tomorrow?" Lucy asked.

"Yes. If I'm right, they'll want to get there early and take away the risk of a random person buying the box by mistake, like at Bellini's last summer. My guess is within an hour of the store's opening."

"I can do it," Mary said.

"Me, too," Kerrie agreed.

"Okay, then, get this back for the delivery. After staking out the market for an hour or so, come to the warehouse to tell me what you've noticed."

They all got up to leave, but Eric waved them to stop. "Please, Kerrie and Mary, be very careful on your surveillance mission. Don't get involved in conversation with anyone at the market. Oh, and one more thing to all of you: Don't say anything about this to anyone until we have an idea what's going on. If this package gets picked up, then we'll know it's for real."

"Okay, but we'd better get going now if we're going to make it back to the warehouse in time," Katie said.

Eric walked out into the hall to see them off. He noticed several office doors open, and he stood for a moment in the hallway wondering if their conversation had been overheard.

• • •

Chapter 39
ARE THOSE NEW SOCKS?

April 29, 1966

In the spring of my second year in admissions I interviewed with an advertising agency in New York: Hedges, Winslow, and Reed. A fraternity brother's father ran the place, and he got me in the door. Julie had already been accepted to med school at Penn, so I dreamed of being somewhat close to her. I bought tickets on the New Haven rail line, pulled out my one clean Robert Hall suit, and invested in a new pair of dark socks, called Midnight Blue, Penney's premium label. Penney's actually had two different price points on their socks, and I spent most of one morning debating which way to go. I ended up going with the slightly more expensive pair because they had a nicer feel and were only a dollar more. Plus I figured they might not need to be washed as often. Julie listened to my argument while driving me to the station, but strongly disagreed.

"That's more flawed logic, Peter," she said, missing her turn-off for the Providence station.

"You know how I feel about this job," she offered.

"Good?"

"No, no. Keep guessing."

"Julie, I'm sorry to disappoint you. Too bad. Maybe this doesn't work. I probably won't get the job anyway, but this is what I want to do for now, and I have to try something. So be happy for me. We can't all save the world."

"That's where you're wrong, Peter. You used to think you could. You're too old just to be trying things. You need direction. You can be something great, if you apply yourself," she said, sounding eerily like my father.

"I don't always measure up, but I try. I really do try."

She kissed me in the parking lot and waved goodbye. Once on the train I picked up a section of *The New York Times* lying on the seat beside me and noticed a job opening at the UN. I wondered if it might be the Secretary General position. Staring out the train window, I thought about applying. It would make Julie's dad proud, and since they'd never picked anyone from Florida, I figured my chances had to be as good as anyone else's.

> "That's quite a feather in your son-in-law's cap," one of Carl's golfing buddies would say to him on the fifth tee soon after my appointment. "The top spot at the UN and only twenty-three? That's very impressive. You must be proud."
>
> "Thanks, Hubert. Of course, we're awfully proud of him. He just walked in the front door, and they gave him the job. What balls."
>
> My membership at Carl's country club would be on the fast track, especially if I could snag somebody famous, like Sandra Dee, into playing mixed doubles with me in the member-guest tournament. *People are such celebrity snobs. It's so sad.*

The advertising agency was not big by New York standards, but they did good work and battled for a number of big accounts. The reception area walls were filled with posters of recently completed print campaigns. The receptionist was very friendly, and we shot the breeze when she wasn't answering the phone, which was most of the time. She had been working at the agency for six months, starting right out of college.

At one point I crossed my legs. She smiled and said, "Nice socks."

"Thanks, they're new!" *Isn't it great when you make a connection with people, find that benchmark and start exploring new things together—and really, what better place to start than at the ankle?*

Shortly after I arrived, two young hotshots about my age entered the lobby. They were both very confident, and I felt a little overwhelmed. My new associates seemed busy, and both were carrying briefcases, no doubt stuffed with important documents. I wished I had brought mine as well. *I read somewhere that a fully loaded briefcase can add up to twenty years of meaning to your professional persona.*

Just as I was about to ask if they wanted to play the briefcase game with me, an assistant came through the dark wooden doors and called out a name. "Mr. Big Shot, Mrs. Walton will see you now," she said, and they both got up. I wasn't sure which one was Mr. Shot and which one was Mr. Toady, but at this point it didn't really matter.

I was pissed and started to say, "Hey, lady, can't you see we're about to play the briefcase game? Come back in an hour. Hold my calls. Extra cream, no sugar, fire Johnson. Get me a three o'clock tee time at the club. I need a foot massage. What the hell happened to the Cosgrove papers? For God's sake, am I the only one working around this place?"

Instead I just picked up a copy of *Advertising Age* sitting on the table beside me and pretended to understand the meaning of a "skewed demographic."

October 23, 1943

The Wallace Market opened at nine. That was the good news. The bad news: Kerrie was driving, and they were lost with less than ten minutes to go. Mary told her to pull over to look at the map. "Here's the problem: you needed to turn right on Main, not left."

"How far back?" Kerrie asked.

"Well, it's a ways, eight, maybe ten blocks. But if you hurry, I think we can still make it. Just make a U-turn."

"Sorry about that," Kerrie said turning her mother's black Plymouth around. Still, her fast driving put them in front of the store with a couple of minutes to spare.

"Phew. That was a close."

"No kidding, but at least we made it," Mary said, trying hard to think of something positive to say that didn't include Kerrie's driving.

They parked across the street and waited. It was quiet for a Saturday morning. The market was in an older residential part of town, with small houses and shops lining the narrow street. Two young boys on bikes came towards them. The older one was carrying a stick and knocking off trash can lids in front of a store. Neither girl paid much attention until the bigger boy pushed back the rearview mirror on the driver's door as he passed.

"Hey, come back here, you little squirt," Kerrie said trying to grab his arm but catching only air. Kerrie had an easygoing nature, but even though she was petite, she knew how to stand up for herself. The boys laughed and continued down the street. Kerrie started to open the door, but Mary grabbed her arm.

"Wait. It doesn't matter. We don't want to call attention to ourselves, not now. I hope nobody asks us what we're doing here," Mary said.

"It's not a problem. You worry too much. We'll tell them that we're a quality control undercover unit to make sure everyone's happy with our berries. See, that wasn't so hard."

"Whatever. I just hope we don't have to wait long."

"Me, too. I'll take the first shift; you can study. Ten-minute shifts?"

"Sure, fine. Say, by the way, what did you make on Mays's math quiz?" Mary asked.

"What did you make?" Kerrie shot back.

"Asked you first," Mary replied.

"Look, if you want to use up your whole ten-minute study window arguing, fine with me, but that seems stupid, don't you think?"

"You're right—I got an 89, by the way," Mary said.

"That's great. I got a 93, but 89 is a really good score."

"Oh, shut up. I wasn't feeling well."

"Yep, that's what you said last time. Only eight more minutes to go," Kerrie said, tapping her nail on the windowsill.

"Got it." Mary pulled out some of her English homework.

Kerrie reached down and picked up a pair of binoculars from under the seat.

"This is sort of creepy, spying like this. But I guess it's our only choice," Mary said.

"Well, we could go ask the clerk to wave a wet hand towel when he sells a box, but that might look strange, don't you think? There are now seven minutes."

"Okay. Enough. I'm studying."

During the first shift only a high school girl came out from the store, adding fresh fruits to the wooden stand before going back inside.

"Okay, your turn." Kerrie dropped the glasses on the seat. "Good luck."

Mary's tour was also uneventful. A woman pushing a shopping cart went in and bought eggs and milk, and two children bought a pack of chewing gum, but no one came close to the boxes on the counter.

Mary looked at her watch. It was 9:22. She handed the glasses back over to Kerrie.

"Your turn."

"No, wait," Kerrie said. "I'm going to the café to get some juice," pointing next to the general store. "You want anything?"

"No, thanks. Well, maybe a good suspect, if they have any."

"I'll see if I can get one for you," Kerrie nodded. Before she could get all the way across the street, an old black truck pulled up in front of the store. A man with brown hair and a brown ball cap got out. Wearing a dark green jacket and faded blue jeans, he seemed older than Eric, but still not much over thirty. Something about him clicked, and Mary honked the horn before realizing her mistake. The man looked over at the car, but Mary recovered quickly by waving Kerrie back to the car.

"Hey, Kerrie," she said in a loud voice, "I've changed my mind. I want you to get me something after all. Come back here for a second."

"What now?" Kerrie asked.

"That's him," Mary said in a firm whisper.

"That's who?" Kerrie asked, not seeing the truck or the man.

"The man we're looking for just went into Wallace's," she said impatiently.

"You're sure?" Kerrie questioned.

"Of course, I'm sure. He came over and introduced himself and asked if the new boxes had arrived yet. And I said, 'Yes, and they've got some really nice ones. Pick any one you like and get a prize inside.' Now follow him before it's too late."

·   ·   ·

Chapter 40
DANCING WITH STRANGERS

April 29, 1966

A few minutes later a secretary of Hedges, Winslow, and Reed came to the reception area, called my name, and took me back for my appointment. Halfway down the hall, a middle-aged woman came running towards us, her arms waving above her head. At first I couldn't understand what she was saying because she was gasping for air. Obviously she had received some life-changing news.

"We got it," she cheered, as she continued waving her arms. "We got Enchanted Gas."

People around her started shouting, "We got gas. We got gas." I cocked my head. It seemed a strange thing to raise your voice over in public. If anything a simple "I'm sorry, or "Looks like Mr. Bean Burrito has gotten fussy again," would have been the appropriate response. But they were dancing in the halls.

I waved my hands giving the two thumbs up sign. A box of T-shirts sitting on a desktop nearby was ripped open, and shirts were tossed wildly in all directions. My hands caught one flying by me. It was a plain shirt with a logo reading, "Land of Enchantment Gas Transmission:: Providing New Mexico's energy needs." *Suddenly it was all becoming clear. Corporate America is one giant toga party, where everyone wears suits and new socks. And they get paid. This totally rocks!*

The secretary grabbed me tightly around my waist, wrinkling my dark blue jacket, her hands squeezing my stomach.

"Easy, girl," I said to her, "I paid eighty-five dollars for this suit, and I'm getting at least two more years out of it."

"Sorry," she said, "we've been holding our breath for eight weeks waiting to hear about this account."

"Really?" I questioned, not buying that answer. Growing up, I found swimming across our neighborhood pool underwater a major accomplishment and not really attainable without a fair amount of cheating. And yet these people had been holding their collective breath for eight weeks? Seriously, it sounded like a tall tale to me, unless they had mastered some ancient Hindu technique, which they would share with me once I was hired. Now I simply had to have this job, no matter what.

Outside Mr. Whellis's office I took a bold step. I slipped my new T-shirt over my suit and entered. Mr. Whellis must have had heard the commotion but not the news.

We met in the middle of the room. I gave him a big bear hug, saying, "Guess what. We got gas! We got gas!"

"Are you serious?" his eyes aching with hopefulness.

"Of course! I never kid about gas—well, at least not after it happens," I replied.

He hugged me back and lifted me off the floor like one of Fred Astaire's dance partners. And that began our whirlwind courtship to every corner of his office. Suddenly every piece of furniture became a prop. We pirouetted over a small coffee table. With short light steps, we made it halfway up one side of the wall before coming to rest in the center of the room. It wasn't my best performance, not by a long shot, but I tried following his lead. After all, he was the boss. *You lead. I follow. The laws of the business jungle are very straightforward.* Then, realizing the moment was no longer magic, we separated in front of his desk.

"Peter Dreeton, Henry's fraternity brother." I said holding out my hand.

I couldn't have wiped the smile off his face faster by revealing his wife's torrid two-year affair with their pool-cleaning guy, the older one, who walked with a limp and had really hairy ears.

"Please have a seat," he said patting me firmly on the shoulder. "I'll be right back."

He went out into the hall and gave the woman bringing the news a generous hug. Of course, seeing his crass display of affection only made me feel cheap, even used. But I tried overlooking it. My mission, a real job, was dead ahead, and nothing was stopping me now.

"Cathy, this is simply great. I'm so proud of you. I've got to talk with the kid, but come back after lunch, and let's go over strategy," he said.

I felt like saying, "Hey, buster, I'm no kid. I'm your dance partner, your lucky charm, your shaman, the butt boy, reporting for duty. Oh, go ahead. Call me whatever you like; just call me hired."

As he turned to come back into his office, he said to his secretary, "Get Winslow on the phone. We need to schedule those aerial shoots for Friday noon at the latest."

"Got it," she said.

After he sat back down, we talked for a few minutes about the sort of getting-to-know-you stuff one goes over in a hard-nosed interview.

"What's your favorite movie scene? Chocolate or vanilla? Scrambled or fried? Who's the best third baseman in the National League?"

"Eddie Matthews." How simple was that one, and how great life was now that we all had gas.

He asked what my major was in college, how I liked working at the university, and why I wanted to work at an ad agency. *Ah, the trick question. I could smell it coming from a mile off and jumped right in.*

"Well, sir, I may not be the smartest guy in this room. In fact, we both know I'm not. But I'm second and considering my competition, that's not a bad place to be. I'm clever, and I see connections between things other people don't always see."

"That's a great answer. Can you give me an example?'

"Well, half an hour ago, you guys were hoping for gas. Then I walked in and look what you've got? Now maybe that was a coincidence, and maybe not, but do you really want to take that chance? You seem too smart to run that kind of a risk."' I crossed my legs. He jumped on the bait.

"Peter, are those new socks you're wearing?" He leaned forward over the front of his desk.

"Yes, sir, Midnight Blue, Penney's premium brand. I like dressing for success."

"No kidding. That's good to hear.

They were hiring now. We both knew it. The new sock story had become obsolete. In fact I shouldn't have wasted my money and wondered about Penney's return policy for one time wearings.

"They're almost brand new," I would say to the salesclerk when I got home. "Look, I even put the wrapper around them so they don't look worn."

"Say, did you wash these?" he'd ask picking up a faint scent from my trip.

"Not yet, but I can. Does that make a difference?"

What did it matter now? The job was mine. The question was would I be getting the corner office with the view of the Brooklyn Bridge? We settled on $10,500.00, plus expenses, and the use of a telephone.

On my way back to the hotel I bought a hot dog, a soda, and a bag of chips from a vendor and slathered the dog with spicy mustard. When I got back to the room, I called Julie. She asked how it went.

"Well, I got gas."

"During the interview?"

"Yes, and it was good."

I told her my gas story, and she seemed excited for me and laughed when I made silly comments about all the people I had met. It was as if our argument on the way to the train station had never happened.

"So you can see yourself at the ad agency, Peter?" she asked.

"Yes, Julie, I can. I really can."

I guess she realized that we were going in different directions, and maybe it was time to let go, even if she didn't approve.

"I love you," I blurted out. It was something I didn't say very often, because she didn't like mushy crap.

"I know, Peter. That's sweet. I am happy for you."

"Hey, maybe I can do some ads for the Peace Corps, even if I'm not in it."

"Yeah, maybe you can. That would be great."

Happy was all around us now. Lying on the bed, I realized two things. I had forgotten to take off my Land of Enchantment Gas Transmission shirt, so I had been a walking billboard all afternoon. Second, my gas logo had spicy mustard stains over their slogan. I needed to get the stains off quickly, before they set. I took cubes of ice from my soda cup and laid them down on top of my bed of mustard.

Julie talked on about school for a while until my chest got very cold, and then we said goodbye.

I got a towel from the tiny bathroom to dry up the mustard spill and called my folks. Mom answered the phone. She seemed pleased, but I could tell she wanted me back in Florida. Dad said, "That's great, son," but what he really meant was: "Peter, are you fucking nuts?"

The answer as always was: "Yes."

October 23, 1943

Kerrie entered the Wallace Market. She didn't believe Mary but did what she was told. Inside, she spotted the display of cranberry boxes still undisturbed. A girl in her twenties, working behind the counter putting packs of cigarettes on the shelves, smiled at Kerrie. A teenager was sweeping the floor at the far end of the store. An Andrews Sisters' song came from the radio behind the counter.

Kerrie, not wanting to appear out of place, picked up one of the handbaskets and headed down the first aisle closest to the window. The aisle was empty, but she put a can of Campbell's tomato soup in her basket and moved to the second aisle, which was also empty. She added a box of saltines wondering where he was in the store. Kerrie felt stupid because she was always getting herself into stuff that didn't make sense, and she suspected the same was happening here. She turned onto the third aisle, about to give up her search before she knocked into him. She fell forward. He grabbed her shoulders and said, "Careful."

"Oh, I'm so sorry," she said, startled and mad at the same time.

"Don't worry," he said in an accent she didn't recognize. "These aisles are very narrow."

"Maybe, but it was still my fault."

He looked down in her basket, and she felt the need to say something else.

"I'm getting a few things for my mother," she replied.

He nodded letting go of her arms and said, "That's nice."

Kerrie looked in his basket and thought he must have been making the same run. His selection included a can of green beans, a bottle of ketchup, and a can of tuna. She wasn't quite sure how to handle her close encounter and started fixing her hair. Unconcerned with her stage fright, he had already left the aisle. She had to do something fast. She went to the end and stopped at a display of sunglasses. A small mirror was affixed to the wall, and she tried on a couple of frames, waiting for him to make his move. He was already at the counter for his big finish.

"Oh, the lid on this bottle seems to be broken, maybe you should get another one?" the check-out girl said, holding up the bottle of ketchup.

"Sure, that sounds good." He left the counter and walked by Kerrie in mid-pose.

"Those for your mother as well?" he asked.

Kerrie shook her head and replied, "No, just looking."

He headed down the last aisle, picked up another bottle, and passed her a second time on his way back to the counter.

"Here," he said to the check-out girl. She rang up the amount and asked, "Will there be anything else?"

He said, "No," as Kerrie moved in line behind him. He was not their suspect after all. He handed the clerk five dollars and waited for his change, but just as she was about to give him it, he reached down and picked the cranberry box with a Clam out of the case of Cods. He looked up and saw Kerrie standing behind him.

"Oh, yes, and a box of these as well." He put a nickel down on the counter.

"Have you tried them?" he asked Kerrie. His question caught her by surprise.

"No. Are they good?"

"Yes, very good." His question gave her an opening, and she took it.

"Would you mind? I'd love to," she said hoping he'd open his box and share. He looked surprised by the request and said they were a present for his wife.

"Thanks, anyway," Kerrie said, "and it looks as if you got the lucky one."

"How's that?" he asked.

"You picked the only Clam out of a school of Cods," she said pointing down to the other boxes below.

"I guess you're right. That does make them lucky," he smiled and headed out the door. Mary's intuition had been right.

. . .

Chapter 41

HOWLING WAS ENCOURGAGED

August, 1966

In August, I left USJ and made the big move from Whitfield to New York City. My supervisor at the advertising agency put me right to work on the gas account. Money aside, Land of Enchantment Gas was not the creative highlight of my stay at the agency, but absolutely it was the easiest money we earned. Their people came to New York, and Cathy, the account manager, insisted we be as southwestern as possible. Little handwritten notes started appearing on desk tops: "Think cactus." *Did we ever think of anything else?*

"Reconnect with the bird, the rock, and the hard place," the cryptic message in the office pantry instructed us. Potato chips in the snack room were replaced with salsa and corn chips. Posters of the Taos skyline at sunset adorned the office walls, and a small collection of smooth stones mysteriously showed up in the center of the men's room floor, though no one seemed to know where they came from, or exactly what it meant. One afternoon I almost dropped thirty-stories from the open bathroom window after running headlong into the rock pile. "Look out below; I'm reconnecting with the hard place." I considered filing a workman's comp claim for my badly stubbed toe, until Bettie, our human resources manager explained, "Impervious doesn't pay claims." *You may think this looks bad for Impervious, and they wouldn't want such an unpleasant detail included in the story, but you'd be so wrong. Because they never honor claims, no matter the circumstances or how grave the injury, they're able to pass some of those enormous cost savings to you. At Impervious you pay only a fraction of what you would if you actually had coverage! No one else in the industry can make that claim, at least not with a straight face.*

Shortly after my accident, the coyote was named the official stuffed animal of the agency, beating out a respected two-term incumbent, Prairie Dog, who lost in what most of us saw as a tainted election.

Cathy came up with the idea of piping Native American music over the sound system, to get us in the right mood. It was fine for an hour or two, almost relaxing in fact, but by late afternoon, their chants became as unwelcome as the wails of a sick pet. Everyone began looking for reasons to check out of work early, any reason at all.

"Can I run by your place and pick up your dry cleaning, Lou? Your suits have been looking sort of scruffy. Trouble at home, something you'd like to talk about? Remember, that's what friends are for."

Or to Maureen in graphic design, I'd suggest, "Hey, I'll bet Elvis, your pet snake, would like to bake in the park after all the rain this week. Toss me your keys. You know how much I love reptiles."

No excuse was too far-fetched or out of order. Fortunately, these "themed periods" of extreme New Mexican overload only lasted a few days at a time. But once in a while, we'd get a call about an unscheduled visit, and all hell would break loose. Caught completely off guard, we were required to double our inspirational treatments to insure total submersion into the Indian spirit. Howling was encouraged.

During these periods you couldn't make it out the front door at night without seeing her mind-blowing note… "Don't forget your tapes… Love, Cathy," a smiley face totem pole drawn next to her name. We conjured up a better location for her pole to reside, but it wouldn't be polite for me to repeat it here. Soon notes began appearing on my desk.

"I need to bitch, meet me in the custodial closet, five minutes. Bring weed… Rhonda."

Outwardly, we acted as if we couldn't get enough of New Mexico, Land of Enchantment. Inside we were seething. Upper management execs even organized a spy ring to make sure we carried out their homework assignments to their liking. They called it Operation Desert Fox. Without a score card, it was hard to know who was on which side, and the motto of the day became "trust no one."

But in spite of the headaches, the gas people were actually easy to deal with, and their lives seemed close to perfect. They could write off all the advertising expenses, plus charge a bundle per cubic foot for gas. Who cared if the ads did any good? It was the customers in Cotton Mouth or Dry Heaves, New Mexico, who'd be paying the tab, and that was all that mattered. There was no alternative energy source. *It is Land of Enchantment Gas or firewood, my friend. Take your choice.*

October 23, 1943

Eric was halfway through his shift as a Starfish when Kerrie and Mary showed up.

"He got it," Kerrie said in a loud voice. A couple of co-workers at the same table looked up at the sound of Kerrie's voice.

Katie, who had been working at the next table, quickly joined them. "Can we talk in the office?" Katie asked, putting her hand across Kerrie's shoulder. She realized this was a conversation best done in private. Eric nodded and got up from his wooden stool and followed the girls into the office at the front. When they passed the Lobster station, a member of her team pulled Mary aside to ask her a question. By the time she got away and came into the office, Kerrie had already explained about how they had picked the man out, and how she had followed him into the store.

"So has she asked for the Bronze Star yet?" Mary asked, smiling.

"Not yet, but that was great work by both of you, I have to say." Eric took his wire glasses off and laid them on the table. "This is great news. But now we have to try and figure out whether this tampered box was a random occurrence, or whether there is some method of keying off when information is to be passed. At this point I have no idea how they might be making connections. There are thousands of boxes shipped out of here, and you'd have to know where to look. Any thoughts?" he asked.

"What's odd," Katie said, "is that the name of that store seems familiar to me, and I don't know why. I've never been there, but when I saw the shipping label, it rang a bell. Kind of like a phone number you've dialed before. But I can't say from where."

"Well, this is going to take time. Let's keep our eyes open and see if anything turns up. I have to go to a conference this week in New York, so don't do anything to rock the boat until I get back. Remember, ladies, these people mean business, and they'll do whatever it takes to keep this information safe," Eric said. "But until we come up with something, there isn't much more we can do."

· · ·

Chapter 42
THE JOURNEY OF A THOUSAND CASES OF ITTY BITTIES BEGINS WITH ONE BOX

August, 1966

At the ad agency the pressure was on to perform, to outdo their unattainable sales goals, to gain more market share while fighting off the evil forces of skewed demographics. The account supervisors would be waiting to see how many boxes of Itty Bitties, "the delightful chocolate mint," we sold the Monday after our new TV campaign broke, and if it didn't meet our sales target, the second-guessing was rampant. Should we have chosen a more peppermint friendly actor? Was *Lassie* not the best media buy for America's favorite chocolate mint or did the melting box in Timmy's back pocket look like an unfortunate accident? Who knew? But by 9 the next morning, the client rep would be storming the building to find out how we could make it up to them.

"How 'bout we flog ourselves ten times with this leather strap, Andrea, while listening to four hours of rain clouds? Trust me that will be punishment enough. People will be firing Itty Bitties out their asses by the time we're done with this campaign. No question about it."

If we missed our sales target by a whopping margin, I excused myself from the collective finger pointing and went down to the concession stand in the lobby to load up.

"Yes, Hamdeesh, that's correct, fifty-three boxes, please," I'd say in spite of the weird look coming from a sales clerk who spoke only broken English.

"You must really like these," he said while loading them into two large paper bags.

"America's favorite mint, doesn't everyone?" I replied.

Sure it was only a couple of cases or so, but it was a start. And those numbers would show up on next month's sales tallies. Plus the sugary rush should get everyone's creative juices flowing again until we figured out what went wrong and how to fix it. There is a famous old Chinese proverb that brings peace to me during times of turmoil, and I paraphrased it for my co-workers: "The journey of a thousand cases of Itty Bitties begins with one box." *So inspirational, don't you think?* The wisdom of the East is as timeless and meaningful today as a thousand summers ago. With my purchase, we could honestly tell Andrea, the account rep, "Sales are up sharply in Manhattan. Clearly people are hearing our message. Let's give it a little more time, shall we?"

Our most creative work was for the Bog's Best Cranberries account. We never had to do any of the silly stuff that we did for the gas company because so many of us drank cranberry juice around the office and understood its natural goodness. At one of the executive meetings, they talked about holding a cranberry stomping event at the company picnic, and I was disappointed when that idea got voted down. I had already chosen a partner to share the stomping experience with, a new hire named Rebecca Billings, with small but happy feet. She worked as a media buyer, and I found any lame excuse to go hang out in front of her desk, hoping to be noticed. I'd run copy down for an upcoming spot buy and say, "Hi there...do you have time for me?"

Since her job was buying time and placing commercials, I assumed she found me wildly charming in a strange sort of way. "What do you want?" she shot back, not raising her head to see who it was. "I'm busy." Maybe she didn't want to appear too interested until she knew me better. But I hoped she was starting to feel a certain chemistry developing between us, not quite tension yet, but something close to it.

The afternoon the event was mentioned I spent hours daydreaming about the article for the company newsletter.

> "Rebecca Billings and Peter Dreeton of our New York office stomped out the competition at the first annual Cranberry Crush." Our photo was taken on the edge of the big wooden bin. We were wearing shorts and T-shirts with bright red-stained feet dangling over the side of the bin. Appearing in uniforms might be seen as boorish, unsportsmanlike or déclassé to the other teams, who just considered this an afternoon of fun. The caption beneath our picture read, "These two attractive additions to our New York office were caught "red-footed" after winning the first annual Cranberry Crush. Good luck at next year's event." *Good luck, my ass. Rebecca and I were talking three-peat.*

Becs' real boyfriend, Bowie, was traded from the Rangers to the Bruins three weeks later, and she left town with her red shoes still on her feet.

For the cranberry ad campaign the agency hired an NYU photography professor, who freelanced for *National Geographic*. She shot stills of the cranberry in various stages of undress. Her photographs were haunting, the ads simple and clean. The copy lovingly discussed the care and attention all Bog's Best growers put into bringing the product to market. One of the photos showed off a whole field of berries lying on top of dark blue water. The copy read, "Rich, Red, and Ready." Another ad had a small girl sampling juice at a fair, her arms around her dad. She was cute, around Casey's age, and it made me sad to think about those times again.

October 23-30, 1943

The idea came to Kerrie later that day while looking at the movie section of the newspaper.

"What time does the movie start?" asked Lucy, who was sitting beside Kerrie on the sofa.

"I haven't found it yet," Kerrie responded. As she glanced over the page, she noticed the small box in the far column. "Oh, my goodness. Look at this: 'Support the Cape Cod Reds: these fine stores already have.' And, bam, right there at the top of the list of stores is 'Wallace Market, Chatham, Mass.' with a Cod drawing beside it. Why that little stink pot," she smiled. "He's been stealing the store name and team from the list on the warehouse bulletin board, before it goes to print in the newspaper. He takes the first name and puts an odd box in with that order. Then the person on the other end just has to look in the newspaper at the first store listed to know where to go."

"Kerrie, I don't like that gleam in your eye. Don't do anything rash. Remember what Eric said about being careful," Lucy admonished.

"Oh, I won't. I won't. Anyway, it's just a theory," Kerrie rebutted.

The next Wednesday after school, when Sister Margaret, as usual, posted the list for the coming Saturday's paper on the warehouse bulletin board, Kerrie was there to look it over. The first store named was the Festival Market in Falmouth, and it was followed by a Starfish symbol. Kerrie wasn't certain she was on the right track, but it was worth a try, and she'd know on Thursday evening. It had been a simple logic problem really, the sort of thing that her teachers would have been proud that she had applied to everyday living.

The orders would be going out on Friday, so late Thursday she dropped by the warehouse and opened the case of Starfish going to Falmouth. She found the out-of-place Whale box on the bottom row. "It's all too easy," she thought, but she knew that Eric would be proud of her when she gave him this week's supply of state secrets. She opened the Whale box and found the piece of notebook paper. She took it and put it in her purse. "There now, little fella, you're coming home with me," she said, treating it as if it were a family pet. Then she inserted her own "Kilroy was here" doodle into the Whale box. Now all she had to do was to find a friend to go to this party with her.

At first Mary said no, and repeated the warning Eric had given them. But Kerrie bribed her by saying that she could stay by the car.

"All I need you to do is to take a couple of pictures of the guy when he gets out of his truck. Oh, and write down his license plate, and take another photo of me holding up the evidence when I leave the store. Pleeeeeeeeeeeease!"

"That sounds easy. Shall I bring handcuffs and a nightstick, too?" Mary asked.

"Come on now. Get serious. Anyway, you owe me for helping you on that science paper. So it's settled. I'll pick you up at 8. This store is much closer. We'll be back by 9:30 at the latest. Plus, it's fun spending time with me, right?"

Kerrie was always looking for confirmation of her importance, and this time Mary gave in, providing she could do the driving.

The Festival Market in Falmouth opened at 8:30 on Saturday. Mary parked next to the front door and waited. Kerrie went inside and looked over some of the specials being advertised. He was early this time, his truck pulling up across the street. Mary nodded to Kerrie through the picture window, and Kerrie picked up a basket. She made a couple of small selections, things her mother would want, and then just on a whim, she noticed a similar display of sunglasses. She walked over and picked up the pair like the ones she had seen the week before at Wallace Market. The man entered and asked where the toothbrushes were. The counter lady pointed to the second aisle, and he picked one up along with a tube of Pepsodent toothpaste.

"Why not?" Kerrie said out loud. "After all today is going to be my lucky day." And she was right. The glasses were thirty cents less than the ones at last week's market. He looked at her, not making the connection at first.

"Small world," he said when he realized, trying to cover up his surprise.

"Excuse me?" Kerrie said. She looked behind her pretending he was speaking to someone else.

"I saw you in another store last week, remember?" he added.

"Oh, yeah, that's crazy," she smiled. "This time I decided to get myself those sunglasses after all," she said holding them up for him to see.

"That's nice," he said picking up a basket. She had him where she wanted. She was in perfect position to make the rebound. She could get to the counter before he could, giving her first pick on the cranberries. She figured that maybe he'd try to wait her out to see if she would leave, but that wasn't going to work either. She pulled a magazine off the rack below the checkout counter and started reading an article about Clark Gable. The counter lady asked if she was ready, but she explained, "Not yet." Kerrie was prepared to wait all day if she had to. She looked over a couple of fashion magazines, and just as she was putting the second one down, he forced her hand by moving toward the checkout counter.

"I'm ready now," she said putting her basket on the counter, blocking his path. The counter lady rang her total. Kerrie paid and turned to leave, but while still blocking the display, she said, "Oh, wait. I'll guess I'll take these." She laid her nickel on the counter and dug into the case of cranberries, pulling out the box she had prepared on Thursday.

"Arr, mateys, it's Captain Ahab. Look what I've harpooned in a school of Starfish?" she said as she held up the Whale box to show to the man behind her. "This is crazy, don't you think? Who knew, two weeks in a row? Those people must not have very good quality control." She smiled at the counter lady and turned to leave.

"Last week I got the lucky box, and this week you did," the man behind her said.

"That's true."

"Would you like to switch?" he asked, as he held out a Starfish box. "My wife has been wanting to get a Whale."

"Okay, I don't care," Kerrie said. "Here." She put the box in his outstretched hand.

"Thanks, that's nice of you." He seemed genuinely pleased with his good fortune.

"Thanks. I try being a good sport when I can. And speaking of that, if I see you next Saturday, we can go for two out of three."

The man laughed and said "It's a deal."

Kerrie headed out to car, and they watched the man come out of the store. He got in his truck but before he left he opened his box to find Kerrie's Kilroy note. The two girls watched him get back out of his truck and walk to the pay phone booth on the corner.

"He doesn't look happy does he?" Mary said as their car drove past the phone booth.

"No, I guess he didn't like my art work," Kerrie replied.

.   .   .

Chapter 43
THE ANSWERS ARE BLOWING IN THE WIND

Summer, 1967

My best friend at the agency was a guy named Robert Talbot, who wrote ad copy. Shortly after I started, he was assigned a toilet tissue account: Baby's Bottom: Baby knows Best.

Robert and I went to bars after work, and he introduced himself to ladies as "Robert, the toilet tissue guy." He told them that he'd been absorbed in his work, but now he was on a roll, and that it was hard tearing himself away from it all. The girls at the bar were howling; drinks were flowing. We had two favorite bars near the office, and we'd settle in around 8 at one of them if we didn't have some special assignment to finish.

Robert competed with another copywriter, Mindy Orenstein, for the best writing assignments. She got a big shipping account about the same time Robert landed Baby's Bottom. I can't say who was better. Their writing styles were just different; that's all. A lesser person might have seen the toilet tissue account for what it was: a demotion; a step down; beneath his dignity. Robert saw it for what it could be: an opportunity; a chance to work his way up from the bottom. The day they started he told the account manager, "Tear us off a couple of sheets, and let's make some magic." *That's the spirit, Robert. A can-do attitude works every time.*

• • •

I didn't make much more than it cost me to live in New York, but then who does really? I figured if I was ever going to travel, this was my chance. Robert and I often talked about going to Europe. A girl named Mary Haskell in graphic design wanted to go, too. The three of us got along well. She had gone to Rhode Island School of Design, so we talked some about her school since it was close to Whitfield. She had vacation time due, and after the May television sweeps things got quiet for the summer. We decided to travel to Europe for a couple of weeks. The three of us started meeting for dinner once a week at restaurants in the Village. Our first meeting was at a hamburger joint several blocks off Houston Street. We decided to start in West Germany for no reason other than it was sort of in the center of things. Our plan was to spend a few days enjoying the sights. We'd take a ride down the Rhine and then head to the beer gardens. The next morning we'd catch the train through Switzerland and on to Italy.

"How 'bout dinner with the Pope?" I suggested on our first planning night out. Robert seemed skeptical of my ability to deliver.

"Please, Robert, it won't be a problem. I worked at a Catholic school, attended mass twice a year. He'll be waiting for us at the train station with bells on. You have my word on it."

"You're sure, Peter?"

"Absolutely."

"If you say so," Robert replied.

Once we agreed on the general itinerary, we started going to restaurants for each country we were planning to visit. I had been busy at work the week we did France and didn't have time to complete my assigned list of must-see things to do. At the last minute I snatched a picture of the Eiffel Tower from Cyndi's desk and brought it along with me. Robert and

Mary seemed amused by my efforts, and they gave me a hard time about the quality of my research.

"What? You people want to go to Paris and not see this place? Are you fucking nuts?"

"No, Peter, it's not that," Mary said.

"Well, what then?"

"Never mind. What did you bring?" Robert asked turning to Mary. She dumped a box load of materials out on the table—everything from information on small galleries, to out of the way bookstores and quaint restaurants—and then they both looked back at me.

"Yeah, Mary, your stuff looks nice, too, but I still feel pretty good about my pick."

"And you should, Peter," she said, patting my hand the way mothers do when their child finishes dead last in a school-sponsored event.

Robert found cheap airfares on Pam Am, and we practiced seeing how much we could put into one backpack. The answer was not nearly enough, so to save space Robert came up with a plan to bring a total of six pairs of underwear and rotate them among us on two-day shifts.

Robert was bringing a journal, Mary an ink pen and sketchpad, and I had gotten a good camera from a secondhand store on Third Avenue. Robert's middle name was Paul, so one night at a German restaurant we decided to call ourselves Peter, Paul, and Mary. *Life is wonderful when you are young and think there's no one else as funny as you are on the face of the earth. Later in life you learn the cruel lesson that your humor is as lame as that of your parents. I hate to say it, but sometimes reality sucks.*

The restaurant in the Village had a German band playing the night we went, and we got wasted early in the evening. This was not a good sign. If we were unable to hold our beer in the East Village, how would we do when our training wheels came off in the Marienplatz, and we had our Bavarian butts against the wall, yodeling for mercy?

Between sets, Mary talked the band into letting the three of us sing "Blowing in the Wind." I think "three sheets in the wind" would have been more like it, but Mary had a beautiful voice even if we were lousy backup. After the song was over, everyone told Robert and me to sit down, and Mary did another number by herself. Caught in the footlights of fame, she belted out "Somewhere over the rainbow, birds will fly…." And soon enough we did.

The Rhine was beautiful, the beer gardens flowing, the cocoa creamy in Lucerne, but in Rome disappointment awaited us.

"Let's give him a few more minutes. The traffic is really bad here," I suggested. It started raining as we stood outside the train station. Mary shook her head.

"No, Peter. He's not coming. He has a motorcade. There is no traffic. The Pope is like Charlton Heston. He can part the ocean or walk on water if he needs to. Let's take a cab and get the hell out of here. These shoes are killing me." A car rushed by us, splashing unholy water on our pants, and Mary frowned.

"Oh, so he's not coming?" Robert said, trying to rub it in as much as possible. "Thanks a lot, Peter. I get it now."

We took the next cab we found to a cheap hotel near the Spanish Steps. Later I read in the American paper that the Pope had gone to his summer home outside the city, and I took no end of grief when I brought it up to the others.

"Boy, is there going to be hell to pay when he gets back to the Vatican and sees that Peter called."

"Unless it's Saint Peter, I'm not sure he's going to care too much. Face it; he has thousands more just like you working at crappy little Catholic colleges trying to imagine their new enrollees naked. You're nothing special, my friend," Mary said lying on top of one of the twin beds, painting her toenails a bright red.

"Maybe the Pope got his dates wrong. But when I say wrong, I mean it in the most modest sense since he is infallible. Well, at least up until now."

"Hey, we all make mistakes. Leave it at that," Robert added. "Like our decision to bring you along, Peter."

"That's cold. I'm telling the Queen when you take us by for tea, Robert."

Mary jumped in and told us both to stop. Even without the big guy, we had fun. We had our picture taken at the coliseum in gladiator costumes, holding Mary sideways, our plastic swords drawn, ready to defend her honor.

The food was wonderful and so were the people. We spent time jumping into water fountains to cool off and walking through beautiful gardens near the Via Veneto. We watched children playing on the worn summer grass in front of the Borghese Gallery and listened to the wind catch the leaves of the cypress trees above our heads. That night we crossed the river to the old part of Rome and dined in a sidewalk café with children playing ball in the street.

In Paris we did all the stuff on Mary's list and still had time to visit the Eiffel Tower, my hot spot. Climbing all the steps, we got a wonderful view overlooking Paris in late afternoon.

"Are you going to thank me now?" I said in a self-satisfied voice.

"Yes, Peter. This is a great find. What's it called again?" Robert asked. And I felt vindicated.

With all of the questions about what Europe would be like, our answers were now blowing in the wind.

November 3, 1943

Sister Margaret was meeting with a freshmen student and her mother about a discipline problem when the knocking began.

"Excuse me, Mrs. O'Malley," she said, raising her head to look at the closed door.

"Come in."

The door tentatively opened halfway, and the face of her secretary peeked in. "Sorry, Sister, but the mail just arrived, and I thought you'd want to see this." She held up a magazine with a Camel cigarette advertisement on the back cover.

"Yes, thank you, dear." She waved for the secretary to come in. "Please."

The secretary smiled at the parent and laid the copy of *Life* magazine on the desk, and started to close the door on her way out.

"That's okay, Ellen. Just leave it open. I feel certain that Polly won't try to burn the school down again with her smoking."

"No, Sister Margaret, I promise this won't happen again, and I've never smoked a Camel," Polly answered.

"You can be sure this will never happen again," Mrs. O'Malley reaffirmed, with an icy stare in the direction of her daughter.

"Before you go, let's look at this piece of history together." Sister Margaret picked up the magazine and walked around to the other side of her desk. She pulled up another chair and opened the magazine to look at the Cape Cod Reds article. It was three pages, with beautiful photographs and quotes about all the hard work that had gone into making the program a success.

Mrs. O'Malley smiled when she picked Polly's face out of a group at the Starfish's workbench. "Look, Polly. There you are with the Starfish."

"It just makes me feel really good about all we're doing," Polly said to the nun.

"Yes, dear, that's how life works. The reminder of one good we've done makes the next one possible. We should all be proud of what we're accomplishing."

A second knock on the door made them look up. Katie peeked her head into the room.

"Sorry to bother you, Sister, but we're going to be leaving soon for the program, and I need to get the keys to the car and the gas voucher," Katie said.

"Certainly, come in and see the photos. *Life* magazine just got here."

"Oh, really, that's so exciting!" she replied. "Hey Polly, do they make us look good?" Katie asked her teammate.

"Yeah, amazing, especially the Starfish," Polly said, her mood lightening.

"You girls are probably a little prejudiced on that point, but I have to agree with you," Polly's mom said chuckling to herself.

Katie went over the pictures with Polly, and Mrs. O'Malley got up to say goodbye. "Thank you, Sister Margaret, for meeting with us. Well, I'll see you at home, Polly," she said to her daughter. "Good to see you, Katie. Please give my best to your mother."

Katie had her head buried in the photographs, and she looked up and said, "Oh, yes, I will. Thanks."

Katie looked for another minute and then needed to go. Sister Margaret handed her the envelope with the keys and the gas ration coupon and wished Katie luck.

"Thanks! We're looking forward to it, and I know the other girls will be jealous that I've gotten to see the photos first."

Sister Margaret laughed and replied, "You ladies are so competitive."

"It's all in good fun," Katie smiled.

•   •   •

Chapter 44
PIECES OF NINE

School year, 1951–1952

Every Friday afternoon when I was in fourth grade, our teacher, Mrs. Grayson, told us to get out our notebooks, and we wrote stories until the go-home bell rang at three. We could write about whatever we chose. Sheila McCurry, who sat in front of me always wrote about her neighbor, Mr. Willard, a man with an unusually large nose. Sheila lived a good ways from my house, so I knew very little about her, other than she was a quiet girl who kept to herself. At lunch she picked a table near the fire exit and laid out her sandwich and thermos neatly in front of her. On the playground she spent most of her time in solitude hanging upside down from the jungle gym while the rest of the girls jumped rope or chased the boys, and she rarely showed up at birthday parties. But Sheila was smart, and we all knew she was Mrs. Grayson's favorite writer. We didn't mind so much because her stories were our favorites as well. Our stories were all up against whatever predicament in which Mr. Big Schnozz found himself. We laughed or held our breath waiting for some happy resolution.

Mr. Schnozz showed up on the first page of Sheila's Big Chief tablet and returned every week until Valentine's Day, when she announced that Mr. Schnozz was moving to Cleveland to take care of his ailing mother. Her substitute story that week dealt with making mud pies, and while it wasn't bad, it wasn't the same. We were all devastated, and it didn't help any when she explained that he didn't exist. *Says who Sheila? You've been playing us for a fool all this time, haven't you? We had an emotional investment in what calamity he might get into next, especially after his car accident in the Sears parking lot. Who didn't love that one? What I learned from her writing was this: if you tell the right story, even if it's made up, people will make it their own.*

Listening to Sheila's words made we want to be a writer someday, and one day after class I shared my dream with Mrs. Grayson. She seemed surprised by my announcement, or maybe confused. After a brief pause, she threw her arms around me quickly as if discovering my clothes had burst into flames, and she needed to cover me with a wool blanket. She hugged and held me for the longest time, her lungs filling up with air and then releasing, and when she finally let me out of her love cave, she looked me in the eye and said, "You do?" Mrs. Grayson was a large woman who long ago had thrown up the white surrender flag of personal eating habits, but she had a wonderfully kind manner. She found any reason to smother students in the warm underbelly of her flabby arms and soft breasts. Sometimes when she took one of us into her grasp, he would be lost from sight in her great caverns, and we wondered if we would ever see him again.

If Sheila was the brains of our class, Mrs. Grayson was our compass. She gave us direction and directions, although sometimes her wise but ambiguous comments left us more confused than ever.

Every week I was the next to be called on after Sheila finished her story. But most times Mrs. Grayson would have to interrupt before my second paragraph was done to remind the class, "Please, children, be courteous, and let Peter finish."

I worked hard on my stories putting great care into character development and storylines. Some weeks Mrs. Grayson said something encouraging which gave me a sweet glimmer of hope, and somehow that seemed enough. If we had time before the writing session began, she read comments on creative writing from a worn book she kept in her top drawer. The book was titled *Helping Children Grow: A Guide to Creative Writing*. Then she would pass out writing samples on freshly mimeographed purple-inked sheets, still moist with the aroma of creativity.

I wrote pirate stories. A few weeks after Mr. Schnozz's departure, I wrote my best work. The adventure took place on Parrot Island, an uninhabited spit of land, where my pirates were endlessly searching for buried treasure, like pieces of eight. The stories centered on Oscar De La Fuentes, a pirate with a debilitating speech impediment.

My story was titled "Oscar and the *Nine Maidens*," which was the name of his pirate ship. Even before it ended, I knew I had nailed it, knocked it out of the park. I began my slow trot around the bases to the hushed glow of victory, and after touching home plate was met with a thunderous round of applause. Mrs. Grayson gave an approving nod and said, "Very nice, Peter, that's your best work ever."

After class she stopped me as I was leaving. "You know, Peter, I may have been wrong about you."

"Wrong, Mrs. Grayson, how's that?" I asked.

"Oh, never mind. It's not important." She smiled to herself while putting her head back down to correct papers.

. . .

Fall, 1965

My last fall in Whitfield Nate's class had a regular writing assignment, similar to the one I had had in the fourth grade. At first his stories were about his life and friends in Washington. Caroline was worried that he wasn't moving forward, and one day after I had biked home from work, she asked what I thought about the situation. She was hanging bed sheets on the line. One of the sheets unfurled, covering her entire body just as she finished asking her question.

"Oops, still there?" I asked.

"I think so," she laughed, pulling the white cloth off her face. "If the sheet monster doesn't eat me up."

"You'll be fine, and I wouldn't worry about Nate either. It's just his way of not forgetting things and people, you know what I mean? It's hard being nine and having to move."

"You know, Peter, you have such a fertile imagination. Maybe you could help him some with his story ideas."

"Sure, that would be fun."

And with her invitation came my second journey into "Pieces of Nine." Nate was a smart nine-year-old, and over time his stories would have ventured out, even without my suggestions, usually on a pirating theme. But we had fun kicking around ideas. Some of my best ones came on nights when the Pendletons headed off to the park. I would sit on my back deck, drinking beer and trying to come up with something for the following week's adventure. So I guess it was no surprise that many of the characters ended up with names familiar to me. Bud, Pabst, Schaefer, and their English cousin, Falstaff, all made regular appearances. It didn't matter really. What mattered was that Nate's class loved his stories the way our class loved Sheila's. Beer was my creative source, but the stories were always Nate's, first to last.

November 3, 1943

Katie took the car keys and the gas ration coupon and went to the locker hallway. There she was meeting Kerrie and Mary, who were going with her to do a Cape Cod Reds presentation at another school. Lucy couldn't go because she was in charge of hosting the Simplicity patterns lady, who was giving an after-school lesson on sewing. Penny couldn't go because she was having a singing lesson. Kerrie was supposed to go, but she was running late, of course. Mary was waiting by her locker when Katie walked up.

"Guess what I just saw?" Katie said with a big smile on her face.

"Clark Gable acting in a movie scene with Kerrie?" Mary guessed.

"No, even better than that," Katie answered.

"Nothing would be better than that as far as Kerrie's concerned," Mary responded.

"Oh, you're probably right, *but I saw our pictures in* Life *magazine!"* Katie shouted.

Penny was coming down the hall when she heard Katie's excited squeals. "Oh, my God, you cad, where?" Penny asked.

"In Sister Margaret's office while I was picking up these," Katie responded as she dangled the school car keys in her hand. "They are so amazing, especially of our group."

"Oh, shut up, but I can't wait to see them," Mary squealed.

"Well, you're going to have to hold your horses. We're supposed to be on the road by now," Katie informed her.

"You ladies have fun," Penny said, pulling her books out of her locker.

"We can't go yet. We're waiting for someone. Care to guess?" Mary remarked.

"Anne Boleyn?" Penny answered.

"No, but she'd probably be here sooner," Mary laughed.

"Of course, but let's get real. If you ladies need help, I can go after all. My voice lesson got cancelled," Penny volunteered.

"Absolutely," Katie replied.

"Okay, then. Let me call my mom and tell the student desk that I'm going instead of Kerrie."

"Sure. What fun!" Katie said. "We're off to dazzle another crowd with our amazing feats."

. . .

Walking up to her locker, Kerrie noticed that Mary and Katie were nowhere to be seen. "Could I have gotten here before them?" she wondered to herself.

Then she saw a note stuck to her locker. She yanked it off and read, "Kerrie, we waited a few minutes for you, but we needed to get going. Penny was available after all, so she went in your place. Have fun studying. Hugs and kisses, Katie, Mary and Penny."

"Those little Miss Perfects couldn't wait a few minutes for me. That's just my bad luck. Now I'll have to go home and study for my Latin test," Kerrie complained.

. . .

Katie pulled into the Sinclair station a few miles before the bridge. She spent the entire time on the road talking about the article and the photos, and the other two girls were tired of hearing about it. She handed the attendant, a young man wearing green overalls, the gas ration coupon Sister Margaret had given her. Whenever they made these trips, they always took the school car, a five-year-old Ford. The attendant zipped his jacket up to his neck and took it. He smiled through the foggy glass and said, "You ladies be careful out here. The weather's getting worse."

"We will," Katie said.

Mary opened the door, and Katie asked, "Where are you going?"

"I'll be right back," she said closing the door before too much cold air could get in. She raced across the parking lot and into the small market next to the gas station. She was gone a minute before coming back with something covered up inside her jacket.

"Look what I got!" she said, beaming as she got back in the car.

"What?" Katie asked starting the engine.

"Pictures of me in a magazine," she replied.

"Hey, I want to see too!" Penny cried.

"You will, girl. Just relax. I couldn't let Katie get the upper hand," Mary said. Mary looked at the photos for a minute and then tossed the magazine over the seat to Penny.

Rain turned to sleet a couple of miles before they approached the bridge. Fat drops blanketed the front windshield. Mary turned on the radio to try and get the weather report. They heard the tail end of a Lux laundry soap commercial and the start of *The Adventures of Dick Cole,* but Katie asked her to turn it off. The worn blades squeaked crossing the frozen glass. "Maybe we should go back? It looks bad to me," Katie said in a worried voice.

"No, are you kidding me?" Mary said from the seat beside her. "We won't get an excused absence if we don't go, and there's no way I'm taking Sister Agnes's Latin exam in the morning. No way. I haven't even looked at that book for three days."

"I hear you, but the weather's supposed to get even worse," Katie countered.

"Maybe, but not worse than what I'd be making on that test. Listen, Miss Class Valedictorian, you'd make an A in your sleep, but keep going for our sakes" Mary offered.

"Okay, you win, but we'd better not get stuck overnight," Katie responded.

"We won't," Mary said, "and as you all know, I'm never wrong."

"That would make me feel better, except I saw what you made on Kimball's history test," Katie said.

"Hey, that was an off-day, one in a million—or at least close to that." Mary replied. "Let's talk about something else. How about our trip this summer to the ranch in Wyoming? I think I'm going to take some horseback riding lessons before we leave," Mary began the new discussion.

.   .   .

Chapter 45
MYSTERIES FROM THE DEEP

February 28, 1966

On the last day of February, Nate and Marcus, a Cod from his class, went ice skating on one of the ponds near Baker's Landing. Marcus Colvin came to the house around 11. They played in Nate's room while Caroline fixed peanut butter and jelly sandwiches, chips, and hot chocolate, which she put in two thermos bottles. They rode their bikes north of town. Low gray clouds lay over the pond. They left their bikes on a high bank and carried their skates over their shoulders down the steep slope. They made long lazy circles in the ice until almost 1.

Snow dusted the pond and their clothes. Marcus sat finishing his sandwich on a rock while Nate skated to the far end of the pond. He slipped, hitting his head in the fall. The force of the ice left him dizzy, and he lay for a moment stunned before getting up. The ice cracked beneath his legs. He yelled for help, but Marcus could not make out the words, only his voice. The sound of the ice snapping shot back to Marcus, like a car backfiring. Then the soft ice shifted a second time. Nate got halfway up before it gave way under his weight. Marcus raced to help but couldn't reach him. He watched the blues and greens of Nate's scarf swirling in the water. By the time Caroline arrived Nate was gone.

I was in Cincinnati for a college night presentation when I got the call.

"What? What?" I shouted back. "Who is this?" Her words flat and lifeless, I wanted to say, "What the hell are you saying? Is this some sick joke?" I wanted to slam a door hard in someone's face, mostly my own; to put out the international "do not disturb" symbol, a stubby middle finger with the words "bite me" written in four languages. I wanted to order room service for days and leave trays filled with half-eaten BLTs and greasy fries outside my door. Caroline and I sat together on the phone for what seemed minutes, breathing into each other's lives with no words to put there, and then we said goodbye.

When I returned, the house had changed, and all our adventures ended. The town seemed empty in ways I couldn't imagine. Nate was gone, Julie was about to leave, and I still had no idea where life would lead. In the end my father had been right all along; all that I had done was waste more time, floating on the Wow.

We were all changed by Nathan's death, but in different ways. The years took us to different places. The Pendletons never had more children. Casey grew up and learned many more words than "duck" and "Sam," which Nathan had taught her.

I have wondered from time to time about the tree house we built, and if Casey ever played in it when she was older, or if it became sacred ground, revered but not spoken about. During those days of our adventures, I would see out my window the artifacts Nate had left behind from his days of play. One by one these items disappeared. Over time they were given away, as Nathan moved to another part of our lives, not by choice but instinct. It had to be.

When I was growing up, a lady came to clean our house a couple of hours a week, so Mom could help out at the store. Her name was Ruby Mullins. She had two children the same ages as Cory and me. Ruby was a wonderful woman, who made the best of the small hand life dealt blacks in the fifties. On Ruby's right forearm was a wide flat scar from a knife wound she had suffered as a child. How she got it she never said, but the scar was as wide as my thumb and ran several inches up her arm. It must have been one helluva cut is all I can say.

Sometimes when she was sitting at the kitchen table waiting for the damp floor to dry, or having a cup of coffee, I sat with her. She let me run my fingers over the scar. It was smooth and silky to the touch. We talked about matters of great importance: the weather, television shows, even her boys. She told me about growing up in Alabama in a small town and what her life was like. She laid out her stories on the kitchen table, and I picked up some small portion of one and asked her questions. I came to know about her aunts and uncles, and over time it felt as if they were my relatives as well. Sometimes the floor would be dry, or the phone would ring, and we would stop before she had said very much; other times she would go into great detail, and I learned a lot. I asked dumb questions, as kids will do, and she laughed without explaining why.

Ruby liked the gospel hour. I liked *Crusader Rabbit*, a dashing solver of crimes. We couldn't agree on everything, and in the end it was our differences that made us friends. Ruby died the summer I turned fourteen, and it was the hardest lesson I learned growing up.

By the time I left Whitfield the urgency of Nate's loss was gone, and what remained, much like the scar on Ruby's arm, was smooth and hard.

November 3, 1943

A big gust of wind rocked the car, pulling it toward the guardrail. Even inside they felt the temperature drop just as the lights came on over the top of the bridge. The tires slipped a little under the slick icy surface, but Katie adjusted the steering wheel back over the center line. The single suspension bridge was steep and narrow. Even on good days, it was not easy. "At least the bridge is empty," Katie thought. Mary reached over and turned up the radio to listen to the news.

"More fire bombings today over London," the announcer said. "And heavy fighting reported again in northern France near the border. In other news. . ." Mary turned it back down just as the car began its steep assent to the top. "It's just too depressing to listen to."

Katie saw headlights coming from the other side, rising up over the other lane. The lights shot upwards in the support columns and off into the sleet-filled sky. Seeing the lights made her tense. She took her foot off the accelerator, bringing the station wagon almost to a crawl. She wanted to make eye contact with the other vehicle before going over the top section of the bridge. Suddenly the light moved to the center of the bridge, directly in front of them. Katie wondered if it was an older person disoriented by the weather, but a head-on collision at the steepest point wasn't a good choice, so she made a split-second decision to move the car into the lane of oncoming traffic.

"Jesus," she said honking at the unseen source.

"What are you doing?" Mary called out.

"Shut up!" Katie yelled, reacting to the stress.

Just then Mary spotted the truck turning back into his rightful lane and screamed, "Look out."

Katie panicked hearing the noise, turning the wagon as hard to her right as she could. The station wagon hit a patch of new ice and spun completely out of Katie's control. She gripped the wheel with both hands and tried to ignore the screaming around her. She caught a glimpse of the truck and the driver during the rotation and wondered for a split second what he had been doing on her side of the bridge. But then the thought was lost. Their car was now sliding over the top of the bridge, skidding toward the guardrail on the down side, and she had bigger things to worry about. At first Katie felt a sense of relief and release. The car was moving slowly now, and she could feel the brakes starting to take hold.

"It's okay. It's okay," she said, letting out her breath and expecting the car to slide down along the rail before stopping. She pumped the breaks again lightly to make sure they caught, but just as the car hit the side, the guardrail gave way. In one flash she felt the first front tire sliding off the bridge spinning in open air and then the second. The car teetered momentarily on the edge before continuing to tip into the open air. She said, "Oh my God," and nothing more.

The station wagon dropped into the dark water below. The truck came to a stop on the far side of the downhill slope. A second car traveling the same direction as the girls stopped. The driver got out and ran to the truck to check on its driver.

"Are you okay?"

The truck driver nodded, but seemed shaken.

"What happened?"

"I lost control of the truck for a moment on this ice," the truck driver admitted.

The man raced to the other side of the bridge and looked below, but all that was left was the rear bumper and taillights going below the surface. Standing in the freezing rain, he shook his head as he watched the car sink.

"Oh, my God, oh, my God," he shouted while running back to the truck.

Shortly after 5 PM, a nun from St. Thomas's School, where the girls' speaking engagement was to be held, called

St. Anne's to say the girls hadn't arrived. Sister Margaret called the police to report the three girls missing, and an hour later they called her back to report the sad news.

Sister Margaret knew she had to make calls but first needed a minute to herself to gather her thoughts. She hung up the phone, put her hands up to her face, and said quietly, "Lord, hear our prayers."

The sleet turned to snow and from out her convent window the fields turned white and beautiful.

. . .

Chapter 46
ISLAND HOPPING

May 7, 1966

The town held a big celebration when the construction work on Bird Island finished in early May, and the whole town went out to see the results. I went with Julie. We listened to Mayor Martinez's speech, enjoyed a band concert, and everyone got free hot dogs and sodas. Julie wanted to go over to see if the flag Dave had planted was still there, and I am glad to say it was. The flagpole had bent near the base, but Caroline's red and white rendition still waved. We stood for moment thinking about all the fun we had together in cranberry land. Then Julie said, "Come on. Let's go." We walked back across the island to catch one of the shuttles, and Julie, noticing the Mayor and city council huddled next to one of the picnic tables, asked, "Do you think they're planning another pay raise?"

"Of course," I nodded before suggesting, "more beers?"

"Absolutely, sweetie, I'm buying."

"That's my girl."

Let's face it; my favorite name for a girl friend was Julie Mathers.

May 18-19, 1966

In mid-May I had to go to Nantucket for a college roundup. Julie had finished exams by then, and she went with me. Naomi's uncle was part-owner of the Beach and Breakers Inn, and she got us a deal on a room for the weekend. We had stayed there the end of the summer before. On this second trip it was too early for tourists and too late for us. The hotel was just glad to have the business.

We drove to the ferryboat terminal in Hyannis early on Friday morning. It was the first time we'd been away together since Nate had died. Julie had been busy with stuff for Penn and finishing her research project, and I was tied up with fall enrollment. At least that's what we told each other, but we both knew the end coming.

"It's hard to believe we're doing this again," she said as we pulled into the oyster-shelled parking lot next to the wharf.

"Doing what?" I asked.

"Going back to Nantucket. There were so many places we've talked about seeing and never made it."

"So many places to see, so little time… Sydney, Paris, Amarillo."

"Yes! We must go there. I've heard the Texas Panhandle is lovely this time of year. We'll just have to plan to go when we have more time to see Amarillo as it should be seen."

"From thirty-four thousand feet?"

"Peter, that's not nice. Have you even been there?"

"No, and I promise never to go without you."

A number of empty benches at the docks faced the water. Julie picked a bench halfway down the row. In busier times every seat would be packed with small children hanging upside down off the backside. Now there were only a handful of brave souls venturing over for the weekend. I went to buy the tickets.

"What time does the ferry get here?" I asked the man at the ticket stand.

"Another twenty minutes, unless the water is rough."

I paid for the tickets and went back to the bench. The wind kicked up. The half-empty ferry arrived a few minutes early. Tourists and islanders poured off the walkway, carrying bags of goodies. Our departing crowd had grown over the last half hour, but not to any sizable numbers. We took seats on the upper open deck, even knowing it would be chilly.

"I want some sun," Julie said picking a spot at the back of the boat and pulling two chairs over to the rail. She kicked off her shoes and wrapped her toes around the low wooden rail.

"I thought you were cold?"

"I am, but I'm tanning my feet."

She pulled out a book and started to read. I opened my briefcase. Naomi had scheduled several appointments at the high school, and I had to drop off papers for an incoming freshman who was going to play running back.

After a while Julie looked over at me. "Peter, what do you tell people when they ask about our school?"

"I tell them I met the most incredible woman, and we're moving to Amarillo to open a digestive clinic. And if they come to St. Jerome's, they can end up someplace wonderful just like me."

"The small intestine?"

"I was thinking of something larger, but the small one would be a good place to start."

"Seriously, Peter. That's a sweet story."

"I think so."

She began playing with a stray thread on my blue blazer and continued pulling while we talked.

"Really, what do you say?"

"Oh, mostly I talk about the size of the place and how you get to know almost everyone on campus on a personal basis, all the neat stuff. Who wears underwear, and who doesn't."

"You don't mention me by name, do you?"

"Sometimes, but only if I've brought pictures to show everybody. What's a name without a face, right?"

She worked the piece of string loose and pulled it out. "There," she said, pleased with her achievement.

"Let me ask you something, Julie. Do you plan to have kids?"

"Of course! What kind of question is that?

"Just wondering, I mean with your career and all."

"Of course, I do."

I nodded, and we sat silently for a minute watching two gulls chase our boat across the water.

"With me?"

"With you what?"

"The babies; are you having them with me?"

"Is that a proposal?"

Of course it wasn't because I knew that she wouldn't go for it, so I tried to slough it off.

"No, just wondering. A boy and a girl?"

"That would be nice."

"Okay. Would the boy's name be Peter Dreeton, Jr. by any chance?"

"No, Peter, it won't."

I made a long sad face and stared out to the ocean.

"But, I haven't ruled it out for the girl. In fact it might be quite nice."

"Wow, back in the running."

"Yes, you are. I've often thought Peter Dreeton, Jr. would make a pretty girl's name. But that's only happening if you find something important to do with your life."

"Does being a pirate count?"

"No, it doesn't," she replied.

One of the riders standing near us started tossing pieces of torn bread over the side, and out of nowhere gulls appeared. Loud squawking was followed by a food fight. We stopped talking and watched. The sun made me sleepy, and I closed my eyes, listening to their lunchroom chatter. I faded off into a midday nap, hearing the sounds of a family stopping at the rail and then moving on.

Julie nudged me just as we are getting close to the island. The rental car place was near the ferry dock. I dropped Julie at the inn, gave her the letter Naomi had gotten from her uncle, and went directly to the high school.

After my meetings with some prospects in the counselor's office, I had a program in the gym at 3. This wasn't a major event, just a handful of colleges, and a chance to acquaint junior students with next year's options.

The bell went off, and the first wave of students flowed in. As luck would have it, my running back stopped by on his own to sign the form. We talked for a couple of minutes about the coach and the team, and then he left.

When I got back to the inn, Julie was working on a jigsaw puzzle in the lobby. In the summer the space was perfect for reading a good book in one of the oversized chairs, feeling the breeze through the open doorway and watching people come and go to the beach. But for the moment there was nothing to watch except Julie fitting a piece of a brown sleeve into place.

They had given us a deluxe room for the standard room price. It looked out to the water with three large bay windows. After dinner at a small restaurant nearby, we brought two bottles of wine back and lay on top of the bed, looking at the lights out over the water. We talked about small things we had done with our families growing up. I talked about how my mother had told us stories about her own childhood, and we had listened carefully in the dark, as if her words would have some great importance later in life that we could not have possibly understood at that age.

We could see the lighthouse out of the first of the three windows and watched the slow rotation of light on the dark blue water before being lost at sea. Just as we were about to fall asleep, with Julie still resting on top of my shoulder, she said, "Peter, I'm going to miss all of this, the way you miss those days with your family. I'll miss it when we're not together. All that we've had, all that we've done. I want you to know that forever. You do know that, don't you?"

"Yes, Julie, I do," I said, and soon after, we fell asleep.

The next day we rented bikes and biked to the museum and then out to 'Sconset, almost eight miles away. The ride was fun, but it was windy and hard work. We stopped at the general store for something to drink. We went up and down little streets and peered over white fences to see the views of the ocean, trying to decide which was our favorite house and what fun our kids would have playing on the lawn. Then we returned to town with the wind at our backs. Julie wanted to stop at the library to look up something on the whaling industry. Julie was always doing that sort of thing, learning some fact and then having to follow it up by doing research. *Busywork if you ask me. I like leaving space available in my own brain for other stuff down the road, sort of like unused storage.*

The library was almost empty, which wasn't surprising this late on a Saturday. Julie went up to the card catalog and then disappeared into the stacks. I grabbed a magazine from the rack and slumped into one of the cushioned chairs by the windows. I had begun reading an article in *Sports Illustrated* when Julie laid a cookbook on the table next to me.

"What's this?" I said. The book was titled *Cape Cod Reds Cookbook.*

"Just open it," she said. "I got it for your own graduation, so to speak. I decided some time ago to do this but just wasn't sure where. Then I remembered how much fun we had here last summer, and it just seemed like a good place for it. You know what I mean? Someday we'll both come back here again."

"We will Julie," I said, though we both knew she didn't mean together. It was still nice knowing it would be there as a marker of sorts.

I began flipping through pages when she turned to the inside front cover. There was a bookplate from the Nantucket Library which read "Given in Memory of Nate Pendleton, from his friends and family. His favorite recipe is found on page 26."

"Wow, Julie, I don't know what to say. When did you do this?"

"I sent it a couple of weeks ago and told them how I wanted it dedicated."

I turned to page 26, and read about crushed pineapple cranberry upside-down cake, something Nate and I both enjoyed.

Afterwards we walked on the beach in front of the hotel. The lights twinkled from across the harbor. It began raining lightly. Wet sand stuck to the bottoms of our feet, and then we went back inside.

November 3-8, 1943

Eric was listening to the Boston Philharmonic when the announcer broke in with news of a Ford station wagon going off the Cape Cod Bridge. "Stay tuned for news on the hour for any further developments," he said.

Eric could feel something was wrong and called the school. He confirmed his fear with Sister Margaret. The next morning before work he drove out to the bridge to see it firsthand. The roads were frozen over and dangerous. Two officers were directing traffic and state police were down below on the banks looking over the car.

Eric thought for a few days about what to do. He was sure of nothing. It could have been an accident—but maybe not. He had already given the FBI the notes that the girls' had found, photographs of the man from the market, and a few shots of his truck and license plate. Eric decided that he had to do something more, but first he had to go to Washington to make his report to the Audubon Society.

He worked most of a normal day on routine tasks, ordered tickets for the train to Washington. He ate lunch with a couple of colleagues before slipping out shortly after 3.

"Leaving a little early today?" Eddie asked as Eric laid his briefcase down on the table.

"Yes, got some errands to do," Eric replied in a friendly manner.

"Horrible about the girls, wasn't it?"

"Yes, tragic. You never know when things will happen."

Eric went by his apartment, gathered clothes and personal effects, and stuffed them into a small suitcase. He hugged Plankton, giving the dog's belly a good long scratch. Mrs. Venzenna was in the hall downstairs when he was leaving. "I was just coming to look for you," he said.

"Where are you going?" she asked.

"I'm going to Washington on business. I'll be back in about a week," he explained. "Will you be able to watch Plankton for me?"

"I'd be delighted. Plankton and I are great friends. I'd have been disappointed if you hadn't asked me. Have a good trip. Take care."

"Thanks. I will. Bye."

He had to leave time before his bus to make a stop at Bird Island to pick up a piece of equipment off the air-raid tower. He needed the readings to complete his report for the Audubon Society. Eric didn't notice the black Packard trailing him at safe distance as he took the city bus out to Coffers Road. He walked painfully the last quarter mile to the boathouse, as he carried with him his small suitcase and a set of hand tools from the Institute wrapped in a cloth case. Untying one of the small rowboats at the end of the wharf, he rowed the mile over to the island fighting cold winds. It was starting to get dark, and he had to act quickly to get it done while there was still light. Taking his tools, he left his suitcase in the boat, checked his map, and began his short trek across the island. When he passed station seven, he noticed one of the cables that held it in place had come loose, and he stopped to reattach it. He didn't really have time for this distraction, but he couldn't afford having it damaged. Pulling a small hand shovel out of his bag, he began digging in the sand to secure the line. He dug down about twelve inches, unearthing two old beer bottles and several small critters crawling in the sand.

"Look out, guys," he said to them off-handily, and they marched off, upset by the disturbance. By now the light had left the sky. He turned on his small flashlight. It was time to go, and he headed to the air-raid tower nearby to retrieve his control monitor. His flashlight led him over the wet sand, and he left deep tracks. Climbing the tower, he put his flashlight in his back rear pocket and placed his foot on the first rung.

When he got on top, he pulled out the light and tools and began unscrewing his wind monitor. He dropped the screwdriver and pointed the flashlight down to find it near his feet. Eric finished the job and placed the wind gauge inside his tool bag. He looked south at the water and back east at the lights across the bay and decided that it was time to go. He walked back to the steps and placed his foot on the top rung. From twenty-five yards away a man dressed in a black leather jacket and dark jeans pulled the rifle into position. He lined Eric up in the sight and put his finger on the trigger. He would wait for Eric to have both feet on the steps before he released. But the step was wet, and Eric lost his balance. He swung away from the rails and out into open space. The man with the rifle pulled it down and waited. "If he's going to do it for me, all the better," the man said to himself. Eric swung out from the steps and then back in, grabbing the rail above him. He held on tightly.

"Wow, that was close," he said out loud. Eric began his next step down and the one after that. He missed the third step completely, catching nothing but thin air. He tumbled, splitting open the back of his head on the narrow shaft wall and snapping his neck. His body continued down twelve feet below ground level.

The man with the rifle put it down on the sand and said, "Easiest money I've ever earned," and he walked over to the air raid tower to see Eric's body lying at the bottom of the shaft. He retraced Eric's steps to the rowboat. Pulling out Eric's suitcase and briefcase, he pushed the boat out towards the sea. The next day another early nor'easter brought two feet of snow and heavy blowing winds that covered Eric's body and all of the tracks.

.   .   .

Chapter 47
THE LO-O-O-ONG GOODBYE

June 3, 1966

Julie's parents came up for graduation and stayed at the Harbor Inn. They invited me to dinner the second night of their visit. We ate at a round table in the middle of the busy dining room, filled with families coming to reclaim lost children. The room was big and light, and conversations were filled with laughter. Julie's sister Marion had just graduated from high school, and we heard a lot about the ceremonies. She was going to go to Carleton College, majoring in French. She talked about her senior year and how her lacrosse team won the conference championships.

After dinner, we went for a walk out on the pier. It made me wonder how much of this I would remember later in life. Mrs. Mathers said she was getting cold, so Julie's parents said goodnight and went back to their room after discussing a meeting time before the ceremony. The three of us stayed on the pier for a while. Julie and Marion started talking about someone from home, and it reminded me of my visit to Chicago the year before.

Now, standing in the cooling mist of June with only a few weeks left, our paths set in opposite directions, it was a different matter.

The air was getting cooler, and Marion wanted to call her boyfriend. Julie had stuff to do, so we dropped Marion off, and I drove Julie home. We talked little during the ride. When I drove up into her driveway she leaned over and said, "Good night, Peter." Then she gave me a kiss without meaning it. It was one of those courtesy kisses you give someone when accepting an award in middle school or after a neighbor dies. It was not the kind of meaningful kiss you give someone you want to spend the rest of your life with, like Miss Mills, your fifth-grade teacher.

"Good night, little bean," I said. "See you in the morning."

June 4 - July 31, 1966

The shadows of goodbye had been creeping across our lives but now had turned to darkness. Julie was staying after graduation to help one of her professors finish a project, but it didn't matter.

Graduation day was beautiful, with a cool breeze off the water. The speaker was an editor at *The New Yorker* who gave a wonderful talk about finishing your dreams and following your passion. The ceremony was held on the commons in front of the administration building. Julie graduated eighth in the class, but that was probably only because of distractions from me. She received the Margaret Griffin Science Award for excellence. Her life was full; mine only a few nights from empty.

On her last night in Whitfield she slept at my place. I made lasagna, and we drank wine. We didn't talk about our past or my future. She had spent the day cleaning her apartment and shortly after 11 fell asleep on the sofa in front of my bed. I took off her shoes and covered her with a blanket. I stayed up most of the night, listening to music, and drinking beer very slowly.

I sat in the large chair slumped down, watching her mouth open and close with every breath, breathing the way my grandmother did the night she died. I had been in the hospital room as she pulled her bed sheet up high on her chest, folding it over in a neat manner. Grandma talked about my father and life when she was young, and little things Cory and I had done when we were younger. I had no way of knowing at the time—though she must have—that she was going to die so soon.

Julie woke early and poured herself a glass of juice. I heard the refrigerator door and opened my eyes. She was energetic and friendly. The fever of us broken, she was now free to go on with the really important stuff she'd planned.

"Come, sport; I've got a full day of driving ahead." *What was I, her German short-haired pointer about to go fetch?* I got up reluctantly, mumbling. When we got to her place, we loaded boxes in her yellow VW. After we finished, I offered to make one more check, while she was getting boxes arranged in the backseat.

"Thanks, Peter. That would be great."

I wandered through the three rooms of her apartment, and then, with the breath sucked out of me, tears ran down my face.

"You okay, Peter?" she asked looking at my red cheeks.

"Sure, I'm fine."

"Peter," she said softly, "okay?"

"Okay," I said. "Fine."

"Peter, it's going to work out for you. You'll find something you're good at."

"Julie, you're not supposed to end a career with a preposition. Anyway, I already have found something."

"You did? What?" she said, seeming surprised.

"Loving you."

She put her hand flat against my chest and brushed it back and forth as if she was cleaning a window of some unseen dust.

"Oh, Peter, you take care, and make me proud." Of course I still had no plans on making anyone proud but now felt obligated to try to meet her challenge.

"Oh, Julie, I almost forgot. This is for you." I laid a letter-sized cardboard box on her backseat.

"What is it?" she asked.

"It's the book you told me to write that night I came back from the boathouse."

"Really?" She seemed every bit as surprised as Mrs. Grayson had been when I broke my secret in fourth grade.

"It's a novel about five fictional Catholic school girls who worked on the Cape Cod Reds."

"That's great, Peter. I'm already so proud of you. I know it will be good." She patted the box as if it were a small pet.

"Hey, let's not get carried away. It's not finished yet. I just haven't felt like working on it the last few months. What I can promise is lots of misspellings."

"I know, sweetie. I wouldn't have it any other way. I'm excited, and this is a good start for you."

Then she hugged me and again said, "Make me proud."

"I'll try," I said because I felt I owed her that.

She ran her hand down the side of my neck, got in her car, and was gone.

I went back to my apartment and lay on the white bedspread, with the small fuzzy balls. Julie had named each one of them. I fiddled with Camille's white tuff near the middle of the spread and said, "I going to miss her, girl." The white ball nodded back. I spent the whole day shamelessly feeling sorry for myself; feeling guilty about feeling sorry; and starting all over again.

. . .

During my remaining time in Whitfield, I twice thought I saw Julie at the A&P on aisle 8, our personal favorite. I played little mind games, wondering if any of these cans were ones Julie and I might have touched or seen while she was still here, and whether some of her being might be hidden inside an eight-ounce serving of tomato sauce, but mostly I tried to think about moving on. Nothing worked. *I can say that if you find yourself seeing former lovers inside cans of food, get help.*

I only wish I had. But everything I did reminded me of her, and I ached to have her back, or at the very least a generic equivalent.

In my last month in Whitfield, I spent time training the new hire. Naomi had taken some vacation time, so I taught the new guy all the tricks, and we practiced the "Not in that chair, are you fucking crazy?" routine together until he owned it.

I went for some runs and some bike rides but never again to the boathouse. I played tennis with a couple of guys from the PE department, and at night I hung out a lot, mostly at Griff's, drinking beer and watching the Red Sox lose. It was time for me to move on. There was no longer anyone in Whitfield who still knew my name.

My goodbyes both at the school and with the Pendletons were brief, but heartfelt. Then the last part of my life, when it was okay to tell people that what I really, really wanted to be was a pirate, came to an end.

November 18, 1943

FBI agents Morrow and Crosby showed up at Sister Margaret's office a week before Thanksgiving. Agent Morrow explained, "In late October, Dr. Eric Ralston informed us of the passage of information out of the Institute through the cranberry boxes. He also gave us some notes, photographs, and a license plate number, which led to a stolen truck, but nothing more at this point. Now Dr. Ralston himself has been missing for over a week. We are not sure about the source of the leak but feel we are moving in on a likely suspect. Nevertheless, it will be necessary to shut down the Cape Cod Reds to avoid any other problems."

Sister Margaret agreed. "We will stop our operation immediately. How horrible to think that our well-intentioned project has been used so malevolently. While the Cape Cod Reds have brought a lot of joy to a lot of people, there unfortunately has been a lot of sadness and pain in this last month."

. . .

Chapter 48

DO YOU MIND IF I WATCH?

Fall, 1966 – January, 1967

After Julie left, I only saw her twice. The first time was for an afternoon in September when she came to New York to see an exhibit of Post-Impressionists at the Met. She was still getting settled in at Penn and hadn't made new friends yet. Robert, my friend from work, came along for the outing. He had taken some art history classes, and Julie and he got into a serious discussion about Seurat and pointillism, so I headed into the gift shop to buy postcards for my folks. I picked out this funny one that depicted Caribbean women wearing big straw hats. I thought my parents would get a kick out of it but then realized that they might not get it at all.

Afterwards we stopped at a café near the UN and ate sandwiches made for tiny men with big wallets. I put the whole four dollars worth of turkey club in one cheek. When the waiter indifferently asked if we needed anything else, I replied, "The other half of my sandwich."

Julie told me to stop and thanked the waiter for the both of us. We talked about her classes and my work. After we dropped her at Grand Central Station, Robert invited me back to his apartment for a drink.

"Listen, Peter," he said, "Julie is a wonderful girl, and I can see that what you two had was good. But here's the deal. It's gone."

"Do you think she's dating someone else?" I asked.

He shook his head and said, "I have no idea, but she isn't dating you."

The last time I saw Julie was later that fall. She invited me down to Philly for a kiss-your-ass-goodbye weekend. I should have seen it coming.

．　．　．

In the two years I worked at the agency my favorite account was Lupe's, a chain of casual Mexican clothing stores. The slogan we wrote was simple enough: "We're the little bitty store with the jalapeño heart." The ads and the stores had spunk and even received an honorable mention at the New York advertising awards. When a new store opened, we hired a mariachi band and invited everyone with a press pass to come freeload. Lupe served lots of good food, the kind I feasted on at home: tacos, chalupas, enchiladas, and, of course, an open bar.

It was after one of those evenings that I came back to my apartment in late January and called Julie for the last time. It had been snowing since eight. The winds howled down the block in front of my building, moving snow into big wispy bowls on 10th Street. My future had become as shapeless as the melting jalapeño ice sculpture at the party. I stumbled into the apartment with only the hall light on, a six-pack of beer in one hand, a raincoat in the other. I threw the coat on the bed and pulled the phone over to the window. The closing door sucked the remainder of light and all of the hope from the room. I opened a beer, looked down on the quiet street below, and picked up the telephone. Desperate times called for desperate measures, so dialing the last digit of her number I hoped for the best.

"Hi, Julie, it's me, Peter."

"I know." She made no effort to conceal her anger. "You're drunk, Peter," her voice flatly noted.

"Am not," I said gingerly, but the "t" wasn't fastened tightly enough on the end and slipped off while coming out of my mouth.

"Okay," she said mockingly. "You're no." Apparently she was "no" in the mood to argue, but I hadn't called to argue either. I had called to be loved, nurtured back to health.

"Peter," she continued impatiently, "what's up?" her voice cracked back. I pulled the loose skin back off droopy eyelids, trying to focus.

"Whatcha doing?" came my lonely inquiry.

"Studying."

"Oh, can I come over?" This comment was funny the first dozen times it was used but now was as sad as the spot in which I found myself. "Sorry, I guess it's late," I added.

"In more ways than you know, Peter."

God, was I part of a metaphor? Because I was too drunk, and anyway they'd given a last call for metaphors two hours ago at the bar on Lexington.

"Peter," she said, "you think you're still in love with me."

"No," I protested, but meekly. I knew it wasn't good for me to be left without an attendant and was fully prepared to offer her the permanent position. I wanted to say, "I can be fun, really," but it would have sounded weak. So I doubled down with the even weaker "Take me back; take me back. I won't be a pirate or a treasure hunter or a fortune teller. I will be whatever you want me to be, I promise. I'll have goals and dreams like regular people. You'll be proud of me. I'll follow the stock market. We'll go to the opera." *Geez, I must have been drunker than I realized.* "You'll see. You'll see."

My heart ached to touch her in ways I could not describe: for her warm legs to roll over mine; for her to put her arms around me and curl up into the tiniest human ball; for the luxury of time to pad across warm floors and bring back cold beers and with them the hours to share stories so rich and full, about people and faces from each other's pasts, for the two of us to lie on top of hot sheets, to hear the whir of the fan as it clattered another rotation around our lives. I wanted her to talk quietly to me about matters of consequence, big or small, late into the night before fading slowly into sleep, for all the reasons people fall in love, to be cared about, to have their thoughts matter, to finish the puzzle of me.

I didn't want to find a new career, learn how to repair toasters, or make the best out of bad situations for God's sake. I'd read all of those books, some of them twice. What I needed was for Julie to come home again and put our lives back together.

Our lives in Whitfield were filled with moments which couldn't possibly matter to anyone who wasn't there. But here's the deal: I was. I was there when Julie tore the skin off her left heel chasing me down the steps after a day at the beach. I was there after the Bob Dylan concert in Boston when she hovered over the potty for hours from food poisoning. I was there the night she ran her fingers through mine, first up one and then down another, singing a song her grandmother taught her when she was nine. But none of those things were anywhere to be found in Julie's apartment in Philly. She wasn't looking. Gone forever were our days of playing "Name that body part" or "Women's Prison" with the countless strip searches and get acquainted showers, supervised by Warden Peabody, a real stickler for cleanliness.

She had new games to play and new friends with whom to share them. The irreplaceable Peter Dreeton had been moved to the discontinued shelf at the Five and Dime, marked for quick sale. I was the pirate suit she no longer needed.

"Peter, you're not in love with me. There is nothing good about us now. You're in love with what we used to have. I am saying this not to hurt your feelings, but to help."

Somehow I wasn't buying her words, in fact, "Liar, liar, pants on fire" came rushing to my lips, but she continued without me, certain of her course.

"It's time to move on, Peter. I never loved you! At least I did not love you in a way that would last." I waited for her words, afraid of what they would tell me. "I was crazy about you, Peter. You are sweet and good."

"And funny," I added to her list.

"Yes, funny, very funny, Peter," she laughed. "I will always be crazy about you, always… forever," she continued. "But that doesn't change where we are, Peter."

"Yeah, you're studying in Philly. I'm drunk in New York."

"Well, that was your choice, wasn't it? It's time to let this go, Peter. When you are over me, I want to know how you are, but not now." She repeated her words very firmly. "Not now, so don't call with some pretext to make small talk. I'm busy, you're not. That's over. We're over, and anyway, Peter," she paused a second to choose her words carefully, "I'm seeing someone else."

"Really? Can I watch?"

This sounded creepy saying it out loud but still vaguely interesting, especially this late in the evening, and let's be honest, New York is a very lonely place.

"No, Peter you can't. Now do we understand each other?" she firmly asked.

"Yes," I said meekly. I knew it was going to come down to this. The question had always been when, not if. The answer was *"ahora."* I just wanted her to know, to remember what she was turning back to love's lost-and-found, the irreplaceable… me. "You know, Julie, there aren't a lot like me out there. You know that, don't you?"

"I do, Peter. I do know that about you." Her voice was conciliatory, which made me feel good, but it also made me realize she already had weighed her options and found me wanting. Of course, I found myself wanting as well, but we no longer wanted the same thing, and that was the hardest part.

"Julie, I wish that before you go, before I never see you again as anything but a stranger, that… there were words to say to overtake your heart. I know now the distance between us is greater than my words can carry me, but God, oh God, I wish that wasn't so."

From deep inside the phone came Julie's response, in words so tender they made me sober again, "Oh, sweet baby, so do I."

November 18, 1943

Sister Margaret promised the FBI men that the next day she would shutter the warehouse. After the FBI men left her office, Sister Margaret sat solemnly reflecting on the girls she had lost and their surviving friends. She had come to St. Anne's the year their class started first grade. She had watched them grow into strong, smart, young women. Sister Margaret was very proud of them, and all they had become. Now she found herself lost in thought about five sweet little girls dressed as cranberries, a long time ago.

At the cranberry festival in 1933 Sister Margaret had helped organize the dancing cranberries for the parade. The five friends all stood near each other. She watched as one of them nervously fiddled with her costume. "Is my beret on straight?" Mary asked.

"Yes, yes, right on top of your head," Penny answered fixing the stem on top of her own brown beret.

"You're sure?"

"Yes, yes. It's fine."

That year there were twenty-four six-and-seven-year-old girls signed up for the parade. It took the mothers most of a week to sew and construct the outfits, which included: brown berets, red turtleneck shirts, tiny red gloves, red tights, and a soft body shell made of cotton and stuffed with batting material.

Sister Margaret had to get all twenty-four girls organized to have their picture taken in front of town hall where the parade was to begin. The reporter from the *Cape Cod Courier* needed help settling the girls, and the nun did her part. Lucy had parked herself in the front next to Katie. "Lucy, there is a good place for you in the third row," Sister Margaret gently suggested.

Lucy didn't understand why she had to move to the back. "I'm always in the back row, Sister. I want to be up in the front," Lucy requested.

"Maybe another time. Today we need you in the back," Sister Margaret explained.

"I'll save your place here by me for the parade," Katie said encouragingly to her friend. Lucy was not a troublemaker, and she moved to the back row without causing a problem.

"Thank you, dear. We can see you better there," Sister Margaret added. Lucy nodded, doing her best to get over her hurt.

Sister Margaret knew they didn't have a lot of time. "Okay, girls, Mr. Nevins is going to take your picture for the paper, so nice bright cranberry smiles on three."

The photographer smiled and dutifully took the shot after calling the number two. The girls giggled and made comments about how Mr. Nevins couldn't count, and Sister Margaret shook her head, feigning her agreement.

Then the cranberries quickly lined up for the parade. A boy and his big, fat tuba pushed between Penny and Kerrie to take his place in line. Penny frowned but didn't say anything. Kerrie was not so bashful.

"Hey, watch it. You could kill someone with that thing," she said. The boy made a face at Kerrie and took his place next to the piccolo player.

The band began misfiring a few notes to their opening march, and the parade was on its way. Walking along beside the berries, Sister Margaret instructed the girls to begin singing the song she had written for the festival.

> *All the little berries right in a row,*
> *All the little berries, where shall we go?*
> *We may be small, and we may be dark red,*
> *But good to eat when it's time to be fed.*
>
> *We grow in sunshine, we grow in the fog.*
> *And we grow in sand deep down in the bog.*
> *And when it is our time, we sail away*
> *To brighten up each and every new day.*
>
> *All the little berries right in row,*
> *All the little berries, where shall we go?*
> *Some become juice, and some become jelly,*
> *But we all taste good right in your belly.*

The young berries repeated their song at least ten times along the parade route. The March of the Berries was always a highlight of Cranberry Days. It would take the girls, the band, and a handful of floats thirty minutes to march from one end of Main Street out past the wharf and down to the Episcopal Church. By then it would only be 10 o'clock, with a whole day of activities still to come, including a dance contest, funny races, bake sales, rides, and a wonderful fireworks show over the water. Cranberry Days was one of the best days of the year, the little girls all agreed.

Sister Margaret smiled at her reminiscence of the girls as little berries. Then she got back to work. She knew she had much to do to bring the Cape Cod Reds to a close. It took Sister Margaret a month to write each volunteer about how much had been done and how much their help mattered. She got Mr. Walters and his brother-in-law to take down the workbenches and remove the equipment at the warehouse. The building stayed vacant until the end of April when an idea came to Sister Margaret to hold a reunion of sorts there.

• • •

Chapter 49
SWATTING FLIES

Our lives hinge on moments filled with both promise and danger, and we must answer the question, "How lucky do you feel?" Isn't that the paradox we all face? We can see what we are missing; we know where we lost it, and what we need to get back. What I have found is this: it isn't coming. What we get in return is something else. Better, perhaps, because it is not of our choosing. The costumes we thought to be so important, we grew out of, and then gave away. We are left with something far more essential: ourselves.

St. Jerome's was responsible for trying to teach me many things I chose not to learn, and one I did. True happiness comes only from things given up, not from things you hold on to. Take it or leave it. A ball tossed in the air comes barreling back to hit you in the nose. Toss out a kindness, and the results are never so clear. For most of us, we know this simple truth, yet spend much of our lives, our energy, and our hopes trying to put more than fifteen items into our basket of toys. When I find myself overwhelmed with these shallow dreams, I try to remember what is important and what is not, like having the time to spend with friends, solving all the world's problems with just "a few more beers." Then I imagine myself drifting peacefully on top of cold blue water with plump red berries for as far the eye can see. Finally home again; I am floating on the Wow.

· · ·

A couple of months after my last call to Julie, I came home from work to find a small package left in front of my door. I tossed it down on the bed; inside was a Coke bottle from Santa Fe and a note.

"Peter, I found this in a flea market last Sunday and thought you could use it. I hope things are better. I will miss you forever. Cassie Niedimire, Acting Director, Nevada Department of Mines." It should have helped but only made me miss her more.

. . .

I've learned many things during those days between childhood and now. I've made friends and lost them; I've thought I had everything figured out before realizing I didn't. Finally, I found out how unfair life could be and how in the end that was the only way it ever could be.

I left New York in the middle of a rainstorm at the end of June, 1968. It was seed store or bust. In Asheville, North Carolina, I stopped for a night and went to a single-A ballgame, sitting next to a dad and his young son. They talked in deep southern drawls. We swatted flies together while watching white balls soar far out into the nighttime sky. The father asked if I had just graduated from college. I thought about saying how I had worked for a university, and then spent a couple of years in New York, but instead replied, "I guess in a way I have."

Graduation Day, 1944

Lucy became class valedictorian by default. Her speech confessed to her hollow victory. Before she began, she asked five junior girls to come up on the stage and stand behind her. She cleared her throat and smiled.

"Katie and Mary and Penny were always telling me that I talked too much when I was nervous, and I guess they were right. Today I've promised them not to make the same mistake. A year ago, these juniors behind me were us. Next year they will stand ready to face challenges we have already met, to commit to things greater than themselves. The graduating class of '44 wishes the class of '45 as much joy and wisdom as we were given by the faculty and staff, especially the kind of wisdom coming from Sister Dorothy's theology class. That should be loads of fun, ladies."

The seniors laughed, and the juniors moaned. Lucy let the laughter subside before she continued.

"We have returned to this warehouse where we spent so many happy hours, working for a common goal. Now we are here to pay tribute to all that we have learned and shared together over the last year, to new friends we've made and old ones we've lost. Goodbye is not simply a word we say before leaving; it is a commitment to carry all that we have learned from one another, until we meet again. For some graduating seniors, these reunions will come very soon: in stores downtown; out at the beach: or when we return for Christmas holidays; but other reunions will come later. We are better for all we have done, and with God's help, stronger for the lessons our loss left for us. As Sister Margaret told us when we began the Reds, 'The dust of our deeds will be carried to places far away,' and now we all know that it has. Our days of packing berries are gone now, but not the good that came from it. I wish for each of you: a wonderful life; the wisdom to appreciate all you have been given; and the generosity to share your gifts with others. These are hard times, ladies. They may not get better soon, but what we make of these days will make us who we are. So, to all the parents and grandparents, brothers, and sisters, who have come here today, I am proud to present to you the St. Anne's graduating class of 1944."

Lucy turned behind her and nodded to the junior girls, who unfolded the five cranberry banners. Sister Margaret returned to the podium to thunderous applause. Then each graduating student was called to the stage to receive her diploma.

"Before our closing prayer," Sister Margaret said, "I have one final announcement to make. I know how much Katie Welch, Mary Sealy, and Penny Caulkins would have wanted to be here with us today, and thanks to the silver screen they can be."

The lights went off, and the projector turned on. It rolled unedited *MovieTone* footage of the USO program in Newport, with the five girls tumbling out on stage. Cheers of encouragement came from the sailors in the audience. The girls sang their first song, and the sailors called for more. The graduation crowd in the warehouse sat in silence seeing these good friends in such a happy moment. Penny came back to the microphone and with the others behind her she sang Gershwin's "They Can't Take That Away From Me". Her words rose up from the film through the open windows above the large graduation crowd and spilled out to the warm evening air on De Carlo Street. When the song finished, the five "cranberries" tossed their white hats out into the sea of sailors, and the film stopped. Sitting together in the front row, Lucy smiled at Kerrie. It seemed to Lucy that her prayers had been answered. The missing fireflies had come home to light her heart again.

. . .

Made in the USA
Charleston, SC
19 February 2010